MURDER A LA MODE

MURDER A LA MODE

ELEANORE KELLY SELLARS

COACHWHIP PUBLICATIONS
Greenville, Ohio

Murder a la Mode, by Eleanore Kelly Sellars
© 2017 Coachwhip Publications
Introduction © 2017 Curtis Evans

Title published 1941
Eleanore Kelly Sellars (1903-1972)
No claims made on public domain material.

CoachwhipBooks.com

ISBN 1-61646-399-6
ISBN-13 978-1-61646-399-1

MERCHANDISING MURDER
ELEANORE KELLY SELLARS (1903-1972) AND "MURDER A LA MODE" (1941)

CURTIS EVANS

*Fifth Avenue is always exhilarating, often dramatic,
and sometimes tragic.—Murder a la Mode*

Upon Dodd, Mead's fall 1941 publication, under its Red Badge mystery fiction imprint, of Eleanore Kelly Sellars' *Murder a la Mode*, the publisher named the novel the sixth recipient of its $1000 prize for the best mystery by an author not previously published under the Red Badge imprint. With its promise of a cash award, enhanced royalties and added publicity, the Red Badge prize had become a lure to striving mystery authors. At the time *Murder a la Mode* was awarded the Red Badge prize, the best-known previous winners were *Fast Company* (1938), a novel by neophyte mystery novelist Marco Page (screenwriter Harry Kurnitz), and *Cancelled in Red* (1939), a novel published under the name "Hugh Pentecost," a newly-launched pseudonym of prolific crime writer Judson Philips. Contemporary accounts sometimes stated that Sellars, whose "first attempt at fiction in any shape or form" was *Murder a la Mode*, was the first woman to win Dodd, Mead's detective novel prize, but in fact Dodd, Mead earlier in the year had bestowed its award upon Susannah Shane, for her debut mystery, *Lady in Lilac*. (Dodd, Mead that year had commenced the practice of bestowing two prizes annually upon Red Badge mystery authors, one in the spring and one in the fall.)

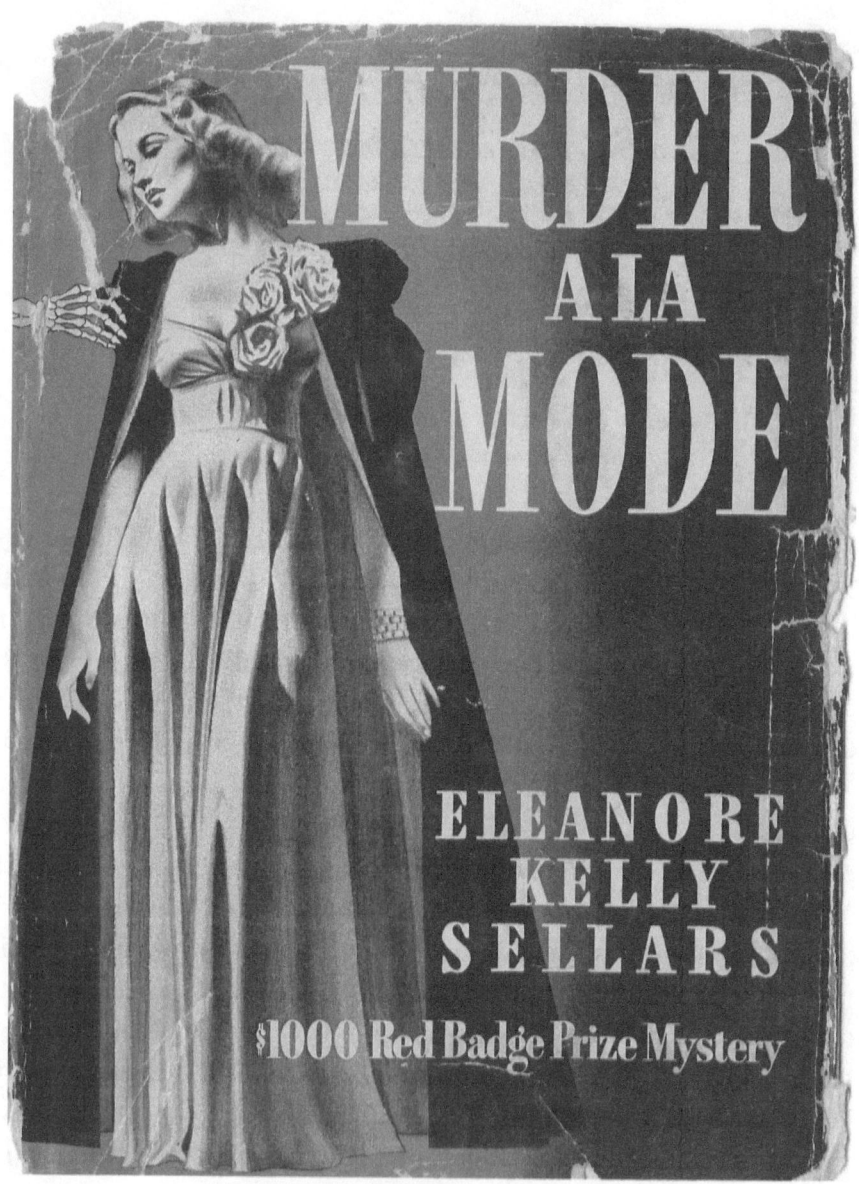

The original cover of *Murder a la Mode*

Eleanore Kelly Sellars may not have been the first woman to receive the Red Badge prize, but with *Murder a la Mode* she worthily represented a rising group of mystery authors in the late 1930s and 1940s: women writers of "manners" mystery, wherein a great part of the appeal lies not in the puzzle plot alone, but in observation of social mores in sophisticated environments. The British Crime Queens Dorothy L. Sayers, Ngaio Marsh, and Margery Allingham in this respect clearly had influence not only in the United Kingdom, but in the United States, where, as in the UK, they enjoyed critical and popular success that other mystery writers hoped to emulate. Between 1939 and 1941, for example, Emma Lou Fetta—a newspaper columnist and founding member of the Fashion Group, a professional organization established in 1930 to promote the New York fashion industry—published a trilogy of detective novels about Susan Yates, a canny dress designer who just happens to find herself frequently involved in toney murder investigations. (It helps that she is romantically involved with the handsome and debonair Lyle Curtis, a New York assistant district attorney.) For her part, Eleanore Kelly Sellars set her own detective novel, which she had originally planned to title *Merchandising Murder*, at a fashionable Fifth Avenue department store, Dexter & Cole's, and peopled it with a range of bright and urbane business executives and executive assistants, male and female, as well as the male executives' spouses. The female professionals are unmarried, though they are still in the hunt for husbands, which can make for social complications.

Murder a la Mode is narrated by Deborah "Debby" Wood, of Dexter & Cole's advertising department, who has amorous feelings (which at the opening of the novel she has not yet admitted to herself) for her not-so-happily-married boss, Ken Holmes. When Martin Cole, Dexter & Cole's aristocratic president (he is "the fourth successive Cole to hold that office"), invites several members of the company, including Debby, Ken and executive vice president Arthur Otis, to his magnificent neoclassical country house above the Hudson River to attend a weekend conference concerning an institutional advertising campaign, Ken tacitly reminds Debby, "Mr. Otis and I are taking our wives, you know," to which Debby tartly responds, "Wives are not a social phenomenon to which I am unaccustomed." Debby may well know how to handle live

TEN—SECOND SECTION   *Book Reviews*—THE PITTSB

Swanky Department Store Is Setting For Suspenseful Mystery

Author Knows Talk, Habits and Problems of People She Casts in Prize Murder Tale

By MAXINE GARRISON

Murderous hi-jinks with an authentic department store background furnish the excitement in Eleanore Kelly Sellars' "Murder a la Mode" (Dodd, Mead), winner of the $1000 Red Badge prize. The book should have special interest locally, since Mrs. Sellars began her writing career as a copywriter for the department store business here in Pittsburgh.

The advertising department of one of New York's swanky Fifth Avenue stores provides the characters in "Murder a la Mode," and its rival ambitions provide more than enough motives for the foul deeds therein.

Martin Cole, president of the store, invites advertising executives to his home for the annual conference on an institutional advertising campaign. Surface friendliness quickly break down to show the hatreds among the writers — the ambitious vice president, the handsome lady-killing vice president in charge of features, the more wealthy office director, the advertising head, the fiction editor, her would-be successor and even Pris Deane Wood, the narrator.

That night Mrs. Cole is murdered, and it turns out that she had wanted to divorce her husband and marry the vice president in charge of features. Two more persons completely demolish any pretense of purpose to the Dodd & Cole advertising department, before the police turn the police's index the culprit.

Mrs. Sellars tells her story very deftly indeed, dramming it with suspense right up to the last page. Her first-hand knowledge of her background is obvious; she knows the chatter, the habits and the problems of her advertising department. And when she writes about clothes, she writes like an authority and not like a novelist but for an adjective. It's a rarely touched field for mysteries, and in "Murder a la Mode," it's done up brown.

Ex-Pittsburgher Writes Novel

Eleanor Kelly Sellars . . . . Writes Prize Mystery

Wohlfahrt Studios

ELEANORE KELLY SELLARS (MRS. RAYMOND G.),
Γ P-*Allegheny*

wives, but dead ones are quite another matter entirely—a fact Debby ruefully realizes at the weekend conference at the Cole mansion, after she discovers Martin Cole's wife Lissa shot dead late at night on the mansion's grand staircase. (Plans of the first and second floors of the Cole mansion are included, and they are pertinent to the puzzle.)

The list of suspects in Lissa Cole's murder is a long one, encompassing the ten other individuals—five men and five women—who were present at the deadly country house gathering. (The servants are "below suspicion," to borrow mystery writer John Dickson Carr's term.) Happily for armchair sleuths—if unhappily for the novel's characters—the list is narrowed over the course of the story, as two more people are fatally and feloniously poisoned. *Murder a La Mode* succeeds both as a witty manners mystery, providing fascinating detail about an early forties workplace where women played leading roles, and as an adroit puzzle, with twist deviously following upon twist; and it is eminently deserving of revival today, seventy-five years after its original publication. The British mystery novelist Patricia Moyes (1923-2000) would use the title *Murder a la Mode* for an excellent 1963 detective novel, but fans of literate manners mystery deserve a chance to see for themselves what we might term the original model.

The author of the first *Murder a la Mode*, a 1925 graduate from Wellesley College who herself worked in Manhattan as a copywriter and retail executive, signaled that the sophisticated manners mysteries of Sayers, Marsh, and Allingham had influenced her own writing when she informed the Kappa Kappa Gamma sorority magazine, *The Key*, that with *Murder a la Mode* she had wished "to write a murder mystery in which all the people were intelligent and logical in their behavior and remained intelligent and logical throughout the book." In her story "everyone did what shrewd, well-bred and practical people would do if they were actually living though the experiences of murder."[1]

A well-bred Eleanore Kelly grew up in comfortable circumstances in Monessen, a steelmaking town founded in 1897 and located in southwestern Pennsylvania's Monongahela River Valley. (The town's name combined the abbreviation for the Monongahela—Mon—with

---

[1] "First Fiction . . . wins Prize Award," *The Key of Kappa Kappa Gamma* 58 (December 1941): 301.

the name of the German industrial city of Essen.) During the first two decades of the twentieth century Monessen experienced substantial growth, with the population expanding from 2197 in 1900 to 18,179 by 1920. Eleanore Kelly's father, James Howard Kelly, was one of the most prominent men of Monessen, serving as president of the town's First National Bank, vice president and general manager of the Monessen Savings and Trust Company, treasurer and director of the Monessen Foundry and Machine Company and superintendent of the Sabbath school at Monessen Presbyterian Church. In 1902 J. Howard Kelly wed Gertrude Pearsall, of the nearby town of Jeanette, where before launching his highly successful business career Kelly, a graduate from Washington and Jefferson College of Washington, Pennsylvania, had served as principal of the high school where Gertrude had been employed as a teacher. The next year, on February 23, Gertrude gave birth to the couple's daughter, Eleanore; a son, George, followed five years later. Gertrude was the daughter of Samuel and Elizabeth (Wooton) Pearsall, a native English couple who had migrated from the West Midlands industrial city of Dudley to the United States in the 1870s. Samuel, the son of a coal miner, worked as a glassblower in the Jeanette Glass Factory.

During the recent presidential campaign of Donald J. Trump, Monessen was one of the Rust Belt locales that the magnate turned politician used to symbolize the decline of the industrialized America that Eleanore Kelly's father had helped to capitalize and her maternal grandfather had helped literally to fashion with his own bare hands. Shortly after Trump delivered a speech at a Monessen aluminum recycling plant with a work force of 35 that formerly had been part of a steel factory, the Monessen Works, employing hundreds of workers, journalist Binjamin Appelbaum in the *New York Times* portrayed Monessen as a dispirited landscape of advanced industrial decay: "The city's population continues to fall, dropping below 7500 last year. The sewer system is collapsing, and erosion is undermining streets and sidewalks. It is getting harder for the high school football team to fill its roster." In his article Appelbaum tellingly noted that just before its near-total demolition in 1987 the Monessen Works (part of the Wheeling-

J. Howard Kelly

Pittsburgh Steel Corporation) was used to film the climactic scenes in the hit dystopian film *RoboCop*.[2]

After attending Washington Female Seminary and graduating from Wellesley at the height of the Jazz Age, Eleanore Kelly left Monessen in the distance behind her, moving to New York, where she worked as a copywriter at a Manhattan department store. In 1929 she married Raymond George Kelly (1905-1966), adding his surname to hers and keeping her job. (The couple apparently had no children.) A native Pennsylvanian like his wife, Raymond Kelly had grown up in Belle Vernon, a small town just a few miles down the river from Monessen. There his widowed native English mother had worked as a dressmaker before marrying Arthur Sellars, who, like Eleanore's maternal grandfather, was employed in a glass factory (the American Window Glass Company). After graduating from high school in 1923, Raymond was hired as a teller by the Monessen Savings and Trust Company, of which, as mentioned above, Eleanore's father was an officer. Raymond later obtained a position in Pittsburgh with the General Motors Acceptance Corporation, the financial services branch of GM. Less than three months before he wed Eleanore, Raymond was transferred to the company's New York office.

There is some indication that Eleanore's parents may not have been overly enthusiastic about the marriage. Certainly the occasion was a distinctly practical affair with little fanfare. The wedding ceremony was conducted at the Fourth Presbyterian Church in New York City, the only guests, the *Monongahela Daily Republican* tersely reported, being "immediate members of the family. The bride was attired in travelling dress." After touring the New England states by car for two weeks, the couple took up residence together in an apartment in the neighborhood of Jackson Heights in Queens.[3]

For a dozen years Eleanore and Raymond resided in the city, but in 1941, the same year that Eleanore published *Murder a la Mode*, the

---

[2] "Struggles in a Steel Town Highlighted by Donald Trump," *New York Times*, 4 July 2016, http://www.nytimes.com/2016/07/05/us/politics/a-towns-past-and-its-future-rest-in-the-husk-of-an-industry-long-gone.html?_r=0; "Trump Delivers Policy Speech at Monessen," *CBS Pittsburgh*, 28 June 2016, at http://pittsburgh.cbslocal.com/2016/06/28/trump-policy-speech-monessen/.

[3] *Monongahela Daily Republican*, 12 October 1929, 4.

couple moved to the small town of Red Oaks Mill, near Poughkeepsie in Dutchess County, New York, where Eleanore had located the country house setting of the first heinous killing in *Murder a la Mode*. Her husband having "an athletic nature," Eleanore explained to *The Key*, she devoted her weekends to a rigorous regimen of skiing, skating, and mountain climbing. Both she and Raymond were members of the Green Mountain Club of Vermont and the Mansfield Ski Club.

Two years later, however, Eleanore and Raymond abandoned rustic rural lanes for the streets of San Francisco, where Raymond was inducted into the army. For the remainder of the Second World War he served as a Technician Fourth Grade in the 55th Quartermaster Depot at Fort Lee, near Richmond, Virginia. During this time, Eleanore, who promptly pronounced herself "enamored" with San Francisco, published some decidedly non-criminous light romantic short stories, including, in *Collier's Weekly*, "Married Ones Are Best" and, in *Liberty*, "Sixty Seconds Are Forever" and "Some One to Belong To."

Eleanore's 1943 *Collier's* story "Married Ones Are Best" (included at the end of this volume) tells the tale of beautiful Tiffany Russell, man-shy on account of her overbearing belle of a mother who, she explains, "wanted me to be the most popular deb in New York and from the time I could talk . . . was coaching me about what to say to boys and how to smile at them and how to be coquettish." Tiffany is only comfortable around attractive young men when these men are married, we learn, because bachelors painfully remind her of those years when her mother repeatedly threw her at any eligible males. Having left New York for wartime San Francisco, where she has taken a copywriting job in a department store, Tiffany's romantic plight attracts the sympathetic interest of her coworker and old Wellesley girlfriend, Mary Ann Carson, who has a handsome unmarried brother, Rohr, in the city on furlough. Mary Ann persuades Rohr to masquerade as their married brother, Raul, in the hope that, with the help of this deception, Tiffany and Rohr might overcome Tiffany's phobia and become a couple. Does Mary Ann's devious plot work? One does not have to be Philip Marlowe to deduce the outcome of this trifling though winsome affair, which obviously draws on some details from the author's own life.

In 1948 a stage play written by Eleanore during a two-month convalescence from major spinal surgery (perhaps necessitated by her

Ex-Monessen Woman
Author of New Play

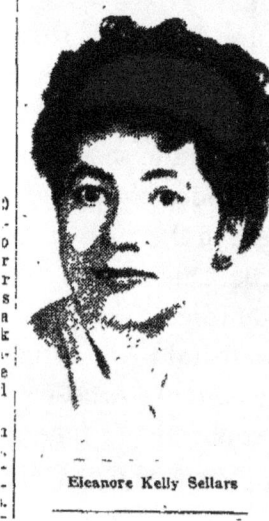

Eleanore Kelly Sellars

Comedy by Eleanore Kelly Sellars to Star Kay Francis; Cleveland Opening

The world premiere of "Favorite Stranger", a comedy of love affairs and marriage, written by Eleanore Kelly Sellars, a former Monessen girl, will be presented at the Hanna Theatre in Cleveland next week, it was learned here today.

Thereafter, with movie actress Kay Francis in the starring role, the play will begin a series of pre-Broadway presentations in Toronto, Jan. 3-8; Erie, Jan. 10; Youngstown, Jan. 11; Akron, Jan. 12; Toledo, Jan. 13-15; and in Detroit, starting Jan. 16.

Born and reared in Monessen, Mrs. Sellars is the daughter of J. Howard Kelly and the late Mrs. Kelly, of this city. She began her writing career at Washington Seminary, Washington, Pa., and Wellesley College, graduating from both institutions. Her first job was writing a fashion column for a large merchandising corporation. She soon branched out to the field of creative writing and later, radio script writing.

Wrote Mystery

In 1941 she wrote her first novel, "Murder a la Mode", which won the Dodd-Mead Red Badge prize of $1,000 for the best mystery novel of that year. This book has subsequently been published in London, Stockholm, Helsinki, Madrid and Sydney, Australia. As a result she has devoted herself exclusively to writing and her short stories have appeared frequently in such publications as Liberty, Collier's and others, and have also seen publication abroad.

Mrs. Sellars is proud that her first effort to write a novel was not merely accepted for publication but was also a prize winner.

"Favorite Stranger", her first effort at playwriting, has not only been accepted, too, but was honored with a prize donated by John Golden. It was written during a two-year convalescence from a major spinal operation and is the first piece written by Mrs. Sellars since her recovery.

Although it is barely a matter of months since "Favorite Stranger" attracted the attention of Miss Francis, who chose it as a vehicle with which to follow up her success in "State of the Union", Mrs. Sellars has already finished a new novel.

Publicity for
Favorite Stranger

past physical exertions) was performed off-Broadway, but, disappoint-
ingly for murder fiction fiends, the four-act play, *Favorite Stranger*, was,
like the short stories, non-criminous. *Favorite Stranger* was a comedy-
romance starring the forty-three year old faded Hollywood film star
Kay Francis as Chalice Chadwick, the "long neglected wife of a man
who has forgotten to return from Paris" after the conclusion of the
Second World War. When a neighboring doctor and a naval command-
er, bachelors both, take an interest in Chalice, she "finds herself in
the enjoyable position of breakfasting with two charming men every
Sunday morning." However, after "her husband returns unexpectedly,
ready to resume his marriage but with one eye cast wistfully toward
the delights of love in Paris," Chalice finds herself faced with a vexing
matrimonial dilemma.[4]

Favorite Stranger opened on Christmas 1948 in Elmira, New York
and closed thirteen weeks later on April 2, 1949 in Pittsburgh, Pennsylvania, not far from Eleanore's home town, never making it to Broad-
way. Much of the attention in reviews of the play focused not so much
on the play itself as on Kay Francis, or more particularly Kay Francis'
wardrobe, the actress having been known in her cinematic heyday as
one of Hollywood's great fashion plates. "Women in the audience were
anxious, and well pleased, to see Miss Francis' $3500 wardrobe," one
reviewer gushed. "She appeared in an especially fetching black dinner
dress of taffeta with a perky bustle of shocking pink roses."[5] Doubtless-
ly detective fiction fans would have preferred screaming blue murder
to shocking pink roses.

A decade later Eleanore experienced rather too much of crime
when Raymond was arrested by police in Corte Madera, north of San
Francisco, and charged with assault with a deadly weapon. According
to contemporary newspaper accounts in the *San Rafael Daily Independent Journal*, Raymond brandished a .32 caliber Colt automatic at
Bob's of Marin restaurant in Corte Madera while boasting of his shooting prowess. Witnesses at the restaurant claimed that Raymond shouted that he could not only "shoot jackrabbits on the run" but "all the

---

4   Quotations are from Lynn Kear and John Rossman, *Kay Francis: A Passionate Life and Career* (Jefferson, NC and London: McFarland, 2006), 149.
5   Ibid.

glasses on the [bar] counter just like that—boom! boom! boom!" Two truckers, who were brothers, told investigating policemen that Raymond pointed the gun specifically at them. During the incident, it was reported, Raymond had confided to a waitress that the brothers "were a couple of hoodlums—that's why I brought in this gun." (One of the policemen countered that the truckers "may have needed a haircut but otherwise looked ordinary enough.") Shortly after his arrest authorities committed Raymond to Napa State Hospital, a psychiatric facility, for a 72-hour evaluation.[6]

How Eleanore fared in this imbroglio is not known to me. Raymond died eight years later, at the age of 60, and was interred in a cemetery in San Francisco. When she passed away in New York City at the age of 69 in 1972, Eleanore from what I can tell does not seem to have been laid to rest beside Raymond, raising the possibility that the couple may have gone their separate ways in the Sixties. Certainly marital disharmony recurs as a theme in Eleanore's Forties fiction (in *Murder a la Mode* none of the marriages she portrays are happy ones), though her public interviews around the time of the publication of *Murder a la Mode* invariably stress the companionability of her and Raymond's union. "Mrs. Sellars gives her husband credit for the finished product," the *Poughkeepsie Eagle-News*, referencing the composition of *Murder a la Mode*, assured its readers, "for it was his encouragement which helped her over the many hard spots."[7]

Eleanore Kelly Sellars' published writing career seems to have lasted less than a decade, leaving only a novel, a play and a mere handful of short stories. (According to the *Monessen Daily Independent*, Eleanore had completed a new novel by the end of 1948, but whatever became of it is unknown to me.) While one surmises that *Favorite Stranger* is unlikely ever to see any modern revival, *Murder a la Mode* merits a renewed readership among fans of classic mystery. Only in the prize-winning *Murder a la Mode* did Eleanore Kelly Sellars deftly dazzle her audience with the dual delights of high fashion and low

---

[6] *San Rafael Daily Independent Journal*: "Boom! Boom! Boom! Customer Pulls Gun in Corte Madera Café" (18 August 1958, 1) and "Pistol-Waver Sent to Napa" (21 August 1958, 4).

[7] *Poughkeepsie Eagle-News*, 17 September 1941, 7.

murder. I will give the final word to publisher Dodd, Mead, who stated of its then-latest $1000 Red Badge Prize Mystery, "*Murder a la Mode* is that rare kind of mystery story which has everything—character, setting, plot, speed, novelty, color. The Red Badge Editors have no hesitation in pronouncing it one of the most distinguished of all the prize winners."

MURDER A LA MODE

1

Fifth Avenue is always exhilarating, often dramatic, and sometimes tragic. Striding, that Saturday morning, down its shadowed canyon with the spring sun tossing an exclamation point of brilliance from each cross street, the exhilarating insistence of life in a great city possessed me. There was a stirring sense of vitality to the scene. Slim girls, their chic black costumes shot through with the brilliance of scarves and gloves and daring, irrepressible hats, darted into the dark austerity of the newly awakened buildings. Haughty facades, by their very restraint and dignity, challenged the spirit. Shop windows glowed with the sheen of costly fabrics, the glitter of jewels, the sleek opulence of priceless furs. A work-a-day fairyland, Fifth Avenue; Mecca to the denizens of the fashion world.

The drama and tragedy of Fifth Avenue is less easy to see. Shrewd mistress that she is, she displays her wares, but seldom her heart; and men and women, blinded by the glitter, sell their souls to possess her. But there is no price mark on a soul and it cannot change hands over a counter. You may think such moralizing observations strangely out of place on a spring morning, but follow me into Dexter and Cole's fashionable department store on upper Fifth Avenue.

When Gloria and I reached Cole's that morning, the front doors were just being thrown open and we entered directly from the Avenue. The first floor had that empty, quiet air peculiar to a store when the doors are first opened: stock fresh and in order, girls exchanging confidences on last night's dates, the pungent smell of leather as you pass the bags and gloves, the pervasive sweetness of the cosmetics counter at the foot of the escalator. A world in itself, this store—filled with luxuries gleaned from the far corners of the earth, brilliant with lights, radiant with color.

But, most of all, it is a world of people. Happy people and people with heartbreaks; girls with driving, ruthless ambitions and girls just marking time until marriage will release them from drudgery; men building and shaping a corporation's destiny and enriching the lives of those who labor there; other men, clutching at power, grasping, and harsh to the helpless. A store is a thrilling and terrifying place to those who have the eyes to see and the heart to feel. For there lie naked the deceits of humanity in the market place.

It was not, however, in a mood of such philosophic contemplation that I arrived at my office on the top floor of Dexter and Cole's and set-tled myself for the usual routine of Saturday in the Advertising Depart-ment. But I had scarcely hung up my coat and hat when the telephone rang and I unwittingly embarked upon adventure.

To my surprise the call was from Martin Cole, President of Dexter and Cole, and fourth successive Cole to hold that office. "Mrs. Wood," his voice came over the wire with the impersonal friendliness which was his particular gift in dealing with the staff, "you doubtless know that Mr. Otis and Mr. Holmes are coming up to my place for the semi-annual meeting on institutional ads. I understand that you are going to write this series. If you can make it for the week-end, perhaps you would like to come, too?"

I could, of course, make it. Added to the fact that I had been dying to attend the conference was my desire to visit the famous Cole man-sion up the Hudson, the splendors of which Gloria had many times recounted. There was no reason for either of us to suspect, as we re-placed our phones in their cradles, that by this thoughtful invitation he was indirectly threatening my life, for although the twenty-four hours which we spent at the Coles' were but a brief introduction to the harrowing events of the following week at the store, nevertheless they ushered in our tragic adventure. My first thought was to tell Ken.

Telling things to Ken was one of the nicer phases about working at Cole's. When I went into his office, next to mine, I found him, tall, thin, impeccably tailored, lowering the Venetian blinds against the morning sun. As always, the mere sight of Ken gave me a sense of satisfaction with life. I told him of Mr. Cole's invitation for the week-end.

"Are you going?" he demanded. His tone implied that he heartily hoped I wasn't. So secure had I always been in his cordial friendliness that his attitude startled me. Ken Holmes was usually as blandly urbane as an advertisement for English tweeds and had never before put me on the defensive.

"It seems to be a command performance. Don't you want me?" My confusion was reflected in my voice.

His lips relaxed into a smile. "It's the best idea that I've heard in a long time. I have always thought that you should be on hand to hear the discussions." Then with what seemed to strike a new high in *non sequitur* remarks, he added, "Mr. Otis and I are taking our wives, you know."

Something in his tone made me say, "Wives are not a social phenomenon to which I am unaccustomed."

It was not, however, until early that afternoon that the conference at the Coles' began to look as if it might be really hard to handle. I had gone to Jim Fenton's office to have him OK some fashion show and millinery advertisements and had arrived just as he returned from what must have been, judging from his expression, a most satisfactory lunch hour.

Jim Fenton was our Vice-President in charge of the Fashion Department and considering his reputation as an irresistible Don Juan, it may surprise you to know that I had never before been aware that he was handsome. Yet, looking at him now, I suddenly realized that his features were not only regular but firmly chiseled, with a squared-off jaw line and a well-proportioned nose. And his eyes were magnificent; deeply blue and fringed with lashes which were the despair of every woman who met him—except for Gloria, whose eyes, as startlingly blue as Jim's, were just as devastatingly fringed. Yes, Jim must have been handsome. I had observed only the dark sullenness of expression when no one was pandering to his insatiable ego, the arrogance of his manner, his gift for treachery. But his good looks had hitherto escaped me.

There was, however, no escaping the fact that Jim lived his life as if he were the only actor on the world's stage. The rest of us constituted the audience and it was in my appointed role as spectator that I sat in his office that afternoon and waited while he went through his famous routine.

In an impressive silence, he made some unnecessary rearrangement of the piles of correspondence on the desk. Then his secretary was called in to receive instructions which could have been easily deferred.

I sat and waited.

He made a telephone call, a one-sided conversation consisting of curt commands and abrupt reprimands. He signed his name to two letters.

I sat and waited.

Then came the crowning touch—the thing which made Jim Fenton's little game of show-off different from that of other executives. He spun around in his chair and picked up from the long conference table behind him the bottle of vichy water which was his prize affection. A second spin and he secured a glass into which the bubbling liquid was leisurely squirted. The siphon was returned to the table behind him and he leaned back in his swivel chair. For at least a moment he twirled the glass meditatively in his fingers.

"You can waken me," I said, "when the show is over."

But nothing could disturb the even flow of his superb self-satisfaction. Eventually he drank the vichy and turned his attention to me and the folder of ads in my hand.

"What have we here?" he asked. His blue eyes were warm, generous, kindly. I recoiled instinctively. It was like seeing a keg of dynamite buried in a bed of violets.

"Nothing you'll like," I replied. "We've given you only a third of the space that you wanted for the next week. And only two small follow-up ads for the fashion show next Wednesday and Thursday."

"It doesn't matter." He smiled.

Speechless—for there is a normal limit to everything, even affability—I pushed the papers across the desk. Where, oh where, was the usual perversity, the forward-thrusting aggressiveness of his heavy shoulders, the quick burst of rage when his requests were denied? He sprawled his usual OK-JLF across the face of the folder.

"I'm afraid," I told him, "that you will have to sign each individual ad."

He looked down at his pagoda-like signature with pleased admiration. "You can't forge it, can you?"

"And I can't be sure that you won't deny having seen the ads after they are published."

He signed each page without a glance at its contents and his smile never wavered. My intimation that he was not above a little treachery was one of the things which he classed as a compliment. "The Advertising Department," he remarked, as I rose to leave, "is in for an overhauling tonight." His tone was so dulcet that, coming from him, I knew it contained a threat.

"On the contrary," I retorted, "tonight's conference is merely the usual meeting about institutional ads."

"That's what it has been before. Tonight I am going."

I attempted to shut off the expression of annoyance which betrayed me. His smile became derisive. "And," he added, leaning back in his chair, the epitome of self-satisfaction, "I have arranged that Jane Kingsley, my stylist, shall be included also."

"That should make any gathering a social success." I grinned. It was well known that only by dint of much self-control did Jane and I manage to keep out of one another's hair, although we habitually exhibited a cordiality that fooled no one. You've seen it—the pat on the back which, with only the slightest shading, becomes a stab in the same place. "Incidentally," I added, "I am going, too. The party is deteriorating in tone."

With that I left him and it was while returning to the Advertising Department from Jim's office that I met Jane Kingsley. Jane was our ready-to-wear stylist, and the first thing of which one was aware when meeting her was, invariably, her costume. She was dressed that afternoon in a simple black suit, product of the designing genius of Philip Mangone. It had what the copy writers were referring to that spring, as the "lengthened limber look" and it did well by Jane's figure. A figure which, in her grandmother's day, would have been described as lanky, but which, in our world, was known as svelte. Over her arm hung a cascade of shimmering silver foxes, voluptuous in their heavy richness. And because pink with black was very knowing just then, and not at all naïve, her handmade blouse and the excuse for a hat which crowned her pompadour were a fragile pink. She looked stunning. But then, Jane always looked stunning. Gloria had summed up the opinion of most of the staff at Cole's when she had remarked, in one of her rarely unflattering comments, that, as a stylist, Jane Kingsley was a magnificent clothes-horse.

But one look at Jane's face was enough to show me that she was, for once, completely oblivious to her appearance. She got off the elevator like a sleepwalker and, turning to the left, went down the corridor to her office, next to Jim Fenton's. In passing, she looked me squarely in the face and walked by without speaking. It was not a snub. She simply didn't know that I was there. If there had ever been any bond of sympathy or understanding between us, her expression would have distressed me. As it was, I forgot the whole episode for the time being.

Ordinarily I could be around the store a week at a time without seeing Garrison Thorpe but, as Jane disappeared into her office, whom should I meet but Garry. He was Dexter and Cole's one and only play-boy and always managed, even in an office-flanked corridor, to look as if he were heading for a Palm Beach cabana.

Margaret Blake, Garry's assistant, was with him that afternoon and they stopped a minute to indulge in the social amenities which were Garry's contribution to the harsh world of business. Then he pleaded an important conference and hurried away.

"Little Boy Blue," said Margaret, "has gone to blow his horn."

"Don't you," I asked her, as we watched his retreating figure, "ever get bored with running a nursery?"

She laughed good-humoredly. "His conferences keep him so busy! He must have read somewhere that an executive is perpetually in conference for he attends any meeting which consists of more than two people."

"He should just stay in café society and let it go at that," I said. "Socially, he's really charming and no one would have ever realized his limitations if he hadn't gone to Harvard Business School and set his heart on becoming a big executive."

Garry and Martin Cole had been inseparable companions since childhood and Martin had set Garry up in the Comparison Department at Dexter and Cole's with all the accoutrements of success—and a capable assistant to do the work. Most of the staff, taking their cue from the President, treated him with a tolerance which was half patronizing, half affectionate. All, that is, except Gloria. For handsome and wealthy bachelors with flawless social connections are not lightly dismissed by redheaded beauties with their way to make in the world.

"But Garry is an enigma," Margaret added. "He's like the deaf people who always hear what wasn't intended for them. He rejects lots of our best reports and passes some of the poorest, but now and then he cracks out with something so shrewd that it leaves me shattered for days."

"Wisdom from the mouths of babes," I said, adding skeptically, "He's probably reciting something which he learned verbatim at Harvard. When he's shrewd it's coincidence."

Back in the Advertising Department, I again stopped in at the office of my boss, Ken Holmes. He looked up and smiled at me in that very special way which meant that I was always welcome. "Sit down," he said, "I want to talk to you."

"Who," I demanded, dropping into the proffered chair, "suggested that Jane Kingsley and Jim Fenton should go to that conference at the Coles' tonight?"

"Jim pulled that one himself," answered Ken half amused, half annoyed. "He was in Martin Cole's office this morning. Apparently Jim can't endure to have company policy decided without his help. Martin had intended, when he decided to include Jim, to have the other two vice-presidents come also. But Jim had outsmarted him on that one. For the other two are out of town."

"Is Jim gunning for Mr. Otis's job as Executive Vice-President?"

"He could be," Ken admitted. "But he won't get it. Martin inherited Arthur Otis just as he inherited the presidency of the store. He can't, under any circumstances, get rid of Mr. Otis until he is thirty-five. What's on your mind?"

"Nothing. Jim is acting so all-fired smug about going tonight that anyone would think that he's just had his name entered in *Who's Who* and the Social Register."

"He's probably working on that, too," replied Ken, a shade of contempt in his cool voice. "He's our outstanding exponent of the genus known as Fourflusher."

"Don't forget Lady Jane Kingsley," I reminded him.

"Runner-up," he conceded. "Now, anything else?"

"If it's all right with you," I told him, "I'd like to take Gloria. Not because she is Mr. Fenton's copy writer, but because she takes rapid shorthand. Both Mr. Fenton and Mr. Otis have a way of thinking that they are strewing pearls of wisdom in my path and that I am not adroit enough to recognize them. I'd like to have what they say tonight on record."

Ken immediately called Martin Cole and arranged that Gloria should be included and then spun his chair around and looked out of the window speculatively. "There's something afoot, Debby," he said. "There is more than egotism in this move of Jim Fenton's. He's a smart strategist and politician. He showed that the first six months that he was in the Fashion Department. But recently there has been a new note. For some reason he dares to move in faster than good judgment would ordinarily warrant."

"How old do you suppose Jim is?" I asked.

"Middle forties, I judge. Are you interested personally?"

"Heavens, no!" I assured him. "Take on an ego like that for a life-time proposition? I'll stay a widow until I meet up with a duplicate for you." And I said it innocently enough. But then, if psychiatrists are to be credited with knowing anything at all, I must have a subconsciousness.

Ken spun his chair back to the desk and regarded me speculative-ly, a half smile in his grey eyes. "A flattering sentiment," he admitted, "although it doesn't speak too highly for your judgment. May I suggest that in the future you refrain from broadcasting it in your casual way?"

"Well!" I declared indignantly, "I wasn't proposing to you! Such conceit! Can't you—"

"*I* can," he interrupted, with emphasis upon the pronoun. Despite an effort to maintain his half playful manner, he was plainly in earnest. "I know that you scatter your declarations of affection with the aban-don of a thoughtless child and, therefore— Oh, what the hell!" he ended helplessly.

I stared at him, hurt and not a little annoyed. Still looking at me, he seemed to be wondering where to take the conversation next. I left that to him. It was his problem from here on.

"Do you girls have transportation for tonight?" he asked, after a long indecisive moment.

"We'll take my car," I told him.

He nodded absently, then rose slowly and crossed the room to the closet where his coat was hanging. "Don't go," he said as I reached the door. Turning, I watched him put on his coat and pick up his hat. Then he came over to where I stood leaning against the door frame. His face, his humorous, kindly, homely face, was troubled. "I have to go over to Jersey and get Louella," he said. "She's still pretty sick. I wish that I didn't have to take her." He stopped, looking down at me as if there was something important which he couldn't bring himself to say. "She's had periodic nervous attacks for some years now." Again he stopped and I felt that he was trying to give me a cue which I couldn't catch.

"Nerves," I ventured, "are tricky."

"Yes, very. You never know when—" Again he hesitated, seemingly unable to break through this habitual reticence regarding his personal life. "I'm going over for her and then will drive her up the Hudson."

I nodded, saying, with an attempted indifference, "We'll see you there."

He still looked disturbed and walked along toward my office. "The elevator is usually in the other direction," I pointed out. And then, in spite of myself, I smiled at him. "We'll keep it a dead secret," I promised, "but I'll still be looking for a carbon of you. And now run along and get your wife and have a nice week-end."

"Thanks," he said, and patted my arm. "Life deals out funny hands, doesn't it?" And with that enigmatic remark he turned abruptly and strode toward the elevator.

Once in my office, I dismissed the thought of Ken and his wife to face the more immediate problem of a dinner dress to wear at the Coles' that night. My available evening attire, at the moment, was more remarkable for its age and durability than for its chic, and so I had Catherine locate Edie Rothman, buyer of evening dresses in the Salon. "Edie," I asked, as her voice came over the wire, "have you a dinner dress down there that I can have right away? I'm unexpectedly going to the Coles' tonight and every evening outfit in my wardrobe looks as if it had been made at home by loving, but work-worn, hands. It must be," I added, "something that will double for both dinner and formal wear—probably something with a jacket."

"Well, let's see." There was a silence while she searched her memory. "There is a gorgeous green," she said, after a moment. "But it is a strong color and I think that it will wash you out unless you put on gobs of make-up."

"I don't wear blues or greens. Try again."

She tried again but with little success. "We're terribly low, Debby," she finally admitted. "We've been working the stock down, because there is a perfect raft of stuff coming in the first of the week—getting ready for the fashion show, you know. Would you have time," she went on, "to run over to Marsh's studio this afternoon? They have one of the best groups of designers in town and they are well stocked right now. I was there this morning and ordered several numbers. I'll phone them to stay open."

She gave me the address and putting it in my bag, I took my wraps from the closet and went down the hall to the copy writers' room—a large unpartitioned section of the northeast corner of the building. Here sprawled in magnificent disorder were a dozen or so desks, some shattered looking file cabinets and the conglomeration of clippings, newspapers, magazines, merchandise and cigarette butts which seem to be a necessary part of writing successful advertising copy.

Gloria was sitting at her desk in the far corner of the room. Seated on the desk was Garry Thorpe, looking like Newport transplanted into the merchandising business. Perched on the window sill was Clive Holland, a blond young giant who wrote copy for the men's wear departments and competed with Garry for Gloria's attention.

"But," Gloria was protesting as I entered the room, "I don't want to get married and have ten red-headed children." She tossed her mane of red-gold hair and widened her eyes, blue as gentians, so that the lashes lay black and curving against her fine skin.

"Scram," said Clive to Garry, "here comes the boss." They all three regarded me with that imperturbable expression indicative of complete lack of discipline in the ranks.

"You probably won't manage to have any red-headed children," I said. "My mother had red hair and where did it get me?"

"Nowhere, apparently," replied Clive with pleasant but devastating accuracy. "I'll bet," he added, "that Gloria was wafted to shore in a shell, like Venus, and is a daughter of the gods."

"You should write poetry—not copy." Garry was plainly put out that this flight of fancy was not his brainchild. "Gloria," he continued, pleased to be the possessor of the information, "had a blond mother and a brunette father."

Knowing Gloria's aversion to her father, who had deserted her mother in Gloria's infancy, I said, "Now that it has been established that she is a compromise of nature and not a product of Olympus, may I interrupt to tell her that she is invited to the Coles' home tonight for the institutional ad conference?"

"Garry has told me." She smiled. "He's going, too."

"It wouldn't be a conference without Garry," I agreed sweetly.

Garry beamed. "I'll drive you and Gloria up," he offered.

"I have to go to Marsh's," I said, "and buy me a rag. Maybe you had better go home early, Gloria, and do some packing for both of us." The matter of evening clothes would, of course, offer Gloria no problem, she being the social butterfly of our ménage. In fact, I sometimes suspected that I had arranged for us to share an apartment that I might indulge in the vicarious pleasure of watching youth and beauty conquer New York.

This is as good a time as any to tell you a little about Gloria. From a copy writing standpoint, she was my special discovery and protégé but she was already well-known as a photographic model when, two years before this story opens, she walked into my office in answer to an ad for a copy writer and wailed, "Now please don't decide that I can't write copy just because I'm a model. Having a straight nose and a photogenic jaw line is no proof of illiteracy."

"Lots of people are literate who can't write copy," I had retorted, a little crisply. She was really too beautiful to make any woman just eager to give her a break. But Gloria was clever and ingratiating, as well as beautiful, and finally I hired her—even agreeing that she could continue her posing for several of the national companies who desired an occasional picture. And, despite the fact that I was nominally the boss, Gloria had been doing a pretty efficient job these two years of managing me.

Some day I am going to try standing in a refrigerator just to see if the atmosphere doesn't seem cozy as compared to that of an elevator with Mr. Otis in it. I met our Executive V. P. going down in the elevator and the feeling of extreme distaste which overcame me was not the product of prescience but of past experience. For Mr. Otis, Executive Vice-President of Dexter and Cole's and second only to Mr. Cole in authority, had the distinction of possessing the most unpleasant personality in that vast organization. He took cold cognizance of the fact that I was dressed for the street and his thin, disapproving lips drew downward. Mr. Otis lived in a state of perpetual fear lest somebody, someday, sneak off and have fun on Saturday afternoon. Had he been in on the writing of the Ten Commandments, one of them unquestionably would have read, "There shall be no levity."

"Mr. Cole has disrupted the whole Advertising Department," I said mischievously, "by inviting me out to his home this week-end. I have to go and buy a dress so that I will be a credit to you."

He opened his mouth but, as the elevator stopped on the sixth floor and several stock girls swarmed into the tiny inclosure, he closed it again. We descended to the street floor in the cold silence of his disapproval and I devoted the brief interval to wondering how a man who wore brown suits—which is a warm color as men's suitings go—and was possessed of a ruddy skin and brown eyes, could emanate such a distinctly chill atmosphere. His eyes, I decided, were the answer. For he possessed the only brown eyes I have ever known which were as cold as steel. And to make matters worse, they matched his voice—a disparaging, accusing voice which flicked like a lash on one's very spirit.

At Marsh Brothers' studio, one of the assistant designers opened the already locked door and assured me eagerly that he had been more than delighted to wait for me and would gladly show me their stock. Such felicity in the middle of Saturday afternoon was most disarming and put me in an unusually receptive and pliant state of mind. After an appraising look, which made me thankful that my suit had been designed by Creed and that my hat was a little thing which Rose Valois had dashed off in one of her more inspired moments, he inquired deferentially, "Do you wish to be glamorous or very elegant?"

There was a choice for any woman! "It will be a little difficult to manage either," I replied, with pretty modesty, "but since you are so nice as to give me a choice, suppose we aim for the elegance."

Each of the four dresses which he brought in from an adjoining room proved to be an achievement in pure, unadulterated chic. "For your coloring," he explained, "I have selected only warm tones. Now this," tenderly gathering up one of the dresses and draping it against his arm, "this is my choice for you."

Of course, being mere putty in the hands of a good salesman, I took the dress he selected. And because I was phoning Andre for a last minute appointment—such a gown deserved better than an everyday hair-do—I paid but scant attention to the designer's happy chatter. The dress had, apparently, been especially designed for one of their best customers and, so he confided, I was the possessor of the only copy, a copy which had been intended for a client in Dallas. "But we will send something else to Dallas," he concluded, expansively. "This one is perfection for you, Madame, and we see perfection all too seldom in this business. Alas," with a sigh, "usually the too old or the too fat buy the most ravishing clothes."

On this frustrated note, he opened the door and bowed me out. "You will be very happy in your dress," he promised me. "I know it! I feel it!" He put his hand over his chest to show just where he knew it and felt it. "And some day, when you are in a mood for glamour, come back and we will find another gown in which you will be equally divine."

As a prognosticator he proved to be a dismal failure but as a salesman he was superb for I left the studio in a rosy glow of flattered femininity. For the first time in six years, even in the remotest corner of my soul, I had lost all consciousness of being a widow. Indeed, settling into a taxi, I murmured with unjustifiable optimism, "Twenty-seven is quite young."

This sense of exhilaration persisted through a manicure, facial and hair-do. Cecily, who took pride in keeping me habitually groomed to that peak of perfection which is imperative to the professional woman, interrupted her afternoon schedule to smuggle me into an empty booth. She ripped back a corner of the box and matched lipstick and powder tones to the rich hue of the dress. She then went vigorously to work on my hands and face.

I was soon ready for Andre's artistic touch and, for once, let my ego have a little work-out in a beauty shop. "Andre," I exhorted, "this is an occasion. My gown expresses the Spirit of Elegance and my hair must do likewise."

"But with your hair," he answered reassuringly, "anything is easy. Most hair I would have to curl especially. But yours! We will lift these curls to the top of your head, these we will draw to the nape of your neck. So!" With dexterous fingers he patted the last hair into place and stepping back, head tilted to one side, appraised his handiwork. "No flowers, no ornaments," he warned me, "the curls are enough. You must not spoil the line. It is sculptured to your features."

Amazing the hooey a woman will swallow and love!

"Behold me," I called to Gloria, bursting into the apartment at ten minutes past five, "I am a spoiled and pampered doll. Do you know of anyone who would like to take a spoiled and pampered doll and set her up permanently in this blissful state?"

"You mean legally?"

"That was my thought," I admitted. "Am I being naïve?" We opened the box and spread the dress across the bed. "I wonder where my gold slippers are?"

"I'll find them," said Gloria. "You go take your bath. That dress is a honey. Maybe, after all these years, we're going to get you out of your shell."

They almost got me to heaven!

2

The ride up to the Cole estate in Garry's convertible, with the windows up and the top down, was cold but exhilarating. We inched through the westbound traffic to the highway and rolled briskly up the Hendrick Hudson Parkway.

"When we come to another high stone wall on the left," Garry said, about two hours after we had left Fifty-seventh Street, "we shall have arrived."

Before many minutes our headlights had picked out the line of the wall and he swung into the open south gate. We rode through a wood and up a long, gently rising slope. Abruptly we rounded a curve and the lights fell full upon the house. The picture was so perfect that it hurt; for the Cole home was one of those stately and classic mansions with which, at the turn of the century, one of America's great architects had dotted the aristocratic banks of the Hudson. Of course, I didn't live in the Age of Pericles but even one who did must have found the facade of that building completely satisfying. Garry slammed on the brakes and brought me back with a jolt to the Twentieth Century. "Well, here we are," he announced, and climbing out of the car, came around to the door on my side.

"You're sure it isn't the Parthenon?" I asked.

Garry turned and regarded it speculatively. "It wasn't when I was here last."

"We might go in and find out," suggested Gloria, who was always practical about such things.

There was a great central hall into which we entered from the portico. This hall, two stories in height, was the dominating feature of the

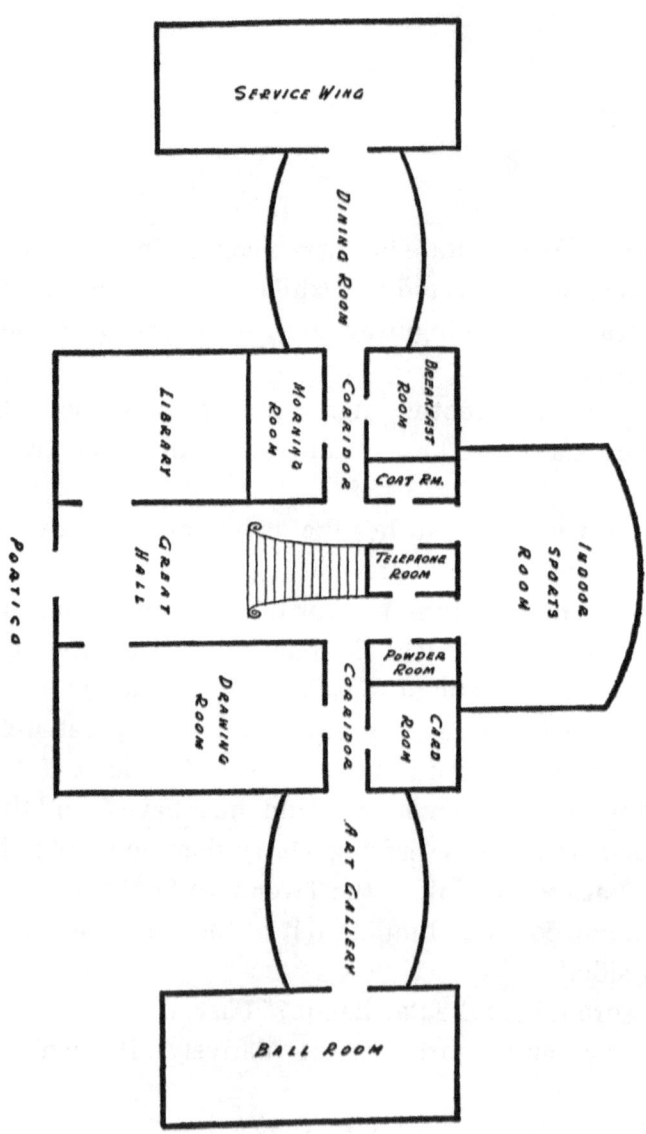

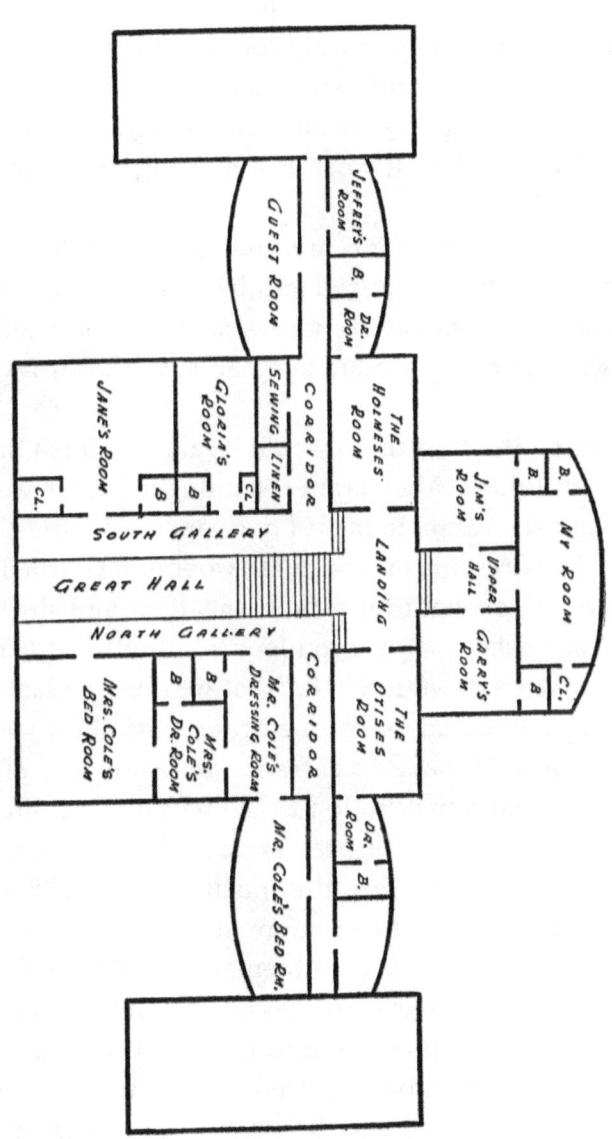

house. Two lines of fluted columns rose the full two stories and, behind each row of columns, second floor galleries extended the length of the hall from front to back. To help you to visualize the disposition of the rooms I have included detailed floor plans.

The crisp maid who entered my room a few minutes after our arrival was as British as an understatement and her name, she told me, was Stebbins. Upon starting to unpack my bags, she explained that one of the maids was ill that week-end and they were, therefore, very shorthanded.

"Mrs. Kingsley arrived a few minutes ago," she added, "and is very anxious to have her hair arranged and be assisted in dressing." It was like Jane Kingsley, I thought, to behave as if she had been brought up with a lady's maid on either hand and had never known what it was to lace a shoe.

I suggested to Stebbins that I would be glad to finish the unpacking if she had other duties. "Miss Trent is coming in before we go down," I concluded, "and she can help me if I have any difficulties in dressing."

I had finished dressing and begun to wonder if Gloria had forgotten me when there came a light rat-a-tat on my door and she looked in.

"Ready?" she asked. "Don't you look scrumptious! I thought," she added, as we started down the hall, "that we'd be the last to reach the drawing room so we could make an entrance and show you off."

"You thought we'd make an entrance and show you off," I corrected, not minding that her devotion to me had never contemplated my possible encroachment on her preserves. In fact, playing backdrop to Gloria constituted my chief role after business hours. "Your heirlooms and your ancestors are so much more substantial than mine," she'd grin, "you don't mind my usurping them, do you?" This time, however, I was destined to outshine even professional competition.

The memory of our entrance into the Coles' magnificent drawing room will always remain a bit confused. The room itself was startlingly large, its high ceiling seemingly borne aloft by white pilasters and a deep cornice molding. Sky blue walls were punctuated by heavy draperies of pale blue damask. The room was at once formal and alive as if the punctilio of tradition had been infused with the freedom and daring of the modern decorating creed. The room glowed with color. Comfortable chairs and sofas in rose red gleamed above an antique

Aubusson carpet which, in turn, reflected the colors of walls and up-holstery.

But the impact of the room itself was as nothing to the sharp stab of horror that was mine when my gaze came to rest upon the rigid forms of the other guests, now grouped about the stately mantel on the opposite side of the room. For there, silhouetted against the dancing flames, stood Lissa Cole, our hostess, wearing my evening gown, her hair, like mine, upswept to a topknot of curls. Or, to be more exact, there stood Lissa Cole staring in mingled rage and astonishment at me, paralyzed in the doorway and dressed in a perfect copy of the exclusive creation especially designed for her.

It was a bad moment for everyone. Then Ken's voice came in cool query, "Where have you two been? At a fire sale?"

You could almost see Mrs. Cole take hold of her temper and put a leash on it. But her voice was unruffled when she said, "I was under the impression that this dress was an exclusive model."

"There really is no such thing as an exclusive model these days," I answered. "If a design is good it finds its way to other markets. When I bought the dress, I was told that it was a copy of a model which had been especially designed for one of their most prominent customers. One of the assistant designers sold it to me and he would probably have had no way of knowing for whom this dress was originally designed."

"Even if he had known," observed Jane Kingsley, upon whose midwestern accent had been super-imposed a practically British accent, "even if he had known that it was Lissa's dress, he'd never have dreamed that you two would be wearing it to the same place."

"Oh, never," I agreed blandly. "It must have hurt the artist in him to have visualized this lovely dress in a dime-a-dance hall. But you know these tradespeople, Jane. No pride. They'll sell to anyone who has the cash. Anyhow," I added, turning back to my hostess, "I hope you won't mind too much. They say that imitation is the sincerest form of flattery."

"And to those of us who are connoisseurs of such matters, fate has been very kind," Garry pointed out. "Two beautiful portraits are better than one in any gallery." This seemed a good point at which to close the subject.

Our host, Martin Cole, blond, good-looking and possessed of that intangible air which bespeaks breeding, came forward. He was tall and slim, with features so finely modeled that one sensed he was primarily a gentleman and only secondarily a merchant. In this one would be wrong for Martin Cole was that rare product, an aristocrat with a trader's instincts.

Mrs. Otis was the first person to whom we were presented. The wife of our Executive Vice President was a short, plumpish woman with a high pitched, gushing voice. Her manner was a cross between Mary Boland at her most effusive and a waitress's conception of Lady Vere de Vere. And, as if to contradict this appalling lack of social poise, Mrs. Otis wore, and wore with distinction and character, a gown which had unquestionably come to life under the gifted hand of Molyneux.

"Mrs. Wood, our advertising manager," said Mr. Cole, "and Miss Trent who does our fashion copy."

"Ah," cried Mrs. Otis, dramatically clasping her hands over her breast, "ah, how wonderful! To write! To create!" She stopped to get a new angle on the handclasp and her voice lowered confidentially. "My friends have always said that I should write." Pausing to let that shaft sink in, she took my hand and murmured, "It is so bitter to know that you could send words soaring out into the world, words—"

"Yes," I agreed, thus bringing into play my remarkable gift for repartee.

Then it was time to meet Ken's wife.

Since his inexplicable behavior in the office that afternoon I had been most eager to meet his wife. One glance was enough to show that Mrs. Holmes was definitely an outsider in that little group of ultra-clothes-conscious women. She wore a dark green dress of indefinite lines and, sartorially speaking, looked as if she might have dropped into the Coles' while enroute to a church social. But her strongly chiseled features were arresting, if not beautiful, and she was plainly both intelligent and well bred.

She moved a step or two toward me, her black eyes blazing with what might have passed for the ardor of a fanatic, had the occasion demanded fanaticism, and acknowledged the introduction with a coldness that startled me. "Why, she hates me," I thought aghast.

To Gloria, Mrs. Holmes was more gracious and her rudeness to me apparently slipped by unnoticed, for Mrs. Otis was informing the others that all her English teachers had said that she really should write.

Cocktails offered a welcome diversion from Mrs. Otis's literary talents and the group around the fireplace took up the discussion of racing which had apparently been in progress when we entered the room. Lissa and Garry were both ardent track fans and Lissa played in a desultory way with the idea of having stables of her own. I sank into a chair and watched the merry-go-round go 'round. An acute psyche was not necessary to sense an extraordinary tension in the entire group, despite an apparently congenial and general conversation. The women's voices were keyed too high, the men's mirth lacked spontaneity. And certainly I, rebuffed by Louella Holmes's curt manner, and uncomfortable in Mrs. Cole's new dress, felt that the evening would prove socially difficult.

The best show, at the moment, was being staged by Jim Fenton and Jane Kingsley who were eagerly proving that they, too, belonged in that elite group to which the columnists refer as "horsey." Mr. Fenton was showing a completely, to me at least, new side of his nature. Gone was the truculent aggressiveness of his business manner. His personality, always dominating, was now actually charged with magnetism. His conversation was quick, witty, gay. So charmed was I by his almost puckish humor and so delighted by the deft way in which he shifted the conversation to keep it always flowing toward himself, that for the first time in our acquaintance, I felt a real admiration for the man. In fact, I was inclined to concede him the right to fourflush—he did it so magnificently. "That's what they mean when they say 'A devil with women'," I thought, and was startled by the sudden realization of his dynamic attractiveness.

Jane was holding up her end of the conversation with less marked ability. Her repertoire consisted chiefly of bewailing the fact that she no longer had time to attend the races unless they were comparatively near New York. "It makes one feel so out of touch," she was saying, apparently under the impression that this created the illusion of a background fraught with the costly things of life.

Mrs. Otis, plainly intent upon deflecting attention from Jane, turned to me and asked if I loved the races, too, implying that, of course, she loved them. Loving the races was one of the accepted social graces at the moment.

"I've only been to one, and then I didn't see anything," I replied.

"How in the world," demanded Jane, "could anyone go to the races and not see anything?"

"I was working for one of the fashion analysts and he sent me out to take a fashion count on shoes. I spent the afternoon walking around under the stands looking at people's feet."

"Debby has such a negative approach to her social life," commented Ken dryly.

That seemed to finish racing as a topic so we all had a second cocktail and transferred our attention to the subject of skeet shooting. Garry, Jim Fenton and both Martin and Lissa Cole were all expert, it seemed. Jane displayed a pretty timidity at the whole idea of shooting, intimating that a too feminine temperament, and not lack of sporting ancestry, accounted for her ignorance of the sport.

"Martin's the shot," confessed Garry generously. "He can beat me any time he sets out to do it."

"You are most disarmingly modest," said Martin.

"If that was intended as a pun," commented his wife, "I hope you are a better store president."

Her husband's lips tightened. "It was not so intended," he replied quietly. It dawned on me then that they had neither looked at nor spoken to one another since we had entered the room.

Mr. Otis admitted to a passion for target shooting in his youth and Mrs. Holmes, who had not spoken since acknowledging her introduction to Gloria, startled us all by saying that as a girl she could hit the bull's-eye at fifty paces. "And with a revolver," she added. "I've never tried skeet."

"That's some shooting," exclaimed Mr. Otis, startled into a show of enthusiasm. "How did you happen to take it up so seriously?"

Mrs. Holmes then explained, in her well modulated but hesitant voice, that as a child she had spent her summers at a mountain resort. Some lumbermen in a nearby loggers' camp had taught her target shooting. "I got so proficient," she concluded, "that Father had the lieutenant of the state troopers coach me at home, and while going to college, I won first or second place in several national amateur meets. The only woman in them, too." She hesitated a little. "It was my only accomplishment," she finished, suddenly shy.

"Underneath, she's sweet," I thought, and said impulsively, "It must give one a sense of great satisfaction to do something well enough to win a prize."

She turned toward me and again her eyes took on that fanatical glow. "As long as the prize," and her low voice dropped the words like separate drops of vitriol, "as long as the prize is not another woman's husband."

3

Dinner was uneventful, at least on the surface, and there was plenty of time to think during it, what with Ken on one side, not daring to acknowledge my presence and Jim Fenton on my right, completely oblivious to my existence. Time to observe and to wonder, for there were enough electric currents running around that table to have powered the City Subway System. However, they were baffling currents which emanated from various sources and flowed toward no one objective. Beneath a surface affability lay bitter hatred, desperation, greed, vindictive triumph. I know all this now. But even then, surrounded by the too brittle conversation of seven business associates and their wives, one sensed that more than the petty jealousies of professional life pressed upon us.

Lissa Cole, seated at the head of her crystal and gilt-embellished table, bestowed upon her guests a graciousness which just missed condescension and as the meal progressed it became increasingly apparent that Lissa was not above tossing off an occasional neat little snub. I found in her none of the naturalness and generosity of spirit which were her husband's chief assets. For Lissa Cole was selfish to the core, without the redeeming grace of humor or tolerance. Like so many women of her class, the search for sophistication and the paralysis of encroaching boredom had nullified what might have become a vigorous personality and keen intelligence. Her grooming was so meticulous as to create the impression that she may have had even her soul manicured.

Engrossing as was the behavior of those about me, my thoughts returned persistently to the inexplicable behavior of Ken's wife. So Mrs.

Holmes thought that I loved her husband? Sitting there, surrounded by the tossing emotions of ten other people, I flushed hotly. For I had made the startling discovery that Mrs. Holmes was right!

It was a relief when we had finished coffee—which, at Mr. Cole's request, had been served at the table—and had followed our hostess from the room. At the foot of the stairs she paused in the circle of light thrown by the candelabra flanking the staircase and turned toward us for an instant. Looking at her was so much like looking into a mirror that I gasped audibly.

"Seeing ghosts?" asked Jane. "The resemblance is astonishing, isn't it? You're about the same height and have the same coloring. But your hair is naturally curly, isn't it, Deborah?"

Gloria and I went ahead into the library. "So the cat has stopped purring at Lissa and is now showing her claws," murmured Gloria and we both laughed.

The others soon followed us into the library, leaving Lissa to the entertainment of Mrs. Otis and Mrs. Holmes—a task which I did not envy her.

If I could have just one room out of the Cole mansion for my very own, I'd choose the library. The walls were covered with walnut paneling, lifted bodily, so Mr. Cole told me, from an old English castle. Dominating the long wall on the south of the room were two identical fireplaces with over-mantel carvings executed by Grinling Gibbons. Across from the French windows, which were curtained in yellow damask, the bookcases reached to the ceiling, their arched tops displaying antique Chinese figurines of rare beauty. The tawny coloring of the Oriental rug merged into the rich brown of the woodwork and was repeated in the background of a Chinese screen with delicate floral designs.

Despite the size of the room and the formality of its background, there was a sense of intimacy and solid comfort, due probably to the comfortable, overstuffed furniture and a pleasant sense of worn and shabby books. For here was no row on row of glittering bindings that would creak at the touch of a human hand. For long years these books had been lived with and loved.

"I marvel at how completely you have succeeded in translating a mansion into a home," I said to Mr. Cole as he seated himself.

He looked up at me with a quick appreciative smile. "I love this place almost as much as I love the store," he said. And then suddenly his whole face changed, grew flushed and tense. He looked like a man who has thoughtlessly betrayed himself before unsympathetic eyes. "Suppose you sit here," he suggested briefly, and pointed to the chair on his right.

Ken sat down on the other side of me, spreading before us the material on which he had worked that morning. Gloria was on Mr. Cole's left, preparing to take notes on the pulled out shelf. The others drew up chairs and faced us.

"I have here," said Ken, "a summary of the themes covered by our institutional advertising during the past ten years. I thought—" he paused.

Martin Cole, hunting a pencil for Gloria, had jerked at the center drawer of the desk and it suddenly shot out into his lap. Gloria and I helped him to gather up the scattered contents and put them back and Ken picked up some pencils which had rolled under his chair. Lying in the drawer, plainly visible to all, was an automatic.

"Better call Mrs. Holmes," suggested Jim Fenton facetiously. "She could do a little target practice while we are working."

"That's like him," I thought with annoyance, "sneering at other people's little vanities."

But Martin Cole was saying very quietly, "Won't you come in, Mrs. Holmes? Do you want something?"

I looked up to see Louella Holmes standing in the doorway of the library, her eyes wild with accusation as she took passionate note of the fact that one of her husband's hands rested on the back of my chair and that, as a result of his efforts to pass the rescued pencils back to Mr. Cole with his other hand, I was practically in his arms.

"We were just saying," spoke up Jane, enjoying the tableau as only she could, "we were just saying that you could do a little target practicing with this pistol that we've found in Mr. Cole's drawer."

Mrs. Holmes pulled her tortured eyes away from us and looked at Jane. "Oh, I couldn't do that," she said, in a horrified whisper.

Ken sprang to his feet and even Jane looked frightened as the implication of the words dawned upon her. "But I didn't mean—" the words hung breathlessly in the still room.

"Did you women get bored over there without any masculine company?" asked Garry, as naturally as if nothing had happened. "Why don't you let me come and make a fourth for bridge?" He went to her and took her arm with such easy gallantry that I blessed the woman who had taught him that gracious gesture. "Let these lowly grubs do their work. We butterflies shall be gay." And patting the thin hand that lay on his arm, he led her quietly from the room.

The instant that Garry and Louella Holmes left the room, Martin Cole reached across my paralyzed body and, gathering up the papers under Ken's hand, said, "We'll go over these previous themes first, then we can consider several new approaches." He read slowly, in a voice so quiet, so matter-of-fact, that my numbed faculties gradually returned. The room, which had become a blur, came back into focus. But the group was well launched into a general discussion before I got around to following the thread of thought.

"That's too vague," Ken was saying. "You fellows make generalized statements about the spirit of the store being progressive, but you don't give us a peg to hang anything on."

"It's our tradition that is most important," declared Mr. Otis. "We are the only store on the Avenue which has handed down the presidency to four successive generations."

"That doesn't sell merchandise," scoffed Jim Fenton.

"What does?" countered Ken.

But Martin Cole interrupted, saying, "Go ahead, Ken, give us whatever you have there, then we'll join the others."

It took scarcely ten minutes for Ken, taking his cue from the President, to skim through the plans he had outlined and we were soon sorting out our papers and pushing back our chairs.

"Keep your mind on that relation-with-the-employee angle," Ken instructed me as we prepared to leave the room. "It's the best idea we have yet. And now you had better scram. You are an anathema to me tonight."

He dropped behind with the men and I joined Jane and Gloria who had walked down the hall and entered the small cardroom. The four players were just finishing a rubber and looked up with evident relief at the interruption.

"Who wants to play?" asked Lissa. "We can have two tables."

"I don't play bridge," I said.

"Bingo your game?" asked Garry. "Lissa, don't you have a bingo set?"

"That's over my head, too," I assured him pleasantly.

"Perhaps you'd enjoy looking at some of the things in the art gallery," suggested Mr. Cole, who had come into the cardroom behind me, adding with the deprecatory air which was his greatest charm, "A few of the portraits are supposed to be quite good."

We went into the corridor as Mrs. Holmes rose and, pleading a headache, asked to be excused. Ken went upstairs with her and Mr. Otis took his place at the card table opposite his wife. Garry offered Jane his chair, declaring that he had had enough cards for the evening, and Jim Fenton said to Gloria, "I'll beat you at pingpong."

"Too strenuous," replied Gloria, "but maybe we can find something to play standing still." They disappeared around the corner in the direction of the mammoth play room which was situated beneath my bedroom and those of Garry and Jim Fenton.

Mr. Cole and I continued on our way to the art gallery.

Some day I would like again to visit the Coles' beautiful oval art gallery, for it is now, in my disturbed recollection, only a blur of ancestral portraits. There were of course more recent works, for I do remember a magnificent portrait of Letitia Cole, Martin's grandmother, by the incomparable Renoir and one of Degas' delightful pastels drawn with the verve and subtlety for which he was so justly famous. But, for the most part, both my host and I saw the gold-framed canvasses through a haze of diversified emotions.

When we turned from a delightful Copley portrait of his great-great-great-great-grandmother—Mr. Cole having whimsically counted off the greats on his fingers and concluded with a shrug to indicate that it made little difference anyhow—I demanded suddenly, "Am I having a nightmare? Evenings like this evening just don't happen."

"You don't know the half of it, little girl," he answered bitterly. "So much is happening in this house tonight—" he broke off, as startled as I by this unprecedented departure from his habitual reticence.

We regarded the bronze head of a child in silence and then walked to another painting. "You mustn't let Louella Holmes disturb you too much," he continued. "She lost a baby about five years ago and, of course, can never have any more. Since then she's been under the care of a psychiatrist. She's older than Ken, you know, and since her illness she's had periodic attacks of believing him unfaithful. They always pass and then she goes through equally intense periods of remorse."

This revelation shocked me into a realization that there were whole facets of Ken's life which had never been turned toward me, and as I thus caught my first glimpse of them, a renewed awareness of him overwhelmed me. He wasn't just an astute and kindly publicity director. He was a man. But he was a married man. And he was unhappy. The thought hurt.

"Why did he let me come?" I asked.

"He told me as we were leaving the dining room, that he had phoned her psychiatrist this morning, and the doctor was inclined to think that the actual sight of you, especially in your normal business role, might dispel the illusion. He evidently underestimated how worthy a rival you would appear."

"In your wife's dress," I supplemented, smiling. "I'm really awfully sorry about it."

His face grew so suddenly tense at the mention of his wife that I again realized our host and hostess had spoken but once since our arrival, and then with ill-concealed antagonism. Was that what he had meant by "so much is happening in this house tonight"? But why tonight? Wouldn't trouble between him and his wife be the same just about any night and how could the entertaining of his business associates precipitate any particular crisis? It was all too hard. I gave up with an audible sigh.

"Maybe a drink would help?" He looked down at me, a solicitous frown puckering the brows above his dark eyes; so dark beneath his light hair that the contrast was always startling. "You're really knocked out, aren't you?"

We returned to the drawing room. Jim Fenton and Gloria, apparently having found no game to their liking, were standing before the fire, Gloria, as usual, playing her role of beautiful and entranced listener. Before we had advanced more than a few feet into the room, Garry thrust his head through the hall door.

"What kind of a joint is this?" he demanded. "Not a drink in the place."

"I was just going to get Mrs. Wood some brandy," replied Mr. Cole. "I'll ring for drinks for everyone." He got halfway to the bellpull, hanging by the door. "If you'll excuse me," he said, looking back, "I'll go with Garry and we'll get them ourselves."

The two of them left the room. I joined Jim Fenton and Gloria who were discussing the portrait of Benson Cole I, which gazed down upon us from the paneled overmantel.

"Mr. Otis is right," I said, "our store does have tradition. If we could get it on to paper that there have been four generations of Coles heading the store, and at the same time interpret them as the people they are—we'd have not only an advertising theme but a full length historical novel."

"Line's thinning out," Fenton assured me. He strutted over to the French windows and, drawing back the curtains, threw them open. A gust of cold air blew across to where I stood. "Inherited wealth weakens the fibre. Makes 'em soft. It takes a self-made man to hold his own these days."

"A self-made man suffering from jealousy," I thought. But, looking at him as he stood staring out into the black night, his head flung back, his nostrils distended like a highly strung race horse waiting for the starter's signal, I was suddenly afraid. He was too vital, too powerful, too sure. As Ken had said that afternoon, his insolence was more than egotism, it was based on something of which the rest of us were ignorant.

Gloria stood watching him with an expression of disdain which approached loathing. For the first time in our acquaintance, I saw the cool veneer of her composure crack and watched malice creep into the famous smile which could make weak women buy more toothpaste and strong men change their brand of cigarettes.

"What we need for an institutional headline," she said cuttingly, "is something to the effect that having had four generations of Coles is as nothing to the fact that we now have the incomparable Jim Fenton."

"Now that," I agreed, walking past him on to the terrace, "that would sell merchandise."

It was a relief to be on the terrace, cold though the air was, and it took several minutes to rid myself of the memory of the irritating chuckle which showed how much our little jibe amused and pleased him. There was something about his capacity for translating an insult into a compliment that pointed to a distortion of society's accepted ethical values.

Walking along the terrace, I crossed the portico and leaned against one of the immense pillars. Becoming more accustomed to the darkness, my eyes could now distinguish the dim line of the driveway and I walked down the steps and paced slowly back and forth before them. A quarter of an hour may have passed when a man's figure became faintly discernible crossing the portico and I stood and watched him as he ran down the steps toward me.

"You are more beautiful tonight than I have ever seen you," said Garry's voice, and he swept me up into his arms and kissed me.

"Good Lord, Garry," I said, "I'm not Gloria. I'm Debby."

He let me go with an abruptness which was definitely not flattering and said, "Why, so you are. Well, what I said still goes."

"But it doesn't go so far," I suggested dryly.

He laughed, and taking my hand tucked it under his arm, "You're solid ice," he said chidingly. "I have a drink ready for you that's guaranteed to stop the jitters from which Martin says you are suffering, but it's no proof against pneumonia."

We walked quickly around the corner of the house and on to the side terrace. Lissa was leaning against the white balustrade, faintly outlined by the light from the windows.

"I'm dummy," she explained. "I wanted a breath of air. The card room got too stuffy." She looked at me with a half smile and when she spoke there was malice as well as amusement in her voice. "*Femme fatale* of the evening," she said.

With swift resentment, I retorted, "The obvious result of wearing your clothes," and regretted, instantly but futilely, so ungracious a rejoinder.

But to my astonishment, Garry laughed, and, with a half wink at Lissa, murmured, "Touché, Debby."

And Lissa, smiling and plainly rather smug about the whole thing, took Garry's other arm and the three of us walked into the drawing-room.

Our entrance was timed to coincide with that of the card players. Jane and Mrs. Otis were discussing the last hand; Mrs. Otis's manner one of armed neutrality. Mr. Otis, severe and detached, walked behind them. At the opposite end of the room, Gloria and Martin Cole were listening to a news broadcast, their heads bent to catch the words. Jim Fenton stood on the hearth alone. For some reason, he seemed not merely alone, but ignored. I sat down in the big chair to the right of the fireplace and let the comforting brandy and glowing coals do their work.

Once thoroughly warm, I announced that I, for one, was going to bed. The idea proved unanimously popular and in a few minutes we were all trooping up the broad staircase. When we reached the landing there were general, but not too cordial, goodnights.

It was at this moment that Gloria remembered she had left her evening bag in the drawer of the library desk. She decided to go back for it, and thus precipitated a little tableau upon which we were to reflect with much interest.

"It has my compact in it," she said. "I'll need it in the morning so I'd better get it now." She ran lightly down the stairs.

"She surely doesn't use the same powder in the morning that she uses in the evening," murmured Jane, always the stylist. "Why, I use a much lighter shade for evening."

"Gloria's skin is so young," Jim Fenton pointed out, a malicious undercurrent in his voice. "She's young enough to be your daughter, Jane. A girl," he continued, with obvious relish, "doesn't need the detailed cosmetic technique of an older woman."

I thought, "When the women in this business aren't being cats, the men are," and stopped aghast to stare at Jane. She stood on the south gallery, part way to her room in the front corner, half turned toward us, her hand on the wrought iron railing that ran behind the pillars. Her face was livid with rage; her knuckles gleamed white against the black rail. For an instant I thought that she would scream at him, but she spun on her heel and, before we had caught our breath, her door slammed shut.

Surreptitiously I looked at Mr. Otis, wondering if it were his presence which had precipitated such a display of outraged vanity. His expression was as non-committal as ever, but certainly his wife was looking well pleased.

Turning, with the faintest suggestion of a shrug, Jim Fenton continued along the upper hallway to his own door, wearing that satisfied smile which the power to inflict pain brings to the faces of some men. For the second time that night, I was afraid of him.

Gloria came running up the steps, we again said goodnight and dispersed to our rooms.

Alone in my luxurious room with its heavy draperies of ice-blue slipper satin, I slipped out of the disastrous dress and into a zippered red wool robe. Deploring the lack of harmony between the pale satin of the chaise-longue and the vibrant hue of the robe, I entertained myself with wondering what a stylist would choose in the way of a negligee for such a background. It never entered my mind to go to bed. For the brandy had not cured my jitters, as Garry had predicted it would, but rather had stepped up my nervous system until it vibrated like a brittle leaf in a high wind.

The whole evening kept parading through my mind, disconcerting event after disconcerting event. Suddenly I remembered Ken's admonition, "Keep your mind on that relation-with-the-employee angle."

"I'll work on that now," I thought. "I work best when I'm keyed-up anyhow." I looked for a pencil in the desk and found none. There was nothing in my bag but a fountain pen and I never could write copy with a pen. A pencil is bad enough.

"Oh, for a typewriter!" I moaned.

Suddenly the ideas started crystallizing, phrases popped into my mind and were replaced with others still better. A whole battery of lines leaped forward, tumbling one after the other, too fast to be captured, much less remembered.

"Hell!" I said. "I'm going to the library and write. If I can get all this on paper tonight, I can go home and sleep for a week."

My own hall was dark when I slipped into it a second later, but there was a light shining from the candelabra at the foot of the great staircase. As I reached the two steps leading to the landing, a still figure standing at the head of the stairs sent my heart into my mouth and I must have made some sound for Louella Holmes turned and looked directly at me. She had been peering intently into the dim recesses of the lower hall, her negligee-clad figure taut as a tightrope walker's. Now, with no indication of surprise at the sight of me, and with her dark eyes such mirrors of desolation that I had an impulse to try, however awkwardly, to break past the barriers into that agonized soul, she turned abruptly and entered her room, closing the door silently behind her.

Much disturbed, I continued down the stairs and into the library, braving its inky blackness until I reached the desk and found the lamp. The flood of light and the familiar papers lying there brought me back to my errand and, dismissing the thought of Mrs. Holmes' tragedy, I went around to Martin Cole's desk, seated myself and pulled open the drawer for a pencil. Four pencils lay in the tray.

But the gun was gone.

It was inevitable that I should suddenly picture Louella Holmes on the balcony above me with that automatic in her hand. Why, I wondered, hadn't she shot me as I was coming down? Had she lost her courage? Had she been coming to my room, perhaps, and been so startled by my unexpected appearance that she could not go through with it? Was she, even then, bolstering up her courage to utilize that remarkable skill of hers as I returned past her door?

"Good gracious," I whispered, "if Garry were only here with another brandy! I'll never get upstairs under my own power."

Gradually my taut nerves became aware of a sound. Above me someone was pacing the floor—back and forth, back and forth—with tense, nervous footsteps. Somehow it was comforting to know that Jane Kingsley was still awake in the front room, as restless as I had been.

At last, screwing up my courage and determining to scream if the hall revealed so much as a shadow, I turned out the light and fled up the heavily carpeted stairs. Once in bed, the door securely locked, the covers pulled up to my chin, my panic in the library seemed ridiculous.

"I'm crazy," I thought; "people don't just go around murdering other people because they see a gun."

And then it came—a woman's scream, a shot, the thud of something heavy dropped from a height.

4

Exactly in what order the eleven of us reached the stair landing and two galleries was never officially established. But it could not have been more than a full minute before we stood there, a horror stricken silent group, staring down into the great hall below. At the foot of the steps, spotlighted by the candelabra flanking the stairs, Lissa Cole, our hostess, lay in a swirl of diaphanous skirts, looking, from above, like a ballet dancer who has forgotten to rise from her last deep bow. She was still wearing her evening dress, a duplicate of which hung in my closet. Near her quiet body lay an automatic, gleaming dully in the soft light.

Strangely enough, the first sound came from Jim Fenton; a strangled sound, as if an infuriated animal choked back its rage and pain. He had been the first from our corridor to reach the landing, streaking down the hall barefooted and clad only in his sleeping pajamas, a fact which, such is our slavish devotion to custom, was almost as startling as the pistol shot. Now he turned, his face suffused with passion, and stalked back to his room.

His going released the rest of us from the rigidity of our first shocked pause. Garry, beside me, started down the steps, looking so self-possessed in his sashed dressing gown, ascotted at the throat, that the words "breeding does tell" flashed through my mind. To my left, on the landing, stood the Otises, her hand in his. She had momentarily forgotten to play the fool and stood quietly staring at Lissa and, upon recalling that instant, it seemed that her expression was more guarded than startled. Mr. Otis, our Executive Vice-President, evidently felt that his authority carried over to the Cole home, for he said sharply,

"Don't touch the body," and, patting his wife's hand reassuringly, started after Garry.

For the first time I noticed Jeffrey, the butler. He stood on the right-hand gallery at the entrance of the upper south corridor. Clearing his throat with a deferential note, he asked, "If you please, sir, shall I check the door to the north wing?" and upon Mr. Otis's acquiescent nod, he came down to the landing, crossed it and disappeared into the upper north corridor.

Even now Martin Cole did not move. His hands clenched on the gallery rail, he leaned forward, looking down upon his murdered wife with a white face so drained of all feeling that it stood out like a mask in the dim light. Suddenly, on the opposite balcony, Jane Kingsley, who had been leaning against the railing in front of her own door, sank to her knees and, head buried in her arms, began to sob hysterically.

"Gloria," said Mr. Cole, "take her to her room." He came along the gallery, passed me on the landing, and followed the other two men down the steps. An expressionless Jeffrey walked behind him.

And now, at last, I turned and looked at my boss, Kenneth Holmes, and his wife Louella. They, too, stood on the landing before their door. Ken's back was turned toward me and his tall figure so effectually concealed his wife that her presence was betrayed only by the thin, veined hands which clutched his arms. I could only guess that her head was pressed against his shoulder. Suddenly she drew away from him and he stepped back a little so that I saw her face quite clearly.

"I'm so horribly ashamed," she said softly. "Can you ever forgive me?"

That he forgave her I have no doubt, but, to my consternation Mrs. Otis stepped forward and touched my arm. "Shall we go down, my dear?" she asked. She was her old effusive self again. It would not have surprised me to have been told that her friends all said that she should go in for murder, too. "To send bullets soaring through the air" . . .

But what she said was much more distressing. "Now, my dear," she whispered, "whatever do you suppose Louella meant by that?"

By the time we had reached the foot of the stairs, Arthur Otis was in full command and well launched in his routine manner of assuming that everyone was in the wrong. I thought of my encounter with him in the elevator the previous afternoon. Then he had seemed a cold and surly executive, lacking in humor and possessed of the suspicious nature of the unimaginative. Now his assumption of authority took on a sinister tone. He looked at Garry. "Call the police at once." It was said in a manner which implied that Garry should, at the same time, just give himself up. When he demanded, "Jeffrey, where are the other servants?" a stranger would have taken his words to imply that Jeffrey had probably murdered them, too.

And when he turned to me and snapped, "Stay where we can see you and don't touch that gun," I could have sworn that he just escaped uttering the word "again." Always antagonized by, and now a little fearful of his manner, I sat down on the lowest step. Garry had already gone to the telephone booth under the stairs but Mr. Cole called him back.

"Let's get our breath before we do anything," he said, passing a slim hand across his eyes as if to shut out the scene before him. "A few minutes more or less can't matter now."

"But the assailant may be escaping," protested Mrs. Otis dramatically. "Oh, to think that someone stealing through the night, some marauder—"

"Be still," her husband commanded and he flashed her a look of such stern displeasure that she caught her lip between her teeth with a quick intake of breath and, turning, walked heavily to a chair near the library door. Irritating as her manner was, it had certainly deserved no such severity and, as if in direct rebuke, Martin Cole walked quickly over to her and said, with a reassuring pat on her shoulder, "Never mind, Aunt Nora, everything will work out. Don't worry."

There was no doubting the existence of a sympathetic bond between the two as she took his hand between her own little plump ones and pressed it against her cheek, but when she spoke her voice was completely matter-of-fact. "Jeffrey," she said, "had better go at once to the servants' wing and see that everything is all right there. And Cook should be called. We will all need something hot and stimulating. It will be some time before we get back to bed. Also, Martin," her voice took on a new note of authority, "have Garry call Bill Riley. He lives up this way some place and he can stand between us and the reporters. The papers will have the story as soon as the police get the word. Also," she paused and swept her eyes about the room, "get Jack Lawrence down here. And, Martin, I want it strictly understood that you don't speak to a soul until you've consulted with Lawrence. He's your mouth-piece from now on."

She stood up, looking taller and straighter, no longer a fussy little woman humiliated by an overbearing husband, but a general giving orders to a disciplined staff. "Get to that telephone, Garry," she commanded; "we won't gain anything by delay—it will just make them more suspicious. But give Lawrence and Riley a few minutes' start on the police. And," she looked up at Ken who was walking slowly down the stairs, his amazed eyes missing nothing of the startling tableau in the lower hall, "you, Ken, get the others down here, no one should have been permitted to go back to his room." She watched his retreating figure as he went back up the stairs, and then, without a glance at her husband, walked across the hall into the drawing-room.

Garry had gone to the telephone. Martin stood staring at his wife's inert body with a curiously blank expression which held nothing of grief in it—astonishment, rather, and disbelief. I didn't dare look at Mr. Otis, fearing that it would be my lot to pay for his moment of humiliation, but presently he said, in a quite ordinary tone of voice, "I'll check the service wing on this floor." For Jeffrey had returned up the main staircase and disappeared into the upper south corridor.

Perhaps it was the unbearable sight of Martin Cole staring blankly at Lissa's body, perhaps it was a woman's instinct to see behind the scenes in someone's else home, at any rate, I followed Mr. Otis through the dining room and stopped abruptly at the door of the lighted pantry. Mr. Otis was, of all things, industriously washing his hands.

"The light switch was greasy," he explained calmly enough. His manner was so unprecedently bland that I beat a hasty retreat after an ill-concealed attempt to get a look at the offending light switch, an effort which was thwarted by a screen of tea towels. People who are behaving out of character are disconcerting at best, but with a corpse in the house they are positively unnerving. I returned to the front hall and again sat down on the lowest step.

It was but a minute until Mr. Otis rejoined us and walked up to Ken, who was kneeling beside Lissa, making as careful an examination as was possible without touching her. "Well?" he asked.

Ken stood up and, thrusting his hands deep in his pockets, said reluctantly, "I'm pretty sure she was shot from above."

Whether it was Ken's words or whether Arthur Otis had, by now, recovered from the shock of his wife's turning executive, he hurried into the center of the hall and barked, with all his accustomed unpleasantness, "Get everyone into the drawing-room at once, there are some questions which I want to ask."

"Everyone is here," replied Ken coolly. He was the only person in the organization whom Mr. Otis could not perturb.

Looking about me, I saw that he was right. Gloria and Jane had come out of Jane's room and were walking arm in arm along the gallery. Jane was obviously holding her nerves under rigid control. However, with her red-rimmed eyes and disheveled hair, she bore little resemblance to our usually chic stylist. Behind me Louella Holmes had also seated herself on the stairs. She was white and tense, but when her eyes met mine they were clear and unwavering. Jim Fenton stood on the landing, once again sartorially correct, his expression so savage that he looked more like a trapped gangster than a department store executive—though I've occasionally felt that the distinction is chiefly a matter of nomenclature. He started slowly to descend the stairs and, as if it were a signal, we all trooped into the drawing-room behind Mr. Otis—gingerly skirting the limp figure that had been our hostess.

Mrs. Otis, sitting on a large rosy-hued couch in the center of that enormous room, looked small and dejected, as if her moment of glory had been too much for a weakened spirit. "I tried to start a fire," she said to her husband with an abject, almost pleading, little smile. "There isn't enough of anything here."

Our Executive Vice-President stopped short halfway across the room, wheeled sharply and walked over to his wife. He leaned over and whispered a few words into her ear.

"But—" she started to protest.

Her husband straightened up, gave her a look of cold command and then came over to the mantel. "Will you all be seated." It was not a request but a brusque command.

By this time Garry had joined us. "They're all coming," he said. "Jack ought to be here first. He's just a few miles away and I gave him a four-minute start over the police. There's been a serious traffic accident on the Post Road about ten miles north. The state troopers have been called up there. Headquarters will get them over here as soon as possible. The Sheriff, the Coroner and the County District Attorney have also been notified." He looked white and miserable. After all, he'd known Lissa since she was a child. I motioned to the chair beside me.

"Sit down," I whispered. "Mr. Otis is going to hold a third degree. You might want to be among friends."

He sank down beside me and took one of the cigarettes I proffered. "Do you always offer your friends cigarettes out of other people's cases?" he asked, his tone edged with sarcasm.

I stared at the black and gold case in my hand. It looked familiar but was certainly not mine. "I'm sorry," I said uncomfortably, "I must have picked it up without being conscious. Murders always leave me quite unstrung."

He reached out his hand for it. "Thanks," he said, "I'll see that it gets back where it belongs."

"Don't mind Debby," said Gloria. "She's vague about things but she's no klep."

Garry ignored her little pleasantry. "There are plenty of cigarettes in that box on the table if you want any more," he said distantly.

Feeling both tried and convicted of petty larceny, I turned my attention to the activities of the others. Fenton had flung himself into an armchair across the hearth from me and was staring moodily into space, a cigar clenched between his teeth. It struck me that his habitual cigar had not been part of his social equipment when our hostess was alive. Louella Holmes had joined Mrs. Otis on the couch, a coat over her negligee. Ken, crossing the room, sat down on the couch beside his wife, slipping his arm through hers and covering the thin white hands which lay in her lap—a protective gesture which she acknowledged with a grateful upward glance. Jane Kingsley was in the chair across from Garry and beside Jim Fenton. She seemed to have become aware of her untidy appearance and was making futile little gestures toward her hair. Fenton's unkind comment upon her age came back to me. I decided she must have been in her middle forties, although, at the store, one would have guessed her age as not more than thirty-five.

Mr. Otis stood on the hearth, a self-constituted judge and jury and looked accusingly about him. "What little we are able to observe without moving the body"—the ease with which he had fallen into the habit of referring to Lissa as "the body" was nothing short of gruesome—"points to murder. Ken claims to have studied medicine and is under the impression that the shot was fired from above. Martin," turning to our host who was standing by the window, his back to the group, "is there any way by which one of the servants or, let us say, a burglar could have fired on Lissa from the landing or the galleries without being seen?"

"You know the house as well as I do," replied Martin without turning. Then he said, "Here comes a car. It is probably Jack Lawrence." He walked the length of the room to the door leading into the north corridor, pausing as he passed the couch to pat Mrs. Otis's hand. Walking away from us, he came inevitably face to face with a full-length portrait of his wife which dominated the west wall, its colors glowing and vital. The rosy-red, the blue and white which had furnished the color motif of the room, shone resplendent in their gold frame. Lissa's face looked down at him, aloof, arrogant, faintly mocking. But if this image of his wife stirred any emotions within him, there was no betrayal in his bearing. Quietly he opened the door and just as quietly closed it behind him. We turned our attention back to Mr. Otis.

That gentleman seemed to resent even the brief moment which had been required for Martin to cross the room. He jerked his head impatiently and said, "We must try to establish as accurately as possible just where everyone was at the exact moment that the shot was fired." Why, with the police en route to the house, it was his responsibility to learn where we were when the shot was fired, I couldn't see.

He turned first to Jane Kingsley. For some months I had noticed that his manner toward Jane lacked much of the acerbity with which he favored the rest of us. "Where were you, Mrs. Kingsley?"

"I was in bed, asleep," she said. "I fell asleep immediately upon going to bed and didn't hear a sound until the shot. I was very tired." Her smile intimated that he would know she was very tired. After all, hadn't she been working her fingers to the bone for Dexter and Cole? "As soon as the shot was fired, I jumped out of bed and turned on the light on the bedside table. Then I got my dressing gown and slippers and came right on to the balcony. You and Mr. Cole were already on your side of the hall. By that time I had seen Mrs. Cole," she shuddered delicately, "and I was too horrified to notice anything else."

So she's been asleep? Nervously pacing the floor in her sleep! Well, that was her story and she could keep it.

Mrs. Otis was next. She looked definitely jittery but her husband was certainly playing his cards smoothly as far as any visible reaction to her obstreperous behavior was concerned for now he attempted a smile as he said, "I know where you were, my dear."

And there the matter stood. We were left to assume that she had been in bed where she belonged.

It was then Louella Holmes's turn. There was a perceptible increase in the tension of the entire group and it was evident that none of the others had overlooked the possibility that Louella, crazed with jealousy, may well have mistaken Lissa Cole for me. Mr. Otis, with an unexpected sense of the moment's dramatic import, allowed the pause to become long, portentous even.

But before he had spoken, Ken said, in the soft drawl that was his most dangerous tone, "Louella was in bed. I was on the little outside balcony which opens off our bath, smoking a cigarette." He looked calm, almost disinterested, and continued in the same easy voice, "I was starting back into the room when the shot was fired. Louella had just thrown back the covers and was reaching for her negligee when I got to the bedroom."

At last Mr. Otis had something into which he could really get his teeth. The coldness of his manner grew positively deadly. "Then you were not with your wife when the shot was fired," he pointed out with vindictive satisfaction. "Your suite has exactly the same floor plan and furniture arrangement that ours has. And the balcony beyond the bath is farther from the bedroom than the hall door is from the beds. Mrs. Holmes could have—"

"Mrs. Holmes could have done nothing except what she did do, and that was to reach for her negligee and slippers and stand up ready to rush to the door. Even as it was, I reached the door first." Ken's voice matched ice with ice. He paused an instant, not with indecision but rather to make his words more emphatic. "No one," he continued, "has any right to question us except the police. Both Louella and I will be very glad to talk to them when the time comes."

Garry murmured softly, "That's telling him," and Gloria gave my knee a cautious little nudge. Personally, I could have cheered.

I couldn't have cheered for long because Mr. Otis promptly turned his attention to me and I knew that it was no accident that he decided to hear my story immediately following that of Louella Holmes's. I had just about screwed up my courage to the point of following Ken's lead and refusing to submit to questioning when I realized that Mr. Otis would still be Executive Vice-President when we got back to the store on Monday.

"I was in bed when the shot was fired," I informed him grudgingly. "But I hadn't been there very long. Maybe two minutes. I'd been down to the library."

There was a sudden stiffening of attention throughout the room. Eight pairs of eyes focused upon me, some merely curious, some accusing. Mr. Otis was plainly dazzled by the wealth of incriminating possibilities that lay before him.

"And what were you doing in the library?" His tone, as always, was infuriating, carrying as it did unspoken inferences of guilt.

After toying briefly with the idea of replying in an offhand manner, "Oh, I just went down to commit a little mayhem," I explained, courteously enough, that, having been unable to sleep, I had gone to the library to write some copy.

"You couldn't sleep? And why not?" His tone implied that, as everyone knows, people contemplating murder seldom can sleep.

"The brandy that I drank just before going to my room was too stimulating. I often can't sleep after a drink. It affects me as coffee affects some people, only more so."

"Next time we'll give you more," said Garry conversationally, quite as if the ten of us had gotten out of bed at two A.M. to discuss my reaction to alcoholic stimulants. "If you'd had two or three drinks they'd have relaxed you."

I said, "Thank you, I'll remember that."

Mr. Otis, looking somewhat baffled by this excursion into the realm of good fellowship, snarled, "And where is the copy you wrote? You surely have that as evidence of your purpose in going to the library at two o'clock in the morning?"

This was treacherous territory and I advanced cautiously, explaining the sudden influx of ideas, the search for a pencil and the hasty resolution to go down to the desk.

"And you couldn't use a pen to write out your ideas?" This really puzzled him. It was simply beyond his comprehension and therefore any explanation was useless. I shook my head.

"And after you reached the library, what did you do?"

Mr. Cole and his attorney, Jack Lawrence, had come into the room from the hall. Mr. Lawrence looked like a movie director's dream of a society barrister. Approaching fifty, tall and aristocratic in bearing, his strong, regular features and black hair with white winged temples would have been all too perfect had he not also been possessed of a keen, intelligent expression and alert, penetrating grey eyes. Looking at him, I was vaguely comforted to know that he stood between us and the coldly impersonal police—although just who comprised "us" was a little difficult to determine at the moment. The two men stood waiting while I answered.

"I turned on the desk lamp. Then I sat down in Mr. Cole's chair and opened the drawer."

The tension in the room was electric. At least one person knew unequivocally why I hesitated. The others certainly guessed. Mr. Otis, without moving seemed to lean forward a little; but it was of Ken that I was most acutely aware. I couldn't do this to him!

"There were several pencils," I continued, "but by the time I got the drawer open and the light on and everything, my inspiration didn't seem so brilliant as it had seemed upstairs and—"

"Was the gun in the drawer?"

"I didn't see it."

Again the triumphant note in his voice, "And what did you think when you saw that the gun was gone?"

"What she thought," said Martin coldly, "has no bearing on the facts either now or at any future time."

Gratefully, I filed away this cue to my interview with the police. As if completely satisfied with the results of his investigation, his highness on the hearth turned and rested one elbow on the mantel. His whole bearing indicated that the essential points of the case having been ferreted out by a master intelligence, the investigation could now be handed over to lesser minds.

"Debby," asked Ken quietly, "did you see anyone when you were going up or down the steps?"

This was the question for which I had been waiting and the answer was completely spontaneous. "No, I didn't," I told him, calmly.

"Did you," it was Martin Cole speaking now, "did you see any light in the drawing-room, the card room or the dining room?"

"No. The drawing-room door was closed. However, I remember having a vague feeling that it had been open when we went upstairs." It was good to be back on the firmer shores of veracity.

Gloria shifted on her stool so that she was facing Mr. Cole. "The drawing-room door was open when I went back to get my bag," she volunteered. "And it was open again when we came out on to the balcony after Lissa was—after we heard the shot."

Our host nodded abstractedly. "Does anyone know why Lissa came downstairs, presumably to the drawing-room?"

No one ever answered that question. There was a roar of motors on the drive, headlights flashed through the front windows, cars screeched to a stop and heavy masculine footsteps came pounding across the portico.

Arthur Otis's dictatorial powers were ended. The state troopers had arrived.

5

When the hall doors swung inward and Jeffrey stepped across the threshold to announce, "The police have arrived, sir," a young lieutenant in a state trooper's uniform followed closely at his heels. He was a blunt-nosed youngster with sunburned, straw-colored hair, and shoulders which pressed, with no need of padding, against the square lines of his jacket. His manner was unnecessarily authoritative, the determination not to be impressed by his surroundings resulting in a too pronounced swagger.

Mr. Cole advanced toward him. "I am Martin Cole," he said, his manner so natural that the officer relaxed perceptibly. "These are all my house guests." He looked at the young trooper inquiringly. "What can I do to help you in your investigation?"

"You'll all have to stay here together until the Sheriff and Coroner arrive," replied the lieutenant. "My men are checking up on the rest of the house. The sergeant is getting some further information from your butler now. When he's through, I'll ask some questions. I understand that no one has touched the body?"

"Right," answered Martin.

The officer returned to the hall and no one moved or spoke until he again entered the drawing-room and closed the door behind him. He picked up a small chair from against the wall and walked over to the hearth which Mr. Otis was still monopolizing, thereby considerately shutting off the heat from the fire which Jeffrey had unobtrusively built, and planted himself firmly beside that would-be tyrant. They sized one another up and then Mr. Otis introduced himself—not failing to indicate the extent of his importance in the Cole organization. The effect of this was exactly opposite to the effect of Martin's easy manner and the young lieutenant's swagger grew more evident.

"Can't you find a chair?" he asked with studied insolence, and, setting his own down so that he was in the center of our semi-circle, he looked curiously at the group before him.

"I'll question the butler first," he said. "He'll be in in a minute."

We sat in an unnerving silence until Jeffrey entered the room, to stand just inside the door, his shrewd eyes upon the trooper, his deference so bland as to suggest disrespect. "About the upstairs corridors," he was asked, "could anyone have shot Mrs. Cole from either of the galleries and then have escaped along the north or south corridor into the wings?"

"No, sir. That would have been impossible, sir. It is our custom to keep the door of the north corridor always locked unless some of those bedrooms are in use. When I retire I lock the door leading to the servants' wing. The door between the kitchen and the pantry is also locked, as is the door leading to the art gallery. Thus neither of the staircases in the wings can be used to reach the main part of the house."

"Were all of the doors locked as usual tonight?"

"Absolutely, sir. No one could have passed from the galleries into the wings of the house, sir."

"When you came on to the gallery, after the sound of the shot, what did you see?"

"Mr. Otis, sir."

Mr. Otis looked annoyed, "Yes, yes, of course, I went on to the landing at once, as all of us did. In fact, I may even have been the first person on the landing. Although I believe Mr. Cole's door opened simultaneously."

"No, sir," said Jeffrey, definitely, "I beg your pardon, sir. Mr. Cole arrived almost last. His bedroom is beyond his dressing room and he had a greater distance to come than most."

So it was Jeffrey who fired the first gun in Martin Cole's defense. Mr. Otis's look of annoyance increased as this effort to place Mr. Cole near the scene of action backfired. I grew very fond of Jeffrey.

Upon the butler's withdrawal from the room, Arthur Otis sullenly surveyed the group before him and, apparently reaching the conclusion that this brush with Jeffrey had passed unnoticed, turned to the lieutenant. "I see you have a list of all the guests in the house," he said. "I have established a few facts regarding their actions just prior to the murder. If you would be interested—"

"I'll find things out for myself," retorted the blunt-nosed young officer. His voice carried more authority than his face.

"Who," he asked, "was the first to enter the upper hallway?"

I looked at Mr. Fenton. He was staring at the portrait of Benson Cole I, which had occasioned his outburst regarding the impotence of those who inherit their wealth. His expression was puzzled.

"Jim," said Garry brusquely, "snap out of it."

Jim Fenton shifted his eyes to the lieutenant.

"Your name?" demanded the officer.

"Fenton."

The lieutenant made a check mark on his list and asked, "Was there anyone in the hall or on the landing when you came out of your room?"

"There was no one in our hall," Jim frowned a little, searching his memory, "I don't remember anyone on the galleries. I believe Mr. Otis was in front of his door on the landing when I opened mine."

"No," the word shot out venomously. Our Executive Vice-President advanced a step. "You know damn well I wasn't in front of my door when you opened yours. You were already on the top step when I came on to the landing."

Jim shrugged and sank back into his chair, plunging his cigar into his mouth and his hands into his pockets, plainly disinterested in the whole discussion. After a second or two our Executive Vice-President, now thoroughly disgruntled, turned to the young trooper and continued harshly, "Someone might have got down those steps without our seeing him, but I very much doubt it. At any rate I would have heard footsteps. Of course, a very athletic person might have jumped over the railing, but that isn't likely, it being a drop of more than twenty feet. At any rate we would have heard the thud of his landing on the floor below."

"But there was a thud," interrupted Jane eagerly. "Right after the shot." She had recovered herself amazingly and seemed almost animated. Perhaps on second thought she found the situation less appalling than it had at first seemed.

"That thud which we all doubtless heard, was the dropping of the gun. Whoever fired it, then tossed it into the middle of the hall—as you probably noticed." It was Mr. Otis who answered, looking indulgent at this feminine incapacity to reason.

"In that case," said the lieutenant, looking us over with definite distaste, "we seem to narrow the choice down to some member of the house party." We sat and stared at him. I, for one, felt quite ill. Gloria reached up and slipped her hand comfortingly into mine.

The young trooper planted his feet wide apart on the gleaming Aubusson carpet and set a hand on each knee, thumbs turned outward. The pose cocked his elbows to each side, arrogantly. He looked like a schoolboy who has been invited to act as mayor for the day.

He turned to Jim, the first person to his right. "Where were you, Fenton, and exactly what were you doing?"

"I was in bed."

"Asleep?"

Mr. Fenton hesitated, "Awake. I had been asleep. I woke up a few minutes before the shot."

"Something waken you?"

"I thought that I heard a door close. After that it was perfectly quiet. The instant I heard the shot I tore out of bed, across the room and into the hall. I was the first to come into our hall. Mrs. Wood's door was closed and so was Mr. Thorpe's. I ran down to the landing. Mr. Otis was there, as I have said. I was too stunned by what I saw to register the order in which the others arrived."

"Which one is Mrs. Wood?"

"I am," I said.

"Do you agree with his statement, Mrs. Wood?"

"Yes, Officer."

The lieutenant looked around the group. "Which one is Mr. Thorpe?"

"I am," said Garry.

"What's your story, Thorpe?"

"In bed asleep," answered Garry laconically.

"Did you hear any unusual sounds, such as the door closing, which Fenton heard?"

"Not a thing."

"Did you retire immediately upon going to your room?"

Garry hesitated only a split second, yet that brief interval robbed his answer of conviction. "Right away," he said.

"What did you do immediately upon going to your room?" pressed the lieutenant.

"Undressed and went to bed," said Garry, in such a believe-me-or-be-damned tone that we all stared at him.

I thought, "Can he be such a snob that he high-hats the police?"

Plainly disgruntled by such obvious lack of enthusiasm, the youthful officer shifted his inquiring gaze to Gloria and stopped short. It was apparently the first time that he had really looked at our famous beauty and the impact sent him sprawling—emotionally speaking, of course. Gloria said sweetly, "I am Gloria Trent," and smiled. Then she volunteered the simple fact that she had been asleep when the shot rang out, having gone to bed immediately upon reaching her room. Her information was no more illuminating than Garry's but the lieutenant relaxed considerably under her more eager spirit of cooperation, not to mention her other assets.

"Miss Trent went back to the library for her evening bag when we were retiring," said Mr. Otis. "Perhaps she saw the gun in the drawer at that time?"

"I don't know if it was there or not," she told him earnestly. "I didn't open the center drawer. My bag was in the left-hand drawer under the pullout shelf that I had been writing on."

"That's right," Garry volunteered. "I saw her put it in as we sat down."

The trooper looked a little annoyed that this interesting avenue of inquiry should be so promptly closed, but apparently finding no further excuse for looking at Gloria's eyelashes, he forced his attention to less enjoyable details.

"Mrs. Otis," he said. "Which one is Mrs. Otis?" Before the plump little woman on the couch could answer the lieutenant lifted his hand for silence and we all listened.

For the third time there was the sound of racing motors, and two cars swung around the curving driveway and skidded to a stop. "That'll be the Sheriff and the Coroner, most likely," said the young officer. He was plainly relieved and, rising, picked up his chair and carried it back to its place. When he left the room a moment later Martin Cole, Jack Lawrence and Mr. Otis followed him. They left the door open and the rest of us stared into the hall with unconcealed curiosity.

Lissa's body was not visible from where we sat, but the hall was filled with hurrying, efficient looking men, several in uniform, most of them dressed in civilian clothes. Gradually the confusion subsided and after what seemed an interminably long time, two troopers passed the drawing-room door carrying a stretcher on which they bore Lissa Cole from her exquisitely appointed home. Then a bustling young man entered the room with a card table which he set up near the door to the north corridor and proceeded busily to set out his fingerprinting equipment.

"If you'll be kind enough to go over to that little table," the lieutenant said, returning from the hall and motioning toward the card table, "we'll make a record of everyone's fingerprints."

We rose slowly. I was stiff and, suddenly terribly tired. The fear that Ken Holmes might have to suffer the horror of finding that his wife had mistaken Lissa for me, was an intolerable weight. Of all the people in my personal world, Ken was the most generous, the most understanding, the most lovable. Even before the astonishing revelation of my real feeling for him, it had been Ken who had guided and steadied me. For Ken to suffer would be unbearable; to lose this precious friendship, unthinkable.

We had seen Martin Cole for the last time in that long and wearisome night. Months later I learned that he was in the card room undergoing a merciless grilling at the hands of the District Attorney. We were left temporarily to the watchful surveillance of the young lieutenant. Soon Jeffrey entered from the hall. He bore a large tray laden with steaming coffee and luscious looking chicken sandwiches and the manner in which we fell upon that food was an indication that there is nothing more stimulating to the appetite than a good murder in the house. Garry passed a cup of coffee to the lieutenant and then offered him a sandwich. "Did they find anything in our rooms?" he asked genially.

"I wouldn't know," replied the lieutenant. He munched thoughtfully on the sandwich and then, as if not wanting to appear ungrateful for the hospitality, he added, "It's definite that the shot came from upstairs."

Jim Fenton aroused himself from the trance-like state in which he had been immersed since entering the room and asked, "Can they tell from the way she was lying the direction from which the bullet came?"

We all looked at the young officer expectantly. Everyone stopped chewing and coffee cups halted in mid-air. Mr. Otis, who had proved himself superior to the demands of hunger, leaned forward in his chair. "They don't know," said the lieutenant. Then, as if to prove that he was not deliberately withholding information, he continued pleasantly, "The skirt of Mrs. Cole's dress was swirled about her. She undoubtedly spun around when the bullet struck her. She screamed first, according to the evidence, so she may also have been turning to escape. There's no way of guessing how far she turned or where she was facing when she started to turn."

We subsided into silence and finished our sandwiches and coffee. It began to look as if we might spend the rest of our lives in that drawing-room, but eventually there was a tap on the door and the lieutenant opened it. After a whispered consultation he turned back to us. "Mr. Otis," he said, "you will please go to the library."

After that things moved quite rapidly. Mr. Otis could not have been gone longer than fifteen minutes when his wife's name was called and she, too, vanished across the hall. Ken was third, Jane fourth, and Garry fifth. Then the lieutenant called, "Miss Gloria Trent."

Gloria left the room with that easy long-legged stride which characterizes the professional model. The young lieutenant looked after her pensively. "You're next," he said, turning to me as the door closed. "Then Mrs. Holmes. Then Mr. Fenton."

It took Gloria a very few minutes to tell her brief story and then it was my turn to cross the long hall to the library.

Jack Lawrence, the Sheriff and the Coroner—a tobacco-stained creature who looked like some politician's brother-in-law—were alone in the room except for a sallow-faced young man who sat at a little table drawn up beside the desk, his shorthand notebook before him. The high polish of the desk itself was blurred by fingerprint powder which had been too hastily wiped away. Mr. Lawrence introduced me to Sheriff Dodd and the Coroner, whose name escapes me at the moment, and then explained that the information required was merely a statement of my whereabouts at the time of the murder, or any knowledge in my possession bearing directly upon the murder; that he advised brevity and a close adherence to actual fact; and finally, that I had a right to counsel if I so desired. In short, what I said would be used against me.

Sheriff Dodd was heavy set, of slightly more than medium height, undistinguished but intelligent looking, with shrewd eyes which had, as I later discovered with gratitude, the capacity to twinkle. But there was no spark of humor in them now as he looked me over with cold dispassionate appraisal. Inwardly quivering, I seated myself, facing him across the desk. He shuffled through some papers, selected one headed by my name and glanced over it.

"I see that you have already stated that you came down to the library about two o'clock. You claim that the gun was gone from the drawer. There seems to be some question as to just why you found it necessary to come to the library at that time. Suppose you explain that first."

So Mr. Otis had been planting little seeds!

"I don't know how much personal acquaintance you have had with advertising copy writing," I said, preparing to plunge valiantly to my own defense. "It is not an occult art despite the fact that some copy writers would have you so believe. However, each ad must have behind it an idea. Getting that idea and expressing it so succinctly that the reader will not only read but desire to buy—that, in a word, is the job of the copy writer. So much for the merchandise ads. Institutional ads sell, not specific merchandise, but the 'spirit' of the store. They are good will ads. They are the devil to think up and worse to write.

"Thinking up the next group of institutional ads, and writing them, is my job. After I retired to my room I was restless. My mind was, naturally enough, running on the ads we needed and a train of thought began to develop. I earn my salary simply by virtue of the fact that I sometimes have ideas. When they come, and they are no respecter of time or place, they must be written down. It was to write down those ideas that I came to the library."

"Had you nothing to write with in your room?" Arthur Otis again!

"Nothing but a fountain pen and some small size correspondence paper. I am accustomed to a typewriter or, if that is not available, a pencil and large pieces of paper. A bricklayer could, conceivably, set in his mortar with a butcher knife, but he'd work more professionally with a trowel."

The Sheriff's blue eyes twinkled. "We come to a third point," he said amiably. "If the ideas were so valuable to you, why didn't you write them down when you reached the library?"

No amount of thinking had given me any method for dodging this question and its implications. I repeated briefly what I had told Mr. Otis in the drawing-room.

"There was, I believe, an incident which took place in this room last night," his voice was smooth and pleasant, "which might have had some bearing upon your fright at finding the gun gone?"

I shook my head. "There was no sense of fright. I was merely disturbed. Also I would like it clearly understood that no incident took place which is connected in my mind with the subsequent murder of Mrs. Cole."

The Sheriff nodded absently and swung one foot tentatively to the top of the desk. Then, thinking better of it, he shifted his chair a little and perched both feet on the rim of the waste basket. The Coroner leaned forward, whispered something and then subsided into his chair.

"Did you," the Sheriff asked, "see anyone or hear anything which might have any bearing upon the case?"

This was, of course, my cue to tell of having met Louella and of having heard Jane pacing the floor. But, following my impulse of the previous questioning, I replied in the negative. There were other questions about my background and the length of service at the store but nothing which bore any direct relation to the murder of our hostess.

Suddenly, the sallow young man whose head had been bent over his notebook as he took down the conversation let out a little chuckling sound and we all turned to stare at him. But he wasn't laughing.

"Getting worse?" inquired Sheriff Dodd solicitously.

The young man nodded. "I'll finish," he said, between clenched teeth, "it just comes in spasms." Then, in answer to my questioning look, he added, "Chronic appendicitis. Anyhow, chronic up to now."

"One more thing," said the Sheriff, turning back to me. "You and Mrs. Cole were wearing identical dresses, you are approximately the same height and coloring, your hair was dressed much the same."

"Yes." There was nothing else to say.

The secretary's pencil rolled to the floor and he suddenly slumped in his chair. Mr. Lawrence and the Sheriff hurried over to him and, under the interested scrutiny of the Coroner, carefully carried him to the couch between the east windows. The trooper who had been lolling outside the library door came in at Sheriff Dodd's call and phoned for an ambulance. While we waited for it the Sheriff called his headquarters and left instructions for another secretary to be sent out. A few minutes later they called back. There was no one available on short notice, but they'd do their best. A minute later the phone buzzed and Dodd lifted the receiver.

"The devil you say!" he exclaimed after listening for a minute. "Why must everything happen at once? I'll get away from here as soon as possible. Yeah! I'll tell Bill to go over."

He hung up the receiver and turned to the Coroner. "There's been a brawl in a gin mill. One of 'em got stabbed. You better get over there and I'll come as soon as I can manage it."

The Coroner shifted his tobacco from right to left. "Eyetalians," he opined disdainfully and left the room.

The Sheriff picked up the phone again and then twirled about and faced me. "How's your shorthand?" he demanded.

I thought of Gloria's excellent shorthand but my own curiosity overcame me. "Fair. I use it occasionally at the store and take down one or two news broadcasts a week to keep in practice."

They moved the small table a little farther away from the desk and brought the tawny Japanese screen to conceal me. Scarcely were we settled than the trooper tapped on the door and entered, a strapping ambulance driver and dapper intern at his heels. After a cursory examination and a few questions the young secretary, who had regained consciousness, was carried from the room.

Louella Holmes arrived promptly. Mr. Lawrence introduced her to the Sheriff and then gave her the same instructions and advice which he had given me. To the Sheriff's question regarding her whereabouts at the time the shot was fired, she repeated the story Ken had told in the drawing-room, namely that she had been lying in bed waiting for him to come in from the balcony.

"Our dressing room and bath are over the northwest corner of the dining room—if an oval room can be said to have a corner," she explained. "There is a small balcony which opens off the bath room. Kenneth had gone there for a smoke. He couldn't sleep. I was restless too. I was just lying there waiting for him." Her voice, which had begun with a note of assurance, wavered uncertainly as she brought out the last sentence. Brevity would have been more convincing.

"Did you know that he was on the balcony?"

"Yes"—an instant's hesitation—"I did," she added, again ending on a note of uncertainty.

"While he was on the balcony, did you leave your bedroom?"

"No."

I thought, "She doesn't lie very persuasively."

"Think back, Mrs. Holmes," urged the Sheriff, "this is very important."

"I didn't leave the room while he was out," she murmured.

"In that case," the Sheriff's voice was suddenly relentless, "since your finger-prints were found on the center drawer of this desk, we can only assume that your husband knew of your trip downstairs."

"Oh, no," she cried, "there couldn't have been fingerprints. I used a handkerchief to open the drawer." There was a sharp intake of breath and then she sighed resignedly. "I'm afraid that I'm not very clever. I'd better tell the truth, hadn't I?"

"That's safest," agreed Sheriff Dodd more gently. "You see, nervous people are apt to fumble when trying to keep their hands covered with a handkerchief and so betray themselves. I am to understand, then, that your husband knew of your coming downstairs?"

"But I didn't mean that," she protested in horror. "Oh, I didn't realize what I was saying. Kenneth has no idea that I came downstairs." She was sobbing, quick little gasps of terror and remorse.

"Immediately after Mrs. Cole was murdered, you were overheard to say that you were terribly ashamed. Were you ashamed of having committed murder?"

"No, no. Please," she pleaded, "please try to understand. I have done a terrible thing. Kenneth must not be made to suffer for it. I meant that I was ashamed of my jealousy. I had accused him of being in love with Mrs. Wood." She was crying again, but obviously struggling for composure. When the Sheriff spoke again his voice was reassuring.

"I understand that you have been very ill. Suppose you just tell me your story."

She told it haltingly, but with a pathetically earnest effort to be accurate. It summed up, briefly, to this—

She and Ken had retired early and she had accused him of having brought me to the Coles' for the purpose of humiliating her. When she finally fell into a doze, some time after she heard the rest of us come upstairs, Ken was pacing the floor of the bedroom. She awoke later to find herself alone. The bedside lamp was still burning but there was no light in the dressing room or bath. Her first thought was that Ken had gone to some rendezvous with me.

"I was out of my mind," she moaned. "It was an obsession. While I lay there, I remembered what Mrs. Kingsley had said in the library, 'You could do a little target practicing.' The words kept running through my head, 'you could do a little target practicing, you could do a little target practicing.' The next thing I knew, I was going down the stairs."

She told then of her trip to the library. The drawing-room doors were closed and she had been sure that Ken and I were in there. She had gone into the library and snapped on the light at the hall door. Then she had walked across the room and pulled out the desk drawer.

"Well?" prompted the Sheriff.

"The gun was gone," she said. There was such flat finality in her tone that I believed her implicitly. "I stood staring into that drawer and it was as if I were wakening from a horrible nightmare. I saw myself as a woman who had wanted to commit murder. I loathed myself."

She had closed the drawer and gone back upstairs. Upon reaching her room she had sat down on the side of the bed and had been about to lie down when the sound of the shot brought her to her feet.

"Then you were not still in bed when your husband entered the room?"

"No," she admitted. "My bed is very close to the door. I'm afraid I already had my hand on the door when I heard Kenneth speak my name. I turned and saw him coming in from the dressing room. The realization of how terribly I had wronged him nearly paralyzed me. He crossed the room and picked up my robe from the bed and handed it to me. While I was putting it on, he went out on to the landing and I followed him almost immediately."

She sobbed a little and then gently blew her nose. "I was so absorbed in the great injustice which I had done Kenneth that it was some time before I realized the others might consider it mistaken identity. But I didn't do it, Mr. Dodd, I didn't," she concluded piteously.

"You must have reached your room about the time that Mrs. Wood left hers. Did you see her?"

There was a silence. "Don't shake your head," he told her, "I must have a verbal reply."

"No." Poor, tragic, Louella Holmes, trapped by the lie that I had told to shield her!

There was but little more and nothing of importance. When Mrs. Holmes left the room, the trooper came in to report that the young secretary had reached the hospital and would have an appendectomy Sunday afternoon. He then went to call Jim Fenton.

"Sit down," I heard the Sheriff order abruptly.

There was a sound of rustling papers. Overcome by curiosity, I leaned back and peeked between the folds of the screen. Mr. Fenton was sitting opposite the Sheriff and as always, when seated, he appeared a heavier man than he actually was. With massive shoulders thrust slightly forward, he looked definitely ready and able to fight. Gone was the stunned look we had seen earlier that night. His blue eyes narrowed and grew wary as the Sheriff took up a letter, hand written in a massive scrawl on heavy white correspondence paper.

"This letter," said the Sheriff, "was found in Mrs. Cole's possession. It says in part, 'Since you are convinced that Martin will fight to the last ditch any effort on your part to secure a divorce, it is imperative that we continue to keep the whole thing very quiet and attempt to allay any suspicion which may have arisen. There are ways of doing everything and this, like everything else, can be done. You must believe that I know a way out.'"

There was a faint rustle as the letter was tossed back on to the desk. "That letter is signed simply with a J.," Sheriff Dodd continued. "You will probably not deny having written it?"

"I wrote it." His voice was both sullen and defiant.

I turned a little sick. Here was the perfect motive for Martin Cole to have murdered his wife.

6

There was a moment of silence after Jim Fenton made his, to me at least, dramatic admission. Then the Sheriff said, "You are obviously aware that Mr. Cole has, on previous occasions, refused to grant Mrs. Cole a divorce unless she will accede to certain stipulated conditions. Is that right?"

"Right."

"Your letter carries an inference that Mrs. Cole may be able to obtain a divorce without acceding to her husband's demands. On what grounds do you base this assumption?"

There was a long silence. Finally Mr. Fenton said, "I reserve answer for advice of counsel."

Jack Lawrence put in cuttingly, "I can give you the name of a good shyster lawyer."

"Thank you," replied Fenton evenly, "but I have already retained one."

"Score one," I thought. There was a quality about the man that caught the imagination. Much as you might despise his brazen egotism, the very magnitude of it was challenging.

The Sheriff now shifted his questions from the contents of the letter to the subject of Mr. Fenton's whereabouts at the time of the murder. Although knowing, from several disastrous experiences at the store, that Jim could lie convincingly, even charmingly, there was a ring of sincerity in his prompt answers which impressed even me. He repeated substantially what we had already heard in the drawing-room.

Next came a series of questions concerning Mr. Fenton's personal life which traced his career up to the present time. He had come to Dexter and Cole's about a year earlier from a well-known store in Dallas,

Texas. Prior to that, a somewhat checkered career had led him through various mid-western and coastal cities including Chicago, Kansas City, Denver, St. Paul and San Francisco. But he had always been in the fashion business and traced a steadily ascending career to his present post of Vice-President of Fashions at Dexter and Cole's.

A real surprise came, however, when he admitted having been married twice. This was the more astonishing because he was popularly supposed to be a bachelor. Actually he had received his second divorce decree just three months before Lissa Cole was found dead at the foot of her own elegant staircase. However, the decree having been applied for three years previously, and his first meeting with Lissa Cole having taken place only about eight months before she was murdered, the circumstances surrounding his divorce seemed in no way connected with the matters at hand.

"You have no children?" the Sheriff asked.

Fenton laughed, the peculiar laugh which heralds the coming of a salacious story when the men get together in a corner. "That's a hard question for a man to answer," he said, "but neither Mrs. Fenton blessed me with an heir. I would make such a wonderful father, too." The man was incredible in his determination to represent himself as a renegade from the accepted laws of decency. He seemed to glory in calling down upon his arrogant black head the contempt of other men, as if, in some mysterious way, it proclaimed him superior to the standards by which society is bound.

The Sheriff then attempted to elicit further information regarding Mr. Fenton's relationship with Lissa, who, an orphan since childhood, was the last of the Dexter line. Her uncle, William Dexter, had been a debonair man about town who left the running of Dexter and Cole chiefly to the capable and conscientious Benson Cole, Martin's father. All I succeeded in making out of the Sheriff's questions was that the provisions of William Dexter's will had created an impasse in Lissa's divorce plans.

No amount of questioning elicited any further important information from Jim Fenton and the Sheriff soon dismissed him. I came around from behind the screen just as Jack Lawrence, the attorney, started for the door. His hand was on the knob when he turned and said to the Sheriff, "I'll check that trust agreement first thing in the morning. I haven't read it over for a number of years so I'm foggy about the details. But the general drift is that, in the event Martin should die, or be rendered incapable of serving as president of the store—" he stopped and frowned at me as I stood wide-eyed and all ears, eagerly waiting to add this tid-bit to my fund of information. "I forgot that you weren't just a secretary," he said with annoyance.

"Well, you seem to have remembered in time," I pointed out. "That much information won't do anything but keep me awake nights."

"I shall trust you not to repeat even the little that I said."

"Promise," I agreed.

He nodded, still disgruntled by his own thoughtlessness, and left the room.

I was just starting to transcribe my notes when the Sheriff inquired, "Mrs. Wood, maybe you can explain something to me. Mrs. Kingsley gives her occupation as that of stylist. Just what does a stylist do?"

"That," I told him, "has been a matter of conjecture in the merchandising business for a good many years. Theoretically, they scout out new style ideas in the market, or conceive the ideas themselves; they coordinate colors and fabrics in different departments; predict fashion trends; and do various other things; such as, getting on the buyer's nerves. Stylists are highly paid; dress like illustrations out of fashion magazines; and are, as a class, gifted fourflushers. Don't get me wrong on this. Merchandising on Fifth Avenue is a fourflushing business, and a styling job requires a lot more than a good front and a gift for striking clothes. The depression years weeded out most of the oracles who flourished during the twenties. Generally speaking, stylists earn their salaries today."

"But you don't think that Mrs. Kingsley earns hers?"

"I don't know her salary."

He let the matter rest at that. I wanted to ask him more about the will and the trust agreement, but didn't have the courage. With the help of my memory, and occasionally his, the notes were transcribed and the Sheriff hurried away to his gin mill fracas.

Upon leaving the library, both tired and hungry, I discovered with gratitude that a buffet breakfast was awaiting me in the breakfast room. Everyone but Gloria and Mrs. Otis had retired to his or her room. Gloria brought me some fruit juice and then went back to the buffet.

"Are you starving?" she asked.

"Just toast," I told her. "I'm dead for sleep."

Mrs. Otis pressed her plump hands together and murmured something inane about being our hostess in poor, dear Lissa's stead.

It struck me that grief for poor, dear Lissa had been at a premium. Composing my features to what was intended for bereaved concern, I inquired about the funeral arrangements and learned that our hostess was to be buried very privately the following Tuesday. The inquest was to be held Monday morning.

"It is to be very brief," Mrs. Otis confided, in an undertone. "The Coroner and Sheriff Dodd being both county men, have the greatest respect for the Cole family. Of course," she added hastily, "they are most anxious to apprehend the murderer but they agree with—ahem—with my husband, that Mrs. Cole's death need not necessarily be a reflection upon the Cole family." She stopped, flounderingly. "But, of course, you of all people can realize that the death was accidental—that is as far as Lissa was concerned."

So they were convicting Louella Holmes even before the inquest! My blood boiled. "On the contrary," I flared, "in all probability, I know more about the circumstances surrounding the matter of possible mistaken identity than anyone else, and I can prove that such a thing was an impossibility."

Her plump, flushed face slowly drained of all color as she stared at me helplessly. "Then you know something you haven't told us?" She clutched my hand and murmured ingratiatingly, "But, my dear child, why not discuss it frankly? Don't you want to come up to my room? We've had so little chance to get acquainted. We could talk things over." Her panic was pitiful but, still angered by such eager treachery to Louella, I pointed out our need for sleep and hastily ate the toast and jam which Gloria had brought me.

It was broad daylight by the time Gloria and I ascended the stairs, leaving Mrs. Otis in unhappy possession of the honor of pinch-hitting for Lissa Cole. Gloria deserted her own gay little room, despite the lure of its fireplace, to sleep in the extra bed in my chilly, ice-blue room. We pulled down the shades and, too tired to talk, I dropped off my robe and was soon fast asleep—such are the inconsistencies of human behavior.

As Mrs. Otis had promised, we were called at four-thirty that Sunday afternoon and were the last to reach the bright, chintz-hung breakfast room and found that all had finished their combination lunch and afternoon tea except Garry, who was smoking a cigarette and having his third cup of coffee. He greeted us courteously but with an apathy quite foreign to his usual cheerful manner. We selected some food from the sideboard and Gloria, seating herself across from Garry, asked, "Any news?"

"Not that I know of. But Debby must be lousy with it after all she heard."

"Debby is being superior to gossip," said Gloria. She was not a little piqued by my silence regarding the testimony of Louella Holmes and Jim Fenton.

Garry rose. "I may stay up with Martin tonight. If I do we'll have you taken back to town in one of Martin's cars." He excused himself and left the room.

"Discounting the normal shock of murder and the loss of a childhood friend, I still think Garry's overdoing the blues," I said impatiently, as the door closed behind him. "When you marry him you can go to work on all the little mannerisms that get on my nerves."

"Train your own men," she retorted amiably, pouring French dressing on her salad. "As men go, he's really very amenable. And what more does a girl want if she doesn't intend to marry a man. I've told you I'm not planning to marry him."

"I put your protests down to coyness," I explained. "Don't tell me you're letting a fortune slip through your fingers! It shocks me to see anyone behaving so out of character."

"There are other fortunes in New York," she replied coolly. "All I need is time." Such a remark coming from most women would have been the height of arrogance, but Gloria managed to create an impression of nothing more objectionable than easy self-confidence. "Imagine being bored for life," she concluded.

"You could be the power behind the Comparison Department," I pointed out. "There is a career for an ambitious girl. He is so in love with you."

"Garry? In love with me? Guess again, Debby."

"For a man who isn't in love," I challenged, "he puts on the best act I've ever seen. Last night I was walking on the driveway and he mistook me for you—and if that man wasn't in love with the girl he thought he was kissing, then I've never been kissed."

She stared at me wide-eyed. "When you were outside last night? He kissed you?" The room rang with her peal of laughter. "How surprised he must have been," she chuckled. "And he really put dynamite into it?"

"He certainly didn't think I was his mother. Really, Gloria, you underestimate Garry's feeling for you. He's madly in love. It'll be an awful shock if you refuse him."

"I'll turn it into a compliment," she assured me. "He's a glutton for compliments, you know."

"You must teach me the technique," I told her as we rose from the table. "Comes a proposal and I just fuss around about being a sister to him. Shall we go now and find the others?"

At Jeffrey's suggestion we crossed the corridor and entered the morning room, a charmingly intimate little room which, despite its lack of a fireplace, could actually be termed cozy—an adjective that certainly described no other part of the house except, possibly, Gloria's little chintz-hung room.

But the atmosphere of the morning room, with its quaint Victorian furnishings, was anything but cozy. The Otises were there, and Jane, and the Holmeses. The five of them presented the effect of three people, all definitely, but politely, hostile. Mr. and Mrs. Otis sat on either side of a round table, its heavy felt cover reaching to the floor, and divided the Sunday *Times* between them. They looked disconcertingly normal. What they felt of grief or worry had been carefully locked behind his impassive countenance and her ineffectual manner. For Mrs. Otis was not an executive that Sunday afternoon.

Jane, ensconced in a "lady's rocker," which made her seem dashingly modern by contrast, was putting up a good show of reading *Vogue*—her bible and therefore appropriate Sunday, as well as weekday, literature. Stebbins had performed miracles in overcoming the signs of wear and tear which had ravaged our stylist the night before. Once more she apparently had managed to regain her thirties.

Ken and his wife were not making any pretense of reading. He was smoking while she placidly knitted on a dark blue sweater. Intuitively, I realized that the appearance of the Holmeses had been met by a blanket of silence and that they were outwaiting it, apparently calm but unquestionably tense and resentful. As Gloria and I entered, Ken rose and, with his peculiar gift for flashing me whole messages with a single glance, asked for my allegiance. Accordingly, I crossed the room and took the place which he had vacated on the settee.

"Good afternoon," I said, to the world in general and to Louella added, "With a sweater half finished, here I am without my knitting. You haven't a hooked rug or something in your pocket, have you?"

"I haven't even a pocket." She smiled. "What kind of a sweater are you making? This one is for a niece of Kenneth's."

Against the barrage of silence with which the others were bombarding us, we discussed knitting—the cable stitch, the moss stitch—homely details of the world's most innocuous occupation. And through it all ran a current of unreality. For this gentle, sweet-voiced woman had unquestionably wished me dead. Had possibly murdered Lissa. And watching those thin hands as they demonstrated the intricacies of a neckline trimming, I strove to forget the skill they had in the handling of other, more potent, instruments. For I was definitely committed to the defense of Louella against her accusers. That much I could do for her husband.

I said, "Ken tells me you've been sick. When you are well enough, you must come into town and we'll have lunch together. Maybe if we both work on him, he'll give me an afternoon off and we can go to a matinee."

"Not," said Ken, "that I have any control over your afternoon activities. But it's a nice theory." His voice, always indulgent when he spoke to me, had a special note in it. I felt like a child who has had her head patted.

"I'm surprised," said Mr. Otis disapprovingly, "that the advertising staff has time to attend matinees. Perhaps we are overstaffed."

"I've always felt that the position of advertising manager could well be eliminated," agreed Ken, with a deceptively innocent expression.

"Why not eliminate the whole department?" I demanded, in a spirit of ready cooperation. "Think of the money the store would save."

Mr. Otis returned to his paper and Mrs. Otis caroled, "These ads for next Wednesday's fashion show are very smart. Would you like to look at them, Miss Trent? We seem to be keeping the paper to ourselves over here. Of course, you'd like to see this main section." She handed it to Gloria who had been standing by the window staring out into the rainwashed garden. For Sunday had ushered in the first of three stormy days and we were not to see the sun again until Wednesday, the day of the tragic fashion show. Gloria turned and accepted the paper with her most engaging smile.

"I'm so glad you like the ads," she said. "This is the first fashion show series that I have ever handled alone. It is much more elaborate than usual this year."

Dear little Gloria! How like her to forget the three hours we spent together on those selfsame ads the previous Wednesday. But when a girl is on the way up one must permit her a little leeway. And a beautiful girl has especial difficulty in convincing anyone that she accomplishes things with her brains.

The door opened and Garry came in. "I'm going to stay with Martin," he told me. "He'll have you taken home in one of his cars."

It was, however, decided that the Holmeses should drive Gloria and me back to town and when we arrived at the apartment, several hours later, Louella seemed so exhausted that we insisted upon her coming up to rest. Once established on the couch she confessed that nothing ever revived her so well as a cup of good strong tea.

"You're as bad as Debby," said Gloria, "only she drinks hers like water."

"Pale amber," I corrected.

I was making the tea in our infinitesimal kitchen when Ken joined me, closing the door behind him.

"Not a tête-à-tête?" I demanded.

"That's all over," he said, a little ruefully, "though I'd rather have a jealous wife than one in the predicament that Lou's in now. I want to talk to you. Martin gave me a message to pass along.

"You already know that Jim was planning to marry Lissa if she could get a divorce. Every effort will be made to keep that from becoming public. Jim has ten more months before his contract expires and will continue at the store for the time being as if nothing had happened. Martin will try to buy up the contract in the next week or two.

But above all, Martin is anxious to have the rest of the world remain in ignorance as to the identity of Lissa's lover."

"How does the world know that she had one?"

"I wasn't informed of that detail. I received instructions and asked no questions."

"I stand corrected. Nay, even squelched!"

"You must remember to treat him—Jim, I mean—exactly as if nothing had happened," Ken continued, trying to look severe and failing utterly. "That shouldn't be hard. You are already accustomed to concealing an antipathy for vice-presidents."

"And I think that one of them is laying a trap for Louella," I said. "Judging from something Mrs. Otis told me, it looks as if they are planning to have the inquest shoved around so that only Louella's connection with the murder is brought out and all information about Lissa's love affairs suppressed. That doesn't seem like Martin Cole—it bears the Otis stamp."

Ken pulled himself up on to the cabinet and watched me pour boiling water into the tea pot.

"Did you put tea in that pot after you rinsed it?"

"Thanks," I said and got out the canister. "See what having you in my kitchen does to me? I'm sorry," I added contritely. "I'd forgotten we don't tease anymore."

"Debby," he whispered, a world of pain in his voice.

So I said, "What about the inquest?" and put the tea in the pot—lots of it because his wife liked her tea strong.

"Martin discussed that with me, too." His voice was firm and easy again. "As you suspected, it was Otis's idea that the Coroner press home the suspicions about Louella and forget to question Martin on his marital affairs."

"Do the Coles own the Coroner?" I inquired with interest.

"Not quite. The Coroner can make a lot of public rumpus at the inquest or he can establish certain publicly known facts and let the police investigation, which inevitably follows a verdict of murder, supply his further information. The public will then know only what the reporters can find out for them."

"Martin has requested that Louella's unfortunate conduct the previous evening be passed over, although, of course, it is recorded in

Dodd's reports. It is Martin and not Arthur Otis to whom the police will listen."

"All right," I said belligerently, "I'll keep quiet about Lissa Cole and Jim Fenton if no one talks about—"

The swing door opened and Gloria stood before us, her eyes like two blue disks in a white bowl. "Lissa Cole and Jim Fenton," she repeated. "Lissa Cole and Jim Fenton!" All the unbelief of the universe was in her voice.

"Oh, hell," I said. "Did you have to open that door at that minute? Yes, Lissa Cole and Jim Fenton. Now do you know why I wouldn't tell you anything about what I had heard?"

The three of us went back into the living room. Gloria was in such a dazed state that we had to tell Louella about Lissa Cole and Jim Fenton, too, and then Ken went to work on them both to explain the need of secrecy. "But," Gloria kept saying, "this gives Martin a motive. It gives him a motive!"

"Yes," agreed Ken, "it's a bad set up for Martin. The servants heard enough of the quarrel to know that he had refused her demand for a divorce. They don't know who the man is, however."

We spent the rest of the Holmes's visit assuring ourselves that Martin Cole was simply not capable of committing murder. But no matter what we proved to ourselves, there were always the police to be reckoned with.

7

It would have been a comfort during that next week if the newspapers had not eagerly told all that the reporters could find out. By Monday morning even the store had lost its welcoming air. Three photographers sprang forward and clicked their shutters when we walked through the entrance and the doorman had forcibly to remove a reporter barring our path. Across the counters, clerks stared at us agape and the elevator starter's, "Good morning," was fringed about with curiosity. A pall fell over the copywriters' room as Gloria entered and there were an abnormal number of newspapers tucked between dictionaries and hurriedly jammed against the files.

However, we learned only one thing from the Monday papers which we had not already known. That unwelcome fact was that Lissa Dexter Cole had owned half of Dexter and Cole. Upon her death, the stock passed to her husband. Added to his refusal to give her a divorce, this made the whole affair look terrifyingly cut and dried.

Tuesday morning brought a new and disastrous development. The papers were full of the feud supposedly raging between Louella Holmes and me. Martin Cole's magnanimous gesture regarding the Coroner's inquest had gone for naught.

By this time, even Garry's company was welcome—and there was a chance that through his association with Mr. Cole he would have some news. I dropped into his office early Tuesday afternoon where he sat doing nothing and looking so much like a super-executive that it was impossible to resist saying, "If you'd just cultivate the art of talking on two telephones at once, a talent scout would have you in Hollywood in a week."

He frowned ponderously and replied, "I don't get it."

"Skip it then." Remembering Gloria's comment, I added, "It was a compliment. Are the police getting anywhere?"

He shook his head. "Not that I've heard. The papers are doing a bang-up job, aren't they?"

"Too good," I agreed, dropping into a chair with a realization that the weight of suspicion is very exhausting. "Who gave them the story about Louella Holmes and me?"

Garry spun his chair around so that he was directly facing me and said with startling emphasis, "I'd like to know the answer to that one, too. Last night four newspapers got typed letters; there was one original and three carbon copies, giving the whole story. They were typed on plain paper, mailed in plain post office envelopes and were postmarked from Queens Plaza, Long Island City."

"Long Island City? But none of us live out on Long Island."

"Exactly. But yesterday afternoon I drove out to some property that I own on the North Shore. Going through Long Island City I got mixed up with a fruit truck. The police took my name, license number and what have you—including the time of the accident. Of course, the time coincided very closely with the mailing of the letters." His voice was bitter.

"That was tough luck," I admitted. "Have they traced the typewriter?"

"Not yet. The papers notified the police as soon as the letters arrived and last night every typewriter in the organization was checked. None tallied. Now they are checking the ones we have at home."

"If the B's are slightly crooked," I said, "we wrote it. And we use a brown typewriter ribbon—just as an affectation."

"It would look worse for me," Garry continued, "if no one had known that I was going. But while you were still with the Sheriff and everyone else was having breakfast, I said that I had to go to Long Island and even told the exact time when I expected to leave the city. That much is in my favor, anyhow."

"Does Mr. Cole have a decent alibi for Saturday night?"

He shook his head. "It's definitely bad. He went downstairs after we had all retired to our rooms, and got a bottle of Scotch and some soda. That is unfortunate because it will give the papers a chance to claim that he was drunk. Of course, he wasn't. He had a drink in his room—and one or two downstairs. Nobody gets tight on three drinks. But try and tell that to a jury.

"After he'd been in his room for a while he decided to go in and talk things over with Lissa. When he reached her room it was empty. He went then to his own bedroom and an instant later heard the shot. Actually," Garry leaned back in his chair and there was something about the manner in which his chest lifted, something in the squaring of his shoulders which reminded me of the rooster in *Esquire's* barnyard cartoons—those inimitable portrayals of masculine conceit—"actually," he said indulgently, "Lissa had no real intention of marrying Jim. She was just stringing him along."

"She certainly loved to play with fire," I said disgustedly. "Now look, Garry, Mrs. Cole and Mr. Fenton certainly aren't the type of people who string each other along. What makes you think anything so ridiculous?"

"She told me," he said, "just before we went upstairs. While we were getting your brandy, Martin told me about the letter he had found. I asked her about it in the drawing-room and she said the whole thing was just a mild flirtation."

"Did you tell Mr. Cole?"

"I didn't have time. That is, I didn't have time before she was killed. I told him in the morning."

"Have you told the police?"

"Yes. They act as if they don't believe it."

I didn't believe it either but instead of saying so I asked, "If Mr. Cole knew that his wife was planning to marry Jim, why did he let the man come to his home?"

"Martin didn't know of it until just before we all arrived. He found the letter from Jim to Lissa while they were dressing Saturday evening. They had a quarrel. One or more of the servants overheard it—that's how it got to the reporters. When Jim arrived, he was with Jane and the Otises and because Martin didn't want to make a scene, he kept quiet."

"Exactly how much stock did Lissa own?"

"Fifty-one percent. Bad, isn't it?"

"Ghastly," I agreed.

Garry rose and stretched. "Well," he said, "I'll have to throw you out. There's a conference in Bill Jackson's office and then I have to stop by Ken's office." His expression sobered abruptly. "The funeral is this afternoon and we're both going. No one else from the store but sourpuss Otis."

Going down the long corridor through the center of the building, I caught sight of myself in the mirror which some personnel-conscious executive had had placed opposite the entrance to the express elevator and was shocked to see that my appearance was as disheveled as my mental state. Consequently, a few feet farther on, I swung into the narrow passageway which leads to the washrooms. It's a darkish little passage which goes along the side of the elevator shaft and then right-angles to the left and leads to the two washrooms which are situated directly behind the elevators.

At this turn Jim Fenton stood talking to someone who was hidden from my sight by the elevator shaft. His face, seen in profile, was grim and threatening and the right hand, upraised, seemed an involuntary response to the owner's impulse to strike. The other hand must have been grasping his listener for I could see only his taut forearm. I arrived in the passageway just in time to hear him mutter threateningly "—double-crossed me, I'll kill you just as surely as I—"

He saw me. His left arm shot out, hurling away from him the person whom the wall concealed and as he turned toward me his whole personality became charged with that spontaneous charm which the man could summon at will. His instantaneous change of manner was more terrifying than the words which he had just uttered and I stood paralyzed as he advanced toward me, saying in a genial voice, "These stock boys! They are sent up from the selling floors with information and merchandise which I must have at once and they fool around in the washrooms!"

And he was no more astonished than I when my voice, vibrant with distaste, retorted, "Killing stockboys is punishable with death—too."

"The idioms of our everyday speech are rather given to violence, aren't they?" he replied smoothly. "Those were fine ads you people gave us on the fashion show."

"Thanks," abruptly. There was just one thought in my mind and that was to get past Jim Fenton and find out who was in those washrooms. He read the wish in my eyes and mocked me with his own. Then, suddenly, he swung about. One of the washroom doors had again opened and again clicked shut. Ken rounded the corner and stopped to stare at me.

"Debby! Are you sick?" he demanded. "You look like a string of spinach."

"I'm all right now," I assured him. "I'm not accustomed to murders—or murderers—and they unnerve me."

Fenton's eyes flicked sardonically as he stepped aside to let me pass. The two men walked away, talking ads. I went on to the washroom, praying—yes, praying—that it would be empty.

It was.

When, a few minutes later, I reached Ken's office, the art director and two of the copy writers from the house furnishings were at his desk, working on some big first proof sheets. They looked up with tactfully blank expressions. For since the appearance of the morning papers, every move Ken and I made was the object of interested scrutiny. A scandal right in the department! And the two bosses at that!

I pulled up a chair and sat down, knowing that Ken could always read my most inexplicable actions and that he would quickly and tactfully get rid of our audience. Accordingly, we were soon alone. He leaned back in his chair and regarded me quizzically. "Have you no regard for gossip? Or do you just find it impossible to exist without my delightful company?"

"The hell with your company," I retorted. "Who went into the men's washroom just half a minute before you came out?"

He stared at me in complete bewilderment. "No one."

"But someone must have," I insisted.

He listened to the whole story, his expression as bewildered as my own. "Whoever it was," he told me, "must have gone into the women's room. Are you sure there was no one in there?"

"I practically stood on my head looking in all the cubby-holes for feet and there weren't any, unless somebody went down the drain or out the window."

We stared at one another for at least a full minute before Ken's face suddenly lighted. "The janitor's closet," he cried. "It's between the other two doors. That's the only place anyone could have gone. He—or she—hid in there until the coast was clear. He's probably gone on his merry way by now. We can still look, however."

We walked down the hall together and he pulled open the door of the closet which, from habit, I had passed without even registering. Of course, it was empty.

"Bird's flown," said Ken grimly. "But I'll have the inside knob checked for finger-prints. Now exactly what did he say?"

I repeated the words. We went back to Ken's office, putting beginnings and endings to the sentence. The beginning could have been, "If you have double-crossed me" or it could have been, "Since you have double-crossed me." The intended ending might have been, "I'll kill you as surely as I killed Lissa Cole" or it might have been something as meaningless as, "I'll kill you as surely as I stand here."

We parted at his door and I went on to my office where Jane Kingsley, in sleek grey jersey topped by a lithe-lined, mustard-colored jacket, was roaming about the room in what might have been described as a "state."

"Deborah," she cried, as I entered, "you simply must help me out on this fashion show. Jean Turner does most of my routine work on a show and she's out sick. I've gone to pieces." She sank into a chair looking haggard, actually ill.

I sank into another chair and felt like she looked. We regarded each other for several minutes and, sensing my lack of cooperative spirit, she continued, "I can't possibly get anything coherent together for the talk that I have to give at the show. You know I can't ad lib worth a cent. They've just had a rehearsal and I couldn't keep my mind on the costumes enough to take notes."

"Now look here, Jane," I said, "as long as anyone can get away with temperament in her work, I concede her the privilege. But I'm not having any. We were both at the Coles' and we both had a severe nervous shock. I'm managing to do my work, after a fashion, and you'll have to do yours."

She sat slumped in her chair, looking fully ten years older than before our visit to the Coles'. In spite of my irritation, I was sorry for her.

"Why don't you go to an osteopath?" I asked. "Let him give you a good treatment and then go home, take something to make you sleep, and you'll feel equal to the show tomorrow."

Gloria came in with a sheaf of copy in her hand and laid it on my desk. She looked at Jane and then, inquiringly, at me. "Jane wants help on the fashion show tomorrow," I explained, suddenly remembering Gloria's ambition to become a stylist. "If you want to take tomorrow morning to go over the costumes and write up something for her to read, it's all right with me. I'll help you with your copy tonight."

Jane rose. "Thanks a lot," she said, some of her old arrogance returning now that she had won her point. "I'll do something for you some day."

"Conference?" inquired Ken's voice from the doorway. We looked up to see him and Garry, dressed for the street and evidently en route to the funeral.

"Jane's inaugurating a new policy," I explained. "She's going to do something for us some day. In the meantime, however, Gloria is going to write Jane's talk for the fashion show tomorrow."

"That's what I wanted to ask you about," said Ken. "Louella thought she'd like to go backstage at the fashion show. I wondered if she could go with you?"

"If she'll come in by one," I told him, "we'll have lunch first. Then she can stay for Jim's cocktail party afterward. Tell her I'll have tea with her instead of a drink."

"Well," sneered Jane, after the two men had disappeared down the hall, "he's not losing any time proving to the world that you and his wife are on the best of terms. Before long he'll have us thinking that we dreamed about how straight she can shoot and how interested she was in the idea of using you as a target."

"Before long, you'll talk yourself out of having your fashion show written," I retorted. "Better straighten your hat. A stylist owes that much to her public."

Her shrug carried just the slightest hint of regained insolence as she strolled over to the mirror behind the door. With deft fingers her shiny grey sailor was adjusted to the newly smart, straight-across-the-eyes line.

Then she took out a compact and went to work on her face. Next, the too tense outline of her lips were accented. She drew back and regarded herself appraisingly. Abruptly her expression altered.

"Like something God forgot," she murmured bitterly and left the room.

Between the time that Jane departed and Sid Shapiro, buyer of the Drug Department, walked into my office that evening a little after nine,

giving us, indirectly, some information which the police were to scruti-
nize with great interest in the near future, Gloria and I worked through
a haze of increasing fatigue which gradually gave way to a mild form
of hysteria. Anyone to have heard us would have thought we had a jag
on, and in a way we did. A jag compounded of nervous shock and suspicion, of fear, even of panic. Gloria would hold up a woman's sweater
in a novelty knit and murmur, "A new stitch for an old bitch," and we'd
giggle like a couple of high school girls over an ice cream soda. And
the ad for girls' millinery had to be laid aside for future consideration
because, to save our souls, we could think of only two headlines—"Lids
for Kids" and "Hats for Brats"—and neither of these seemed, even in
our exhausted state, quite up to Dexter and Cole standards. However, we did manage to produce some copy that was adequate but unin-
spired; certainly offering no challenge to Margaret Fishback's laurels.

"I'll have to go home by way of the studio," Gloria was saying when
Sid appeared suddenly in the doorway.

"They need a re-take on the bridal picture for silverware."

Sid greeted us and flung himself into a chair, his face a study in disgust. "I was hoping you'd be here," he said. "Mr. Otis has turned down
this whole series of ads." He tossed the sheaf of papers on to my desk.
"He says the Drug Department sells drugs—not glamour."

I nodded wearily, torn between the desire to cry or to throw something. "Yes, I know. List the item and the price. That's how they did it
thirty years ago when he was drug buyer. And that's how we should do
it now. Well?"

He stretched his arms above his head, relaxed suddenly, like a cat,
and lifted his hands in characteristic gesture. "And so I am telling you—
he doesn't like it. I'm down in my office a few minutes ago, checking
invoices, and old man Otis comes snooping through the department,
checking up on things."

"The funeral must have been short and snappy," I observed. "He's
hardly had time to get out there and back."

"Maybe he rides a broomstick," suggested Sid, still the picture of
disgust. "He thought I'd be gone and never know he was around. So I
walk out and see him. That cooks my goose. He has to find something
for me to be wrong about so he picks out the ads. What do I do with
them now?"

"Leave them here. I'll give them to Mr. Holmes and he can resell them to your friend and predecessor."

"Friend, bah," retorted Sid, and walked with us to the elevators.

8

When Louella Holmes joined me at the store the next day, the thought uppermost in our minds was that we must, for the benefit of the observant audience, put on a good act of mutual friendliness. It was not difficult, for we soon found ourselves on easy and cordial terms.

"May I talk to you quite frankly?" she demanded while I was putting on my coat and hat. "May I tell you something? Kenneth believes that I murdered Lissa. I know he does. He won't even let me mention it. But, Mrs. Wood, I didn't kill her. I didn't."

She stood there watching me desperately and, reading the doubt which mingled with the sympathy in my eyes, added pleadingly, "You saw me on the landing. I didn't have a gun with me then, did I? And you looked directly into my eyes. They were sane eyes. You know they were. I was in mental agony but I was sane."

"Of course, you were sane," I agreed, "and you didn't have a gun. You were clutching the railing with both hands. Why didn't I realize that before? You didn't have a pocket in your negligee, did you?"

She shook her head. "It was chiffon. I couldn't have concealed a gun even with a pocket. And I was myself again. Just as much myself as I am this minute. You will talk to Kenneth, won't you?"

"Of course, I'll talk to him," I promised. "Why didn't you tell this to the Sheriff? I would have borne you out in anything you might have said."

She lowered her eyes suddenly and, coming over to the desk, picked up her bag and gloves. "I was confused. I should have talked it over with Kenneth before I went in to see the Sheriff. But I didn't want him to know any more than he already knew. And you had told Mr. Otis that you hadn't seen anybody. You did that as a kindness to me and I didn't like to tell them that you had—" she hesitated.

"Lied," I finished for her. "Well, I did it with the best of intentions but maybe it wasn't such a good idea." I put my arm through hers and we walked down the corridor to the elevator. "But we'll undo the damage as soon as the fashion show is over. We'll talk it all over with Ken."

Contrary to custom, Dexter and Cole were holding their fashion show in the ballroom of one of the big hotels on upper Fifth Avenue. That first day was to be a private showing for our charge account customers and there would be similar shows on the following day for the general public. Louella and I walked up Fifth Avenue through the busy, well dressed, lunch-time crowd. It was one of those days which make even New York exult in the miracle of spring.

"I'm looking forward to seeing how a fashion show is run," she replied. "It will be good to have something to concentrate on besides myself. Isn't Fifth Avenue interesting? I never get over the novelty of it."

"I love Fifth Avenue," I agreed. "It gets in one's blood. It's so gay and extravagant on the surface and behind its magnificent facade, there's such a vicious fight for existence. Handsome women in their self-consciously smart clothes, tense with the struggle to seize upon a new fashion. Sleek men counting costs, appraising values, cold and ruthless in their dealings with one another. And don't overlook the spoiled and pampered customers—most of whom need a good spanking."

She laughed. "You don't make it sound like a place to love."

"Only as one loves the fight for life which in itself is exhilarating—as long as you're winning. And a dramatic background does lend zest. That's probably why Fifth Avenue never loses its fascination."

When we reached the hotel, we found the dining room quite crowded. There were several tables of buyers and executives from the store and an almost equal number of stylists and merchandisers from the other stores on the Avenue. It is sometimes a moot question whether department stores hold their fashion shows to attract customers or to impress competitors. At a table for four near the windows, Arthur Otis was seated with several of the top executives and at a larger table nearby, Jim Fenton was playing host to half a dozen of his buyers. His swarthy face looked sullen but he was maintaining a surface affability which indicated that he was well in control of himself. Other store people were scattered about and we caught sight of Ken and nodded across the room to him.

The head waiter came hurrying up. "How many? Only two? I am afraid we have no table for two left."

In a very short time Mrs. Otis bore down upon us attired in a new spring costume as smart as her manner was confused.

"Louella, my dear, how are you?" she cried effusively. "And Mrs. Wood! Oh, this is such a treat, such a treat! Isn't it crowded? Perhaps I can join you? Will I be intruding?"

Thinking, "I must consult an astrologer and see what sign I'm under and then go to a desert island if I ever come under it again," I said aloud, "Not at all. We were just hoping that you'd see us and come over. Waiter, another menu, please."

Mrs. Otis seemed excited, even more highstrung than she had been at the Coles' the previous week-end. But I watched her warily, for her change of front after Lissa's death had planted a suspicion that something was awry in Mrs. Otis's behavior pattern.

"How thrilling it all is!" she exclaimed, waving a plump hand vaguely toward the dining room in general. "It's so long since I've had any part in it. I just love the store, you know."

"You probably wouldn't love it so if you had ever worked in it," I said, feeling like the voice of experience admonishing impulsive youth.

"My child," she replied, suddenly mature with dignity, "I was a buyer at Dexter and Cole's while you were a child at grade school."

I stared at her in astonishment. She flushed a little, twisting the cord of her eyeglasses in a nervous hand. Her glance, wandering across the room, suddenly encountered that of her husband at his table near the windows. She looked back at us almost guiltily.

"You'll just forget about it, won't you?" she murmured. "It isn't at all important. I've really forgotten all about it myself. We never think of it any more."

"What don't you think about any more?" demanded Garry, coming up behind her and giving her shoulder a playful little pat.

"About the war," said Louella, with a surprising presence of mind.

Garry pulled out the fourth chair and sat down. Turning to Mrs. Otis he said affably, "Quite an idea, this, having the show at a hotel."

"It's been done before by plenty of stores," she retorted coldly. "I think it's silly. What do you have a show for? To attract customers. After the show some of them buy. So you bring them to a hotel to see your wares. And what happens? They come out of the hotel and drop into some other store on the way downtown to see whether your competitors' styles are as smart as yours."

"Which they usually are," I commented.

"Which they too often are," she declared. "Of course, we must remember," in a voice that was suddenly honeyed, "we must remember that our competitors have stylists."

Garry looked at her blankly, "But we do—" his eyes caught mine and he stopped, comprehension dawning. "Jane seemed to think that having the show here would be quite a coup," he said and waited for results, as wary as a cat.

"She has a lot to learn about fashions," answered Mrs. Otis, with a toss of her head. Again her eyes wandered over to her husband across the room. Was it imagination or did they glint vindictively? "Mark my words," she concluded, "they'll lose money on this show, which will be just as well! Teach 'em a lesson."

Garry's slate colored eyes were narrowed, watching her. "Well!" he said, a few minutes later as she hurried away, "was I dreaming or did we stumble on to something?"

"You were probably dreaming," said Louella gently. "I've known the Otises for a good many years and they are completely devoted to one another."

"She certainly hates Jane's guts," he observed inelegantly.

"Don't be vulgar, Garry," I said, "why should we have a gentleman in the merchandising business if he can't lend it a soigné atmosphere? By the way did you know that Mrs. Otis was once a buyer at Dexter and Cole's?"

"And what a buyer!" he said. "She made history there. Don't you know the famous Otis past? Mrs. Otis," said Garry expansively, always pleased to display his close association with the Cole family and its history, "came to Dexter and Cole's as a stock girl almost forty years ago and she climbed slowly but steadily until she was merchandiser for all the fashion departments. In fact, she had Jim Fenton's present job except that she never had the rating of vice-president." He paused while he lit our three cigarettes and blew out the match. "Waiter," he called, "ash tray here."

"She was a merchandiser," I prompted.

So he told us about Mrs. Otis. It was one of Fifth Avenue's typical stories, beginning with success and ending with oblivion. Mrs. Otis, whose name had been Nora Collins, had been an ignorant little stock girl who, with no weapons but persistence and an almost prophetic insight into the vagaries of fashion, had fought slowly from the humble post of stock girl to the dizzy heights of a success granted to but few women of her generation. It was she, in Dexter and Cole's, who had predicted the passing of the private dressmaker and had fought for the ready-made dresses which were coming into being along New York's astonishing Seventh Avenue. She had been a pioneer in that market; driving before her the designers, dragging behind her the reactionaries of a too conservative store, fighting for originality and for style. Nora Collins Otis had had her reward. A great merchandiser, years later she would have been called a great stylist as well, sought after by every big merchant on the Avenue. Nora Collins had become Mrs. Otis, the harassed, plump little woman who gushed aimlessly about nothing!

"What," I asked, "was Mr. Otis's rating in the store when he married her?"

"He was the buyer—head pharmacist, actually—of the Drug Department. No sooner did they get back from their honeymoon than Mr. Otis went to Martin's dad, who was President then, with some swell promotional ideas. Everyone was pretty sure he was picking Nora's brains for he was no nine-day wonder before he married. People got to ribbing him about his new promotional ideas and, of course, he got pretty sore. Rotten sport, Otis. Nobody knows just what happened but one day Nora resigned. That was the end of Nora Collins Otis. That is— she got off the stage. But she still ran the show from the wings."

"And he kept right on going up in the organization?"

"Oh, he wasn't above using her brains if no one could watch him do it. Uncle Benson always said she was the smartest merchant on the Avenue, and it was better to have her working for him through a representative, than not at all."

So it had been Nora Collins who had taken command of the situation when Lissa Cole lay dead at her husband's feet. She had not been stepping out of character, but rather, had been returning to it.

"What's his hold over her?" I demanded.

Garry shrugged. "She was shanty Irish and he had a college diploma. He sold her the idea that she was common and he was a gentleman and, therefore, she should be honored to be his wife. He made her self-conscious and belittled her and now she gushes because she wants to be a lady and doesn't quite know how." He rose to leave us with some casual remark about seeing us later at the show.

It was almost time for the fashion show to start when Louella and I went up to the ballroom where it was being held. At one end was a commodious stage and behind the stage and flanking it on either side were two large L-shaped rooms, being used currently as dressing rooms. Each room had three doors; one leading to the ballroom, one to the stage and the third was a connecting door between the rooms themselves and behind the stage. The models would go on to the stage through the door from the room to the right, walk out a long runway into the middle of the ballroom, and then returning to the stage, leave it by means of the door into the room on the left. There was a line of empty dress racks in this room and it was planned that the models should undress here, leaving their costumes to be hung on these racks by the several attendants. Then they would dash back to the first room and be rushed into their next costume.

Already the ballroom floor was filled with tiny gold and damask chairs which looked alarmingly fragile for the Schrafft-fed women who were pouring from the elevators. Flowers banked the stage and the long runway. A string quartette played softly behind a bank of greens at one corner of the stage.

Fashion shows are fun—when they aren't one's own responsibility. Like any other show, the most amazing thing about them is their gracious unhurried appearance before the audience. Behind the scenes, all is turmoil. Twelve models were dashing about in various stages of dishabille. They crowded around a make-up table, littered with cosmetics, and clamored for the attention of the harassed hairdresser. A ravishing blonde balanced on one foot as she pulled on gossamer hose.

A sloe-eyed beauty with raven, sleeked-back hair was working herself into a tiny pull-on girdle with shrill vocal protests. The dilatory ones were being hustled into their first costumes so that all would be ready before the show started. Several, fully dressed and ready to step upon the stage, preened before the full-length mirrors in unself-conscious admiration of their own youthful beauty.

Gloria, standing near the stage door, was checking each completed costume for detail, making sure that hats, bags and other accessories were according to the schedule in her hand. On the edge of the stage, Jane was shuffling through the pages of the typewritten speech and, even from that distance, I could see the papers trembling. But she was composed and there was a set little smile about her rouged lips.

"You look very chic," I said, as we joined her.

"Like an illustration out of *Vogue* or *Harper's Bazaar*," Louella supplemented.

The two models who were to go on first came up and stood ready. Jane looked over at Gloria who nodded and waved toward the stage. Turning, Jane gave a signal to the orchestra leader and walked out to the microphone. The show had started!

Louella and I slipped through the door on to the platform and, concealed by the draperies and banked greens, watched the show from the wings. The models passed us one by one with that supple grace, that fluid rhythm which is almost poetry in motion. They wore, besides their appointed costumes, the happy eager smile which models summon up, miraculously, as they step from the curtains. They always give me the feeling that there is some delicious secret which they want to share and that if I were not so lacking in perception, I could guess what it is. Consequently, I always find myself returning the smile in an apologetic way. This gets tiresome after the first hour.

Louella leaned over as one of the girls passed us. "That navy with the polka dot scarf and belt," she whispered, "I'd like to see it when the show is over."

As the inevitable bridal party brought the show to a conclusion, we followed Jane back into the now practically deserted dressing room. The models were all in the other room changing into their street clothes and the costumes which had once filled this room were likewise transferred to the other. The assistants who had been helping the models to dress, pushed the empty costume racks into one corner so that the couches and chairs which had been crowded into the background were available. Jane threw herself on a couch and wearily accepted congratulations upon the success of her presentation. All of the buyers and many other executives from the store congregated in the room. Jim Fenton himself soon joined us.

He was in one of his expansive moods. Only with the knowledge of his recent overwhelming disappointment could one detect any flaw in the whole-heartedness of his manner. He was an actor, that man!

"If someone will get hold of a waiter," he said, "I'll order drinks for the crowd. You were superb, Jane, superb."

"She read her talk very well, very well indeed." It was Mrs. Otis's voice. She stood in the doorway, her husband by her side. "I always think it's hard to read convincingly something you haven't written yourself. Yet no one would have guessed from the way you gave it that Miss Trent had done the preparation." She went over to Gloria and patted her arm affectionately. "You have a real insight into the psychology of selling fashions, my dear, and a very excellent gift of expression.

"And I want you"—drawing Gloria with her to the door of the next room—"I want you to help me to select a little outfit for myself. There were several things that were very chic. I want to look at them right away."

"Debby and I are going into the next room," said Louella to her husband. "I want to look at some of the dresses. We won't be long and then you can take me home. I'm getting tired."

But Louella had over-estimated her strength and before we could find the navy blue with polka dot trim, she admitted that she would like to sit down by a window because she was feeling a little faint.

We went at once to a couch from which several of the models obligingly removed their paraphernalia and, after making her lie down, I opened the window and covered her with a coat taken from a nearby rack.

"I'll order tea for both of us," I said. "And I'll have Ken phone for your car."

I returned to the other room, ordered the tea and was telling Ken of his wife's exhaustion when Mrs. Otis and Gloria joined us.

"Louella doesn't look at all well," said the wife of our executive V.-P., in a tone of genuine concern. "Why don't you get her a little brandy?"

"Debby's ordered tea," Ken explained, "and I'm just leaving to phone for the car."

"You haven't had anything to drink." It was Jim Fenton, coming up with a cocktail in either hand. Jane was with him, her cheeks flushed and her eyes a little feverish. She looked like a woman who was on the verge of either getting tight or having a nice little bout of hysterics. Mrs. Otis accepted the drink with excellent grace, though I knew that she could have cheerfully thrown it into Fenton's smiling face. I said, "No, thanks, I'm having tea with Mrs. Holmes in a minute or two."

"You're a sissy," said Jane. Reaching over, she took the second glass from his hand, drained it and returned it to him with an almost imperceptible toss of her head. There was something about the gesture which seemed suddenly to reduce him to the role of a waiter. She turned on her heel and left us abruptly.

"You may be a sissy," commented Mrs. Otis dryly, "but you're not a hussy." With which trenchant observation she, also, left us, taking Gloria with her.

"Well," I asked Jim, "what do we do? Break into animated conversation to prove to the world that we wanted to be alone?"

But Jim Fenton couldn't joke about the little tableau. His sense of humor always stopped just short of himself and his blue eyes darkened with anger.

"We'll have to use more publicity if we want to get this show across," he asserted. "We'd better get working on something right away."

It was easier to humor him than to protest. We went over to the center table, pushed the glasses to one end and sat down. He whipped out a pencil and a notebook and we put on an act indicating deep absorption in an important discussion. He was a strange man! Always playing tricks on himself to build up his ego. But you know his type. Among executives, his name is legion!

A few minutes later a waiter brought in a tray containing a large teapot, hot water jug, two cups and saucers and some melba toast. He walked over to us and set the tray beside me, handing the check over to Mr. Fenton.

"Looks as if you're entertaining us to tea," I said.

He nodded and waving his hand toward the tray, said to the boy, "Take this into the next room. There is a lady in there waiting for it."

"She's lying down," I called after him, "at the other end of the room near the door into the ballroom."

As soon as was possible, I escaped. I found Louella already looking much better, although she had not touched either of the two cups of tea poured out before her. The models had all finished dressing and had left and she was alone in the room.

"Good gracious," I cried. "Tea that strength would take the skin off my tongue."

She laughed. "I always drink it that way you know. I'd forgotten you like yours so weak." Watching me pour more than half the cupful back and fill it up with hot water, she added, "You're a sissy."

"That seems to be the general opinion. I'm sorry you had to stay alone. Mr. Fenton was having a burst of ego dramatics."

"Oh, I had lots of company," she assured me. "Everyone was so solicitous."

We sipped our tea. It tasted bitter, due, I assumed, to the long steeping which Louella had permitted. To avoid drinking it, I munched on the toast. Louella, leaning back against the couch, the coat still over her knees, cradled her cup in both hands and stared aimlessly over my head. I wondered what she was thinking. I wondered about her life with Ken. It was apparent that he wasn't happy in his marriage, hadn't been for years. He was very dear to me and his happiness was important. By what a tragic coincidence, I thought, had his wife's delusions startled me into an awareness of my own feeling for Ken. And yet, I knew that now she trusted me completely. Well, loyalty was still possible. I took a second sip of the bitter tea and closed my eyes. As soon as Ken returned, I would tell him of my conversation with Louella at the store. Although there was no conclusive proof, I could at least restore his confidence in her innocence.

The door which led to the ballroom opened and Ken and Gloria came in. "Here you are," he said. "The car— My God! Louella!"

I looked at her, suddenly aware that I was not focusing well.

A horrible sensation hit the pit of my stomach. Louella gagged, a terrible rasping sound, and her hands clawed madly at the air. I tried to reach for her, dimly aware that Ken had sprung past me to catch her as she toppled forward. Nauseatingly, I felt myself slipping to the floor and heard Gloria crying, "Debby! Debby!" Then she screamed and there was a confused babble of voices from the other room.

Ken said, in a constricted voice, "Lou's dying."

I lost consciousness.

9

If you've ever been poisoned by potassium cyanide, you know all the acute unpleasantness of my next few hours. If you've never had this experience, no detailed explanation is going to make either of us feel any better. Suffice it to say that eventually I lay in bed, exhausted but fully conscious, wondering why so many hospital rooms are painted pale green, as if attempting to reflect the patient's own queasy state.

Gloria came in and sat down on the bed beside me. "Debby," she said quaveringly, "we almost lost you." She put her head down beside mine on the pillow and sobbed a little. It was most gratifying to have aroused all this emotion in Gloria whose cool exterior always made me seem to be, by contrast, in a constant state of dither.

"Louella?" I asked.

"She died almost instantly. It's dreadful to think of, but it is a relief to have all the suspense over."

"What suspense?" I demanded.

She stared at me with startled blue eyes. "Of who killed Lissa Cole, of course. Mrs. Holmes thought that Lissa was you and killed her. Then she tried again to kill you but she knew by this time that the police would be sure she did it so she committed suicide. It's all here in the papers, Debby. Everything is settled."

"Then it will all get unsettled," I said grimly. "I want to see Ken."

"You mustn't," she protested. "Think how it will look. His wife tries to murder you and commits suicide and a few hours later he comes rushing to your bedside. Your cue is just to lie low and keep quiet. You'll just get things into a worse mess."

"There is no such thing as a worse mess," I retorted. "It will look a lot better for him to be at my bedside than to have his wife branded as a murderer."

"Debby," she said, as if she were reasoning with a refractory child, "it's all settled. You can't do anything. Please let it alone."

A nurse came in, all crisp and white in her bobbing cap. "You'll have to go now," she said to Gloria. "The doctor said just two minutes."

"Gloria," I said, "will you get word to Ken that I'm sure Louella was innocent and that I want him and Mr. Cole to come over to the apartment tomorrow night?"

She shrugged resignedly. "All right, Debby, I will if you want me to. How can you be so sure?"

"She told me she was innocent," I explained. The explanation seemed absurdly inadequate and I could see that Gloria felt the same way about it.

For what seemed hours, I lay there drifting just on the edge of consciousness. It was as if, disembodied, I floated back into the days just past, collecting thoughts lost in the confusion, sorting out impressions, listening again to inflections, seeing eyes blaze with anger, lips curl in contempt. Before I fell asleep I tried to summarize it all and had only a jig-saw puzzle, none of whose pieces fitted. A stylist who could be stung to unreasoning fury by a jibe about her age in the presence of Arthur Otis. A society woman so swayed by Jim Fenton that she had betrayed her husband, and in so doing had lost her life. A husband, with every motive for murdering his wife, who, just by being himself, could never be branded by his friends as a murderer. A man whose wife believed him unfaithful. And she too had lost her life.

And where in the turmoil did the Otises fit? She, whose vague manner shielded a viper. He, cold, ruthless and vindictive. And Garry. Garry who had said, "Do you always offer your friends cigarettes out of other people's cases?" There was the black and gold case in my hand. I must have picked it up off the seat of the wing chair. I had been the last person sitting in that chair before we all went to bed. Someone had dropped a cigarette case there while we were upstairs. Louella Holmes had seen a light under the drawing-room door. Presumably Lissa had lit that light. Lissa or someone who carried a black and gold cigarette case.

I drifted off to sleep.

It was inevitable that they would question me regarding the events leading up to Louella's death and my own poisoning. A brisk young man from the District Attorney's office appeared soon after the nurse had carried out my breakfast tray and, whisking a notebook from his pocket, began asking questions. As Gloria had told me the night before, the entire case was solved to the satisfaction of the police and my interrogator plainly saw his task merely as a part of his official routine. His questions were so stereotyped in form that they gave little opportunity beyond straight "yes" and "no" answers. At first, I was filled with the impulse to sweep aside his complacent attitude and challenge this assumption that the case was closed. On second thought, it occurred to me that Louella might be more ably defended by her husband if all the facts were first laid before him and he had an opportunity to formulate some planned offensive. Consequently I said "yes" and "no" obediently in all the proper places and let the matter ride.

They permitted me to leave the hospital by four and Gloria came home that night with a batch of copy for me to O.K. She had also brought a package of my favorite Chinese tea and a gorgeous robe which was designed to do more for a woman than God had figured on when he made me. "You can wear it tonight," she said. "That woodrose tone is grand with the colors in your comforter, and it will give you some color. You looked horrible at the hospital. Sea green."

"The robe's lovely," I assured her gratefully, "but I don't know if it's safe to wear it. The last time you tried to help me make an impression, I had on Lissa's dress—and eventually got poisoned as a consequence."

"It isn't likely that any of the men will be wearing a taffeta robe tonight," she laughed.

"Any? How many?"

"Four. Ken is coming, and with him Martin and Mr. Lawrence, the attorney, and, of course, Garry will be along, too. Two rich bachelors and two widowers don't come every night."

"Bring my comb and get out my purple lipstick," I said. "Though if you're going to wear that new blue whatsis of yours, I might just as well go back to being sea green."

"I'm going to wear it, honey," she assured me. "But I only want one of them. You can have the other three."

We were just finishing dinner when the bell rang. Anna carried out the table on which she had served dinner by my chaise and then went to open the door. The four men all arrived at once, having eaten at a restaurant around the corner. Garry and Jack Lawrence entered the room first, looking cheerful and rather blatantly handsome when teamed together. Ken and Martin bore unmistakable marks of the ordeal of these last five days. They were white-faced and haggard, their eyes betraying intense anxiety.

We wasted no time in coming to the object of the meeting. As soon as the men were all seated and had been assured as to the excellent condition of my health, Mr. Lawrence said to me, "I understand, Mrs. Wood, that we are here because you are of the opinion that Mrs. Holmes did not shoot Mrs. Cole."

I explained that Louella and I had met in the upper hall of the Cole home on that fateful Saturday night and that she had been grasping the rail with both hands so that she could not have been holding a gun, and it was difficult to see how she could have concealed any such heavy object in a pocketless, chiffon negligee.

Ken said quickly, "What were you wearing when you went down to the library?"

"The same red woolen robe that I wore later."

"Then if Lou saw you go downstairs wearing a woolen robe, she wouldn't have shot at Lissa who was still wearing an evening dress."

We all stared at him. "Oh, Ken," I cried remorsefully, "how unpardonably stupid of me. It was bad enough not to have told the truth about meeting her. At least I did that in an effort to shield her. This is just inexcusable stupidity."

"We'll just consider," he replied gently, "that your conscious efforts to shield her cancel any unintentional failure to do so."

Already he looked better. The tight lines about his lips were relaxing and his eyes seemed less haunted. I never knew until later how much self-reproach had been mingled with his fear that Louella had been driven to attempt a double murder and suicide.

"It must be observed," put in Jack Lawrence, "that apparently Mrs. Holmes also failed to realize that the change in Mrs. Wood's costume would have exonerated her."

"But she didn't tell anyone she saw me," I said eagerly. It was unbearable to have that hopeful look go out of Ken's face.

"But she didn't mention it when she talked to you. She based her plea on the fact that she apparently carried no gun and that she had been shocked out of her momentary insanity into complete conscious sanity."

"She had been," I insisted. "She looked unutterably miserable—but she was certainly sane. And that isn't all," I added. "Mrs. Holmes had both cups of tea poured out when I joined her. They were terribly strong and I poured more than half of mine back and filled it with water—which is doubtless why I was not seriously poisoned—that and the fact that I drank mine more slowly and only got a few swallows of it down. Now if she had put the poison in and had wanted me to die, she wouldn't have watched me with complete complacency, even amusement, while I put half of that tea back. And she certainly wouldn't have gulped hers down ahead of me, thereby serving as a warning."

Ken looked at me gratefully and nodded his head. For a homely man he always seemed to be so good looking.

"I think," said Martin Cole, "that Mrs. Wood has given us enough evidence in vindication of Mrs. Holmes that the whole matter should be reopened by the police."

He was a good sport. How good, I did not realize until I turned to him and said, "I'm glad you weren't at the fashion show. If you had been there I would have found myself back in my old state of being torn between two loyalties."

He looked back into the fire with a rueful half smile. "But I was there," he answered quietly.

"Oh, my God," whispered Gloria, as if her world had fallen apart. "Oh, Martin, why didn't you stay home where you belonged?"

It was plain enough now what she had meant when she had said she only wanted one of them. She wanted Martin Cole. It was in her eyes, in every line of her tense young body. He smiled at her now and shrugged his shoulders resignedly.

"I'll know better next time," he said.

"I didn't see you," exclaimed Ken.

"Nobody did. That is, nobody but the police. However, the police very carelessly let me out of their sight for half an hour. Of course, Mrs.

Holmes was murdered during that half hour. There is a row of boxes along one side of the ballroom—you probably saw them—I went into one and watched the last half of the show from there. They had a plain clothes man following me and he went into the adjoining box. Unfortunately for me, he thought the show would last longer than it did and slipped out for a drink. When he got back he met me walking across the lobby, headed for the station. That was at exactly four-seventeen."

"And Lou died at four twenty-three," said Ken. There was no accusation in his voice. He accepted, just as the rest of us did, the fact that murder was simply not a part of Martin Cole's make-up.

"Weren't you with anyone after the show was over?" It was a white-faced Gloria who asked the question.

"No, I was completely alone. Not wanting to get into that mob of women as they poured out of the ballroom, I just sat there in the box. Then I went to the washroom down the corridor. Then I walked down to the lobby—it was only two flights. I didn't see a soul and, apparently, nobody saw me."

"Is there any way of determining," I asked Mr. Lawrence, "exactly how many of us who were at the Cole home last Saturday, were also in the second dressing room after Mrs. Holmes's tea had been served?"

"We have that information pretty well lined up," he answered and flipped the pages of his notebook toward the back. Suddenly Gloria got up and, crossing the room, switched out the lamp beside Martin's chair. "We don't need it," she said, "the others are plenty."

He looked up at her and smiled. "I didn't stay home," he said, quite as if no one had spoken since her startled question, "because it was lonely there—and I wanted to see the show. I haven't missed one of Dexter and Cole's fashion shows since I left college."

She nodded to him and answered forlornly, "I didn't think of that."

Mr. Lawrence waited until she was again curled up in her corner of the couch and then turned to Garry. "Shall we take you first?" he asked. "Let's trace your movements from the time you were served a cocktail in the first dressing room until you left the show."

"Go ahead," said Garry. His voice was more cordial than his expression.

"You were talking to Miss Rothman, one of the buyers, when the tea was carried into the room and put on the table beside Mrs. Wood. It was then carried in to Mrs. Holmes. Within the next three to five minutes, Miss Rothman said she was leaving and you went into the second dressing room. Do you want to continue from here?"

Garry nodded, "I wanted to find Gloria," he took up the story. "When I went into the room, I joined Mrs. Holmes who said that Gloria had gone out with several of the models about ten minutes before. I left her then and went through the door into the ballroom. Gloria was standing by the elevators talking to two of the girls. I told her I'd be over about seven and then left the hotel." He shrugged. "So I had a perfect chance to put the poison into the tea. Providing, of course, I could have persuaded Mrs. Holmes to play sleeping beauty while I did it. You don't suppose she would just lie there and smile resignedly while I doctored up her drink, do you?" His voice was irritable. It made him seem nervous.

"We don't suppose, we simply inquire," replied Lawrence blandly. "Shall we take you next, Ken? You left the scene of action to phone for your car. You went down to the lobby, it seems."

"Yes, I phoned for the car. Bill Riley was in the lobby. We talked for a while and then I took the elevator back to the ballroom. When I got off the elevator Gloria was saying goodbye to her two friends. She and I walked over to the dressing room together. We reached it just as Louella started gagging."

Lawrence looked down at his book. "Right. You're water-tight as to alibi. Now for Gloria." He looked at her expectantly.

"I left the dressing room at least five minutes before the tea was brought in," said Gloria. "Several of the models left when I did and we all went down the corridor to the powder room. Later, when I was coming back to the dressing room I stopped to talk to two of the girls and I was still with them when Mr. Holmes stepped off the elevator."

"That checks," agreed the attorney. "Now Mrs. Wood can tell us what she knows."

"Not much," I told him regretfully and, with careful attention to detail, outlined my movements following the arrival of the tea service. Then I repeated my conversation with Louella, telling them of her remark that everyone had been so solicitous.

Ken turned to Mr. Lawrence and asked, "How many people talked to Lou while she was in the dressing room?"

"As far as we know, Gloria, Garry, Mr. and Mrs. Otis, Mrs. Kingsley and a Miss Burns who is not involved in the case at all."

"Were Mr. and Mrs. Otis together?" asked Garry with a sudden re-birth of interest; almost, it seemed, of optimism.

"No. After the tea was served, Mrs. Otis went into the second dressing room to look for Gloria. Mrs. Holmes was alone, and Mrs. Otis went to the powder room where she found Gloria. Then she came back into the ballroom. Mr. Otis was just coming from the dressing room where he had been looking for her."

"That leaves us with Mrs. Kingsley. She said goodbye to everyone in the first dressing room and then went into the next room to get her coat. She was talking to Louella when the tea was carried in. She and the waiter agree on this. She says she stayed less than two minutes and then went home. No one saw her leave."

"So Garry, the Otises, Jane and I are left holding the well-known bag," I said reflectively.

"Don't leave me out," put in Martin Cole, smiling with more natu-ralness than we had seen before that evening. "That makes six of us."

Suddenly Garry demanded, "Can't somebody find a way to pin it on to Jim Fenton?"

Martin Cole's sensitive lips twitched a little at this mention of the man who had so ruthlessly attempted to appropriate both his wife and his beloved store. But he said, "He had no motive. He, of all people, had no motive."

"Assuming that he had a motive," exclaimed Jack Lawrence, sud-denly turning to me, "was there any possible way in which he could have put the poison into the tea when it was set down beside you?"

Perhaps it was wishful thinking but, upon reflection, it did seem that his hand had fluttered perilously close when he signaled to the waiter to remove the tray. "He might have dropped something in the cups," I admitted thoughtfully," but he certainly didn't pick up the lid and plop something into the teapot. No, I'm sorry to do it, but I'm afraid I must furnish him with the perfect alibi."

We rehashed the whole thing pretty thoroughly but arrived just ex-actly nowhere. At last Ken asked, "Debby, do you keep beer on tap?"

"Not only beer," I said, startled back into my role as hostess. "Why don't you go out with Gloria and see what else you can find? How does alcohol mix with potassium cyanide?"

"You can have some of your new tea," said Gloria. She went into the kitchen followed by Garry, Ken and Jack Lawrence and I heard Ken say, "Well, of course, if you have the mixings for a highball, I'd never argue for beer."

Mr. Lawrence stuck his head through the door. "There's a pretty well stocked cellar out here," he said to Martin, "what'll you have?"

Martin raised his eyes and hesitated, seeming to come back from a long distance. "Scotch and soda," he answered, "long on soda." He looked over at me as if about to speak, his dark eyes still concentrated from the intensity of his thoughts. Then he rose, went over to the fireplace and leaned against the mantel, his gaze on the flaming logs. Suddenly he laughed.

"Somebody," he observed, with evident relish, "is going to get one awful jolt when tomorrow's papers come out. The whole mystery solved and Mrs. Holmes convicted! And now—wham! The murderer is right back where he started from."

I couldn't help wondering which of the four absent people who would learn of our conversation through the papers, he assumed to be the murderer. But instead of asking that question, I asked another.

"Ken once remarked," I said, "that you had inherited Mr. Otis just as you inherited the presidency of the store. If it is something which you don't object to discussing, would you explain that statement to me?"

He frowned, not with annoyance, but with concentration and something akin to regret, as if my question forced an answer which he preferred to disregard. But he replied straightforwardly enough. "There was a trust agreement entered into by my father and Mr. Otis," he explained. "It provides that, in event of my death or of my being rendered incapable of serving as president of the store, the voting power of my stock shall go to Arthur Otis. He would presumably elect himself president in that event. The trust is effective only until my thirty-fifth birthday. My thirty-fifth birthday falls on the fourteenth of next November."

"Then," I said, a great sense of satisfaction overwhelming me, "it would be very definitely to Mr. Otis's advantage for you to be convicted of the death of Mrs. Cole and Mrs. Holmes. That would remove you very neatly from the field of battle."

Mr. Cole swung around and stood on the hearth looking down at me. His face betrayed his extreme concern. "There seems no way of refuting that statement," he admitted reluctantly and then returned to his study of the glowing coals.

The men left before midnight and once we were alone I discovered that being poisoned is an exhausting business and went gratefully to bed. Gloria came in and curled up at my feet, a blanket wrapped around her. Her face was almost sullen. Finally she said, a defiant note in her voice, "I suppose you think that I am after his money."

"Not necessarily," I replied. "It isn't hard for me to understand that a girl could very easily fall in love with Martin Cole. I don't labor under any delusion that you would marry for love alone. But if you can have both love and money, all I can say is that you are luckier than most of us."

She flashed her lovely and ingratiating smile. "You're swell," she said, "to understand. Really, Debby, I'm not meant to be poor and I'd make Martin a wonderful wife. I have brains enough to understand all about his store; I have beauty enough to grace his home; I have wit enough to keep him amused. That's more than he got out of Lissa."

"There are intangibles in marriage," I remarked. "It doesn't seem to me that you have exactly covered them in the summing up of your talents. Anyway, it takes two to make a marriage. Where does Martin stand?"

She shrugged. "He likes me," she said. "He'd rather talk to me than to any girl he has ever known. He'd rather look at me than at any girl he has ever known. All these months that Garry, Lissa, Martin and I have been making a congenial foursome, Garry and Lissa have amused one another and left me a clear field with Martin. I've been making good use of my time!" She paused and sighed a little. "I was counting on a divorce, to tell you the truth. That would have been a lot simpler than all this mess."

"How thoughtless"—and I smiled—"for someone to have interfered with your predatory plans. Well, my child, you've come a long way from that bedraggled Colorado ranch which you hated so. You have both beauty and brains and you've certainly used them. But you'd be bucking something pretty strong when you came up against the Cole family tradition. I suspect that one of the things the Cole men do not do is marry copy writers who work in the store."

"But, Debby, I'm not just a copy writer," she protested. "I'm Gloria Trent, one of the most famous beauties in the country. I took the McMaster's prize for being the outstanding photographic beauty of 1938.

The best artists in America have painted me. My picture hangs in three world famous galleries. I'm a celebrity. That breaks down a lot of this old-family tradition stuff."

Of course she was right. Sighing a little for the old way of selfless love and succumbing to the practical viewpoint of modernity, I said, "Run along to bed and let the police solve the murder. You can't start losing your beauty sleep now."

At the door she turned and said with a seriousness that was unusual for her, "You haven't heard the latest development about those letters that were sent to the papers, have you? Well, the police have traced the typewriter. It belongs to Garry. They found it in his apartment. Garry insists that he isn't a good enough typist to have done those letters. He says he never uses the typewriter any more."

"Any finger-prints?"

"The whole thing was clean as a whistle. Also Garry says he has only two keys, his and his Filipino's. The Filipino is there just part time so the apartment is empty about half of every day. Seto swears that his key never left his pocket and that he can't type and there doesn't seem to be much reason to doubt him. It would be pretty risky for someone to have tried to bribe him. Well, that's all that's happened since you passed out on us. You can draw your own conclusions—I'm lost in the maze."

10

It was the next afternoon, Friday, that Sheriff Dodd came in to see me. A long morning of rest and comparative peace of mind had almost restored me to normal and by the time he arrived, following Anna in from our tiny foyer, I was again installed before the living room fire.

His shrewd intelligent face, softened about the eyes by crinkles of humor, was a welcome sight and our greeting was one of mutual cordiality. "You have in me," I told him, "a much more appreciative, shall we say suspect, than before. Since seeing you at the Coles', I have had a dose of the New York police."

He laughed, releasing my hand from a paralyzing grip. "Did they give you the third degree?"

"They just wouldn't give me time to say more than 'yes' and 'no' and that is hard on a woman. Won't you sit down?"

He shook his head, saying something about wanting to stretch his legs after the long drive into town, and walked over to the rain drenched windows to look down upon the sprawling city. It was our fifth rainy day out of six. Only on Wednesday, the day of the fateful fashion show, had we seen the sun since that glorious morning preceding Lissa Cole's death. At last the Sheriff moved away from the window and wandered restlessly about the room, examining the prints above the bookcase and finally stopping before the corner cupboard to pick up a tiny china compote and examine it carefully.

"Lowestoft," I said. "You can always tell it by the peculiar greyish tinge in the background."

He nodded abstractedly, set the piece down with care and picked up a miniature vase.

"Belleek," I told him. "That piece is particularly nice because—or don't you care?"

"Not much," he acknowledged and came back to the fire to seat himself opposite me. "So Mrs. Holmes didn't shoot Mrs. Cole, nor attempt to poison you, nor commit suicide?"

"I'm sure she didn't."

"Any ideas as to who did?"

"I'm a trader by instinct."

"Oh! Well, what do you want to know?"

"Once I read a story. In it there was a murder—someone was shot. The police examined everyone's hands before they could wash them. Do they just do that in books or did you overlook something last Saturday night?"

"By the time I got to that house," said the Sheriff, "everyone in it had had time to take a bath, let alone wash his hands. Well, who did?"

"I'm a trader," I repeated. "Haven't you anything to offer?"

He threw back his head and laughed. "Yes, I have. Why did Mrs. Cole threaten her husband three years ago with the idea that she could get a divorce by naming you as correspondent?"

"Good Lord!" I sat and stared at him. "You don't mean—why, I never laid eyes on Mr. Cole away from the store until last week-end."

"That seems to be what stymied her efforts," he admitted. "At any rate she soon gave up the whole idea. All right now, who washed his hands?"

"Who told you my hidden scandal?"

We grinned at one another and then said simultaneously, "Mr. Otis." The Sheriff's keen eyes widened. "Well!" he exclaimed. "Mr. Otis is a busy man." He heard my story with interest and asked, "Was the light switch really sticky?"

"My social inhibitions prevented me from looking."

The Sheriff took a few minutes to mull over Mr. Otis and the light switch and then said, in his characteristically straightforward manner, "Of course, you know that I have no official concern with Mrs. Holmes's death except as it is related to the death of Mrs. Cole who died in my own county. There is unquestionably a great deal of circumstantial evidence against Mr. Cole and I am personally convinced that he is not involved. I don't want the case to be rushed to an unfortunate conclusion by the super-efficiency of the New York police."

I assured him that such an attitude was completely understand-able and a great comfort, asking what I could do to help him. "You can gossip," he said, his shrewd eyes on my face. "In an organization as big as Dexter and Cole's there is bound to be talk—talk about rivalries or under-cover romances or personality conflicts."

"Having little aptitude for inquiring into people's private lives," I replied, "my capacity for gossip is limited. And being a naïve soul who persists in believing, against overwhelming evidence to the contrary, that platonic friendships are possible, I don't know an under-cover ro-mance when I see one. But I have been wondering—" and then I told him about Jane and Mr. Otis and his obvious attempts to be playful in her presence, his deference to her opinion at the store and his wife's antagonism and poorly concealed jealousy.

It apparently meant no more to him than it had to me, for who would kill Lissa Cole because Mrs. Otis was jealous of Jane? "Try again," he suggested, and getting up began another restless inspection of the room. The rain continued to beat against the windows. Even the fire and the lighted lamps could not dispel the sense of threat from a too ruthless world. Frantically I searched through my mind for a signif-icant detail which could help him. Then I remembered.

"Still on the subject of Jane Kingsley," I said. "While I was alone in the library, just before Mrs. Cole was shot, I heard her pacing the floor up in her room."

He returned to the hearth and stared down at me, "Are you sure?"

"Positive. She was right over my head, pacing back and forth, ner-vous as a witch."

"Mrs. Kingsley seems to specialize in nerves."

"She does indeed," I replied. "They've been on mine for some months now. Not only her nerves! Mrs. Kingsley can be best described by one word, a word that was taboo in what Gloria refers to as my Vic-torian background. It starts with a 'b.'"

His lips twitched. "Ignoring your upbringing," he asked, "what would you call Mr. Otis?"

"You might say that he is a son of Mrs. Kingsley."

"Two of a kind," he agreed. "But how does she fit in?" He resumed his seat.

At this point, I decided to bring up a subject over which I had done considerable pondering ever since returning to consciousness after an almost lethal dose of potassium cyanide. The Sheriff was evidently reading my face for he said, "Well, go on. What is it?"

"Just in passing, and purely as a matter of intellectual curiosity, have you ever wondered why Dexter and Cole is the only fashionable department store on Fifth Avenue which has a Drug Department?"

"Is it? How do you explain that fact?"

"I wouldn't know," I admitted, "unless it has something to do with the fact that Mr. Otis, our charming and affable Vice-President, is a graduate pharmacist and was at one time—some twenty or thirty years ago—manager of the Drug Department. I've always understood that he is very fussy about everything having to do with the operation of that department. In fact, the night after the funeral and before the fashion show, he stopped in the Drug Department to make one of his periodic inspections."

The Sheriff looked at me speculatively. "H'm'm'm," he said.

"In a fit of annoyance because Mrs. Otis was too obviously anxious to obtain an opinion against Mrs. Holmes," I continued, with what must have appeared obvious relish, "I claimed to be able to prove that Mrs. Holmes was innocent. Mrs. Otis was terribly upset. I can't help wondering if my remark was responsible for the fact that an attempt was also made on my life. Mrs. Otis very likely repeated our conversation to her husband."

The Sheriff regarded me humorously. "You are certainly Mr. Otis's little pal." He grinned. "And you have the courage of your convictions."

"I don't like him," I explained.

The Sheriff shouted with glee. "You're telling me," he chuckled.

We lapsed into silence, each of us trying to sort out the jumbled mass of information which seemed to point in so many directions but which carried me, at least, no appreciable distance along any route. I was stunned by the thought that Lissa Cole had attempted to link my name with her husband's, furious that Mr. Otis had reported the fact to the police. Lissa had, then, been desirous of a divorce as far back as that. And why? Not to marry Jim Fenton whom she had known but a brief eight months. Not, if I was any judge of temperament, to live alone and like it. Into what man's hands had she, at that time, planned to pass her controlling interest of Dexter and Cole? I asked the Sheriff if he knew.

"As far as I can find out," he answered, "nobody knows. Certainly Otis doesn't and if Martin does, he won't tell."

It was after five when he rose to go. It dawned on me that he had provided little news but had efficiently pumped me of all I knew. But I was wrong. One little bit of information lay right there in my mind, although, by no possible stretch of the imagination could I have guessed that it held a clew.

On the way to the door he paused, looking with rapt masculine admiration at a picture of Gloria on the top of the bookcase. "A beautiful girl, Miss Trent," he said almost reverently. "Why isn't she in Hollywood?"

"Too tall," I explained, "and, anyhow, she lost her yen for acting at the age of fourteen when she and another youngster tried to do a sister act—the Dean Twins they called themselves. She has associated the stage with an empty stomach ever since."

His elevator must have passed Gloria's on the way down for the door had scarcely closed upon his stalwart back than her key turned in the lock and an instant later, cheeks tinged with wind-whipped color, she came swinging into the room.

"Hi-yah," she greeted me, flinging herself into a chair and stretching out five feet eight inches of the highest priced photographic material in New York. "Oh, what a day! I wish you and Ken would get back—that place is a madhouse with you both away at the same time. What have you found to do with yourself?"

I told her about Sheriff Dodd's visit, repeating our conversation in detail. When I had finished she said, "So you think there is something between Jane and Otis-of-the-mailed-fist?"

"Don't you?"

"I did," she admitted, "but on the way home I picked up something. And it is something, Debby." Never had I seen Gloria look so serious as when she continued, "I've just found out that Jane Kingsley has been engaged to Jim Fenton for three years. He was to marry her when he got his divorce a few months ago."

Gloria's announcement, rather than startling me, seemed merely a confirmation of something which I must have known but had never put into actual thought. It was the perfect corollary to so many things. There was the fact that Jane's past was more shrouded in mystery than is customary with a person who has been exposed to as much professional publicity as the typical department store stylist. And it explained two other things. First, her determined effort at the Coles' weekend party to compete with her hostess—a bad technique under any circumstances and entirely out of keeping with Jane's normal attitude—there being no more efficient bootlicker than the talented fourflusher. And second, it explained, as nothing else could, her rage at Fenton's taunt regarding her age.

"That man is a brute," I said to Gloria. "How did you come by this interesting tidbit of information?"

"On the way up town I met Tony Barrini. He did those last bridal photographs of me—for the silver flat-wear ads, you know—and we dropped into Longchamps for a cocktail. At the bar we met Adele Bainter. You remember the black-haired, black-eyed model at the show, the one that wore the green suit?"

"Vaguely."

"Well, anyway, we met her and she said, 'I see Jim Fenton and Jane Kingsley Edwards are back together again. Hasn't he his divorce yet?' I said that I didn't know anything about a divorce."

"He got it three months ago," I interrupted. "No wonder Jane's been getting more nervous and jittery these last few months. What woman wouldn't? You didn't leave it at that, did you?"

"I'm having lunch with Adele tomorrow," said Gloria, "and I'll get the details."

I was just preparing to desert my chaise and retire to bed, when Garry arrived to take Gloria out. While he waited for her to finish dressing, he tossed his coat and hat into a chair and insisted upon a detailed account of my state of health. When Garry was being solicitous, a woman's ego couldn't help expanding. Having exhausted the subject of my convalescence, I asked, thoughtlessly, if he had been to Long Island City recently. He flushed with annoyance and shot me a quick suspicious glance.

"I was just kidding," I assured him in a mollifying tone. "If I had really suspected that you mailed those letters, I'd have been much too tactful to have mentioned it."

His face relaxed a little. "The window of my kitchen is only a few feet above the roof of the next building," he said. "I think that someone came in through that window."

I tried to imagine Arthur Otis climbing in a kitchen window. I laughed.

"There's nothing so funny about it," said Garry truculently. "Somebody got into the apartment without a key. And I think that it was Louella Holmes."

"Oh, Garry," I said weakly. "Imagine Louella Holmes scrambling around on strange roofs and climbing into people's apartments by the kitchen window. Or any window, for that matter. And then imagine her telling the papers about that scene in the library."

"She wanted everyone to know," he explained, with a painstaking effort to make it all clear to me, "how jealous she had been so that when she committed suicide and tried to murder you the second time, no one else would be blamed."

"Magnanimous of her," I admitted sarcastically, "but not very practical. She could have written a nice little note to the police from her own home. She's probably managed to express herself in writing before without the use of your typewriter."

Garry shook his head stubbornly and rose to his feet as Gloria entered the room. He looked across at her almost appealingly, a look which betrayed the labored processes of his thinking.

"Debby's being obstinate," he exclaimed petulantly. "I've just been telling her that Mrs. Holmes felt so repentant about murdering Lissa by mistake that she wrote those letters so that when she murdered Debby at the show, there would be no mistake about who did it."

Gloria gave him the smile which she used for her toothpaste photographs—very bright but devoid of expression. "Of course, that's a very good explanation. I wonder why nobody thought of it before?"

"How could they?" I asked. "There is only one mind like Garry's."

Garry strode over to the chair on which his hat and gloves were lying, his face dark with anger, and then spun around, thrashing his gloves violently against the open palm of his left hand to emphasize his words, "I don't know what's wrong with you, Debby. Every time there is any chance to close this case, you fight to keep it open. It must have been Louella Holmes. If she didn't murder Lissa, who did?"

I didn't answer. Gloria said, "Oh, come now, Garry, Debby's just trying to look at it from every angle."

"There isn't anybody who could have done it." He was almost shouting, as he answered his own question. "Yet you spend your time giving Louella alibis."

"I can't help it if people have alibis," I retorted shortly. "There are still eight of us left and several people seem to have a motive and no alibi."

"You two are acting like children," said Gloria chidingly. She slipped her arm through Garry's and smiled up at him. It was against her religion to let a man—any man—be antagonized. Not that it isn't a smart religion for a girl who's on her own in a big city—I'm just an agnostic by nature. So by way of proving that the technique of humoring men was not a monopoly, I said, "Garry, the way you tie your scarf into an ascot so that it always looks as if your valet had just patted it into place two minutes before, has me green with envy. Mine always slithers around."

He was instantly the debonair Garry whom we knew, or at least had always thought we knew, so well. Putting his gloves and hat on the couch beside me, he said, "Most people just loop the scarf over, and then of course it slips. A real ascot is an actual knot." He unfastened his scarf. "You do it like this." Again the scarf was knotted, the folds adjusted, the whole patted into impeccable, masculine lines. Garry stood at attention before me, smiling, pleased, secure in this evidence of his social accomplishments.

"I'll never tie an ascot again without thinking of you," I murmured, avoiding Gloria's dancing eyes. "It takes time, but the results are more than worth an extra minute or two. I noticed your ascot as you were going down the steps the night Lissa—oh, I'm sorry," as his lips tightened, "but I did notice how well-groomed you looked there on the stairs."

It was as if something darted through his eyes, an almost imperceptible cornet of light through that opaque greyness. It was gone in an instant but I had seen it and his easy handshake, his gay banter with Gloria as they went into the foyer, did not dim the memory. For a long time I sat very still and stared into the fire. Where, I wondered, had Garry found the necessary minute or two required to tie his ascot during the sixty seconds between the pistol shot and our arrival at the landing, to stare, aghast, upon our murdered hostess?

11

Even the weather refused to cooperate. Saturday, the third day after the fashion show, dawned bright and clear. There was no howling of wind down the canyons of Manhattan, no blinding sheet of rain, no dank and drifting fog to presage the day's events. In the midst of my breakfast of tea and toast, I realized that during the past week it had rained every day on which we had no murder. It seemed silly to take the sunshine as an omen, but the thought did make me jittery.

That morning at the store was like time spent in a madhouse but about noon two things happened which pulled me away from my desk. In the first place, I managed finally to struggle through the work which kept appearing like magic upon my desk and met a momentary lull in the buzzing of the telephone. In that brief instant of respite, I discovered in my lower drawer the sheaf of drug department ads which Mr. Otis had rejected the previous Tuesday. As I was pulling them out of the drawer, debating the advisability of bearding Mr. Otis in his den or going over his head to Mr. Cole, Jane Kingsley walked into my office.

It was the first time we had met since my disastrous experience at the fashion show; although she had gallantly sent me flowers and a cordial note of sympathy. Now she appeared so sincere in her congratulations upon my prompt recovery that I was moved, unworthily no doubt, to suspicion.

"How about lunch?" she asked.

"That would be grand."

Jane sank into a chair and lit a cigarette. She seemed tired but there was a relaxed quality in her manner utterly at variance with its usual tenseness. I had the feeling that Jane had stopped struggling. Having lost, she appeared more acquiescent than desperate.

Catherine appeared in the doorway. "Miss Trent left you this note," she told me.

Gloria's scrawled note was brief and characteristic.

"Debby," it read, "You were busy and I didn't want to disturb you. Join Adele and me at the usual Schrafft's if you want but I think I can pump her more efficiently alone.

"Took the millinery, dress and coat ads to his nibs, Fenton, for OK and got his hateful signature on all sheets so he can't cheat.

"Hope to come back with clews galore."

"Where shall we eat?" I asked Jane.

"How about Tremaine's?"

"Never heard of it. But I'm always willing to learn."

She sat still while I got my coat and hat. "It's a nice restaurant," she said musingly. "Small, exclusive, with good French cooking." Lost in thought she pulled on the cigarette and then blew the smoke toward the ceiling. "Good murals in the main dining room by a French artist whose name I should remember. I'm not usually thinking of artists when I go there." She rose and joined me at the door. "They have nice private booths at the back if you're ever interested in that sort of thing." Her short laugh was bitter. It wasn't necessary to ask how she happened to know about the private booths.

"Why do you go?" I asked. "There are plenty of other restaurants in New York."

She considered for a moment.

"Because, Debby, it isn't only the murderer who returns to the scene of the crime. The murdered also go back."

"Oh, come, Jane," I said briskly. "You're not dead yet."

She walked down the aisle in silence. "Some people," she said, pressing the elevator's signal button, "are like Rover and die all over. I seem destined to do it in sections."

The restaurant, to which we walked in spring sunshine which was still too brilliant for my peace of mind, was small but perfectly appointed. The head waiter greeted Jane with the deference due a regular patron. "A table?" he asked, standing poised in the center aisle like a dancer about to do an arabesque.

"My usual booth," replied Jane, "if it's empty."

"Madame, it has been empty all week." His heels clicked and he half bowed.

"I missed you last Saturday," said Jane. "You were out?"

"Madame, my eternal regrets. I did not return until Monday."

Jane hesitated a moment before her next question, "Has anyone been here this week?"

"No, madame."

She relaxed perceptibly. "I see." She nodded toward the back of the room and he swooped ahead of us to open the narrow French doors which converted each spacious booth into a private room. She took a ten-dollar bill out of her bag and slipped it into his hand as he closed the doors. I would have gladly given him another to find out why that information was worth so much to her.

"I saw Gloria leaving the building with Adele Bainter." We had ordered lunch, and were sampling a delectable assortment of hors d'oeuvres when she spoke. It was a casual statement as if it were unimportant but worth a passing comment.

"Yes," I agreed. "Am I indebted to that fact for this delightful invitation?"

"No," she replied easily, "not entirely. I want to ask you to do me a favor. How much has Adele already told Gloria?"

"Not much. Merely that, under the name of Jane Edwards, you have been engaged to Jim Fenton for the past three years. She's getting the rest of the story now."

"In that case," said Jane, "I'll save her the trouble of passing it along. Kingsley is my maiden name. I used my married name, Edwards, professionally, until I left my husband. That," with a wry smile, "was when I left the store at St. Louis in which Jim was merchandise manager and I was assistant fashion stylist." She paused, lifting a fork full of anchovies onto her plate. "Oh, well," she continued, with a resigned shrug, "you'll get it anyhow, I might as well be frank. There was something of a scandal, well covered up, of course. His wife sued him for divorce, naming me as correspondent and my husband sued me, naming Jim. I got my divorce almost at once but Jim's took three years."

"Why?"

She hesitated. "There was some litigation about money. His wife was wealthy. It seems he had her money tied up in some way and she tried to get it back. He married her for her money. Jim was quite frank about that." She spoke as if frankness were a virtue under any circumstances. It was easy to imagine Jim Fenton being magnificently above shame.

"Did she get the money?"

"No. He had it in his name. Everything was entirely legal."

"As long as it's legal, what need is there for it to be ethical?"

My sarcasm seemed to startle her. She said, after a moment's pause, "Considering the way he's treated me there's no reason why I should defend him. I really didn't intend to discuss this at all. You know, Debby, Jim can't be judged like other men. I should hate him. But I don't. His wife didn't either. She'd never have gotten a divorce or fought for her money if her brothers hadn't made her.

"But he didn't love me," she leaned back and closed her eyes, resignation etching deeper the fine lines of her face, "he never intended to marry me. I thought he brought me into Dexter and Cole's because he wanted me there, and that he'd marry me as soon as he was free. But he brought me in at a higher salary than I could get anywhere else—nearly double—and he's been helping me invest most of it."

"And is that legally in his name, too?"

"I wouldn't be surprised," she agreed, with that same odd acceptance of his methods. "As long as he could string me along it was very profitable to have me earning a good salary. Of course he wouldn't have needed my contribution if he had married Lissa."

"And you still love him," I marveled. "Can't you despise him instead? It would make things much easier for you."

"It's possible to despise a man and still love him. You wouldn't understand about that, Debby. Jim mesmerizes the women who fall for him. Look at Lissa. She had nothing to gain. His first wife died of a broken heart. He brags about it. His second one would take him back any minute. He stops over in St. Louis every now and then to see her. Just to watch her suffer. And there was another woman—he never married her. She was a soft fragile little blond and she had a baby more than twenty years ago. She trailed him from city to city for years, always hoping he'd marry her when he broke off with his then current wife. She committed suicide three years ago."

I said, "Don't tell me any more. There's been enough murder around lately."

We played with our food in silence. It took my mind some time to work around to the realization that I had left the store feeling half convinced that Jane was our murderer. In that regard there was one thing that I wanted to know.

"Did you know that Jim was planning to marry Lissa?" I looked at her sharply to detect any betrayal in her expression. Unfortunately, however, she had just bent over to retrieve a glove which had slipped to the floor and by the time I could see her face it was wiped clear of any expression whatsoever.

"I had no idea," she replied. She looked as innocent as a school child. She had never looked so innocent before. I didn't believe her but there was no advantage in saying so.

"I thought that it was Otis you were making a play for," I said.

The corner of her lips turned up in a mischievous little quirk. "Now wouldn't he make a sweet sugar daddy? By the way," she continued, with an abrupt change of manner, "there is a position as stylist open at Prescott and Black's Department Store in Kansas City. Carlson Dwight has recently been made fashion merchandiser there and I know you were working with Dwight before you came to Cole's. He's in New York now and I thought you might find a way of suggesting that I could handle the job. I can't apply directly," she continued, "because it would look as if I was on my way out at Cole's and knew it. Of course, I am on my way out and I do know it. But there is no use broadcasting the fact."

"I'll see him," I assured her. "It can easily be done with no loss of prestige to you. But need you go? Jim Fenton certainly won't be with Dexter and Cole's much longer. You might manage to stay on."

She shook her head. "I couldn't make the grade alone, Debby," she confessed. "Whatever his shortcomings may be, Jim is a genius as a merchandiser. He's carried my job, too. But I could manage in a smaller store away from Fifth Avenue competition."

A feeling almost of affection swept over me. So she had known all these months that she wasn't measuring up! Her arrogance was bluff, her cattiness self-defense. She was one more tragic woman who, with inadequate weapons of background and equipment, was fighting desperately for a livelihood. I said, "Whoever thought up this idea of careers for women didn't look ahead."

"They can have mine," she sighed.

We finished our lunch in a companionable silence and after paying the check, rose to leave. Jane was wearing one of the soft feminized suits which smoothed out the tense lines of her figure and over it she slipped a short boxy jacket of platinum tipped blue fox. Standing by the edge of the table, drawing on her gloves she was the perfect example of New York's chicly glamorous woman of fashion. I wondered how many of them had had to pay so high a price for their worldly success.

Abruptly I asked, "Have you told the police that you were pacing the floor in your bedroom just two minutes before Lissa was shot?"

She stared at me in an amazement which certainly seemed genuine. "But I wasn't," she declared. "I told the truth when I said that I was asleep. I was asleep."

There was no point in arguing so I let it go. But some of my new-found sympathy for her vanished. She was obviously too good an actress to be trusted.

"We'd better be getting back," I suggested, "we have to be in Mr. Fenton's office before long."

The first thing to claim attention upon my arrival at the office was the group of Drug Department ads which seemed destined never to reach the press. There being no time in which to rework them, it was imperative that they be accepted in their present form.

Going down the hall I stopped by the water cooler where Miss Phillips, Mr. Otis's secretary, was having herself a drink and a cigarette and asked if his highness were in his office and able to give a girl some time. She regarded me skeptically and said he was in his office but she had her doubts about there being any spare time for the Advertising Department. "He's pretty busy," she added enigmatically. "Mrs. Otis is in his office."

That decided me. Continuing down the corridor, I entered the empty outer office of our Executive Vice-President's suite and stopped before the closed door leading to the inner room. Regarding the closed door with frank curiosity I explained to myself that eavesdropping is one of the lower forms of self-indulgence. Fortunately, the thickness of the door eliminated any need for self-discipline. There simply were no sounds coming through it. Instinct took me to the open window.

Across the sunlit city drifted a gentle shadow. One tiny cloud rode high in that brilliant sky. Its pattern lay against the massive bulk of Radio City and then crept across roof tops, trickled down into street gullies and climbed the skyscrapers. Gradually the sparkle of the ruffled Hudson was blotted out, to reappear again as the shadow mounted the Palisades and slowly vanished over the flats of New Jersey. Once more the sky was as flawlessly blue as an inverted Wedgwood bowl. Hopefully I leaned out of the window and looked in the direction from which the single cloud had come. Perhaps there were more. Perhaps it would rain. Then I'd feel safer. Our murders had occurred on our two clear days—and this was the third. The superstitions of the ages nagged at me.

Leaning out of the window brought the brisk spring breeze against my face. And it brought Mrs. Otis's voice from the next open window. "Blackmail becomes a lifetime proposition," she was saying. "It would be better—"

"What are you trying to do, fall out the window?" Miss Phillips stood beside me, innocently peering down over the sill. I could have gladly pushed her into the street below. Now I might never know what it would be better for the Otises to do.

I consulted my watch judiciously and said, "If I can't see Mr. Otis in the next five minutes, I'll have to talk to Mr. Cole about these ads. They've been delayed by my illness and they must leave my office inside of an hour."

I went down the hall toward the President's office. Blackmail! There was a new note. By whom? For what? Blackmail. My mind almost itched with curiosity. Who needed money? Not Martin. Not Garry. Scarcely Jim Fenton. Jane? Yes, it was conceivable that Jane needed money. But that didn't hold water. If she were blackmailing Arthur Otis it would doubtless take the form of some deal to keep her job at Dexter and Cole's. And she was trying to go to Kansas City. The idea of Ken in the role of blackmailer was too ridiculous to entertain even momentarily. That left Gloria and me and heaven knows we often needed money. I made a mental note to ask Gloria whether or not she was blackmailing the Otises. If she were it would certainly be a pleasure to lend her a hand. In fact, here might lie the answer to a three-year-old prayer: Dear Lord, give me some way of being a nuisance to Mr. Otis.

Engrossed with my nefarious thoughts, I swung around a corner and ran plunk into Margaret Blake, Garry's assistant. After we pumped some wind back into our lungs and recovered a degree of equilibrium, she demanded, "Have you seen my boss?"

"No, I haven't seen him. And he isn't lunching with Gloria."

"Come on in and talk to me," she said. "I'm lonesome."

Now you can get into plenty of mental states while working in a Comparison Department but none of them is loneliness. If she wanted to talk, I wanted to listen. Together we went into the office where her desk stood at right angles to Garry's.

"It was a strange coincidence that Garry should happen to be at Queens Plaza at exactly the time the letters were mailed, wasn't it?" she asked, after we had settled down and lighted a couple of cigarettes. "Especially when they were written on his typewriter."

"If you're implying something," I said, "you'd better just come out and say it."

Her thin intelligent face grew suddenly serious and for an instant I was afraid that she would decide not to reveal the conclusions which she herself had obviously drawn. However, after tapping a pencil against her lips reflectively, she tossed it suddenly to the desk in a gesture of decision and said, "Garry claims that he can't type and those letters were plainly done by a good typist."

Again she paused and regarded his desk thoughtfully as if its presence were a mute reminder of the unwritten but very binding law that one never betrays the boss. "I'm distressed," she said, simply. "An incident occurred last night which proves that he can type like a whiz." She looked again at his desk and then at the typewriter on her own. "I came in last night and he was sitting here at my desk, copying something. When I walked in here he was so absorbed he didn't even hear the door open. I tried to get away without being seen but my bag slipped out from under my arm and went clattering to the floor."

"What did he do?" I asked.

She made a grimace that was a mixture of fear and amusement, as if attempting to disclaim the importance which she unquestionably attached to the incident.

"He lost his Park Avenue manner," she said, "and raised hell as I never dreamed he could and then stormed out of the office."

"He can get mad," I agreed. "He lost his temper at our apartment last night. Whatever he was typing could have been traced to the machine. The machine would have been here day and night, wouldn't it?"

"No, Debby, it wouldn't. The one on my desk had been on the blink for some time and we'd put in a requisition for a new one some months ago. Yesterday mine practically fell apart and Garry went to the Supply Department and raised hell. After all," she grinned, "it reflects upon his prestige to have his requisitions ignored. The supply clerk refused to give us a new one. But he did give the typewriter man instructions to send another typewriter to me. Accordingly, just before five this typewriter," she touched the instrument by her side, "was brought in to me from Mr. Otis's secretary."

"So," I reflected, "when you came in last night Garry was using the typewriter which had, until nearly the end of yesterday's working day been in Mr. Otis's office."

"Precisely," she agreed. "And that isn't all. For the first time since I've worked for Garry, better than four years, he hung around the office until I was ready to leave, walked to the elevator with me, rode down with me and then, my sweet, as if to impress upon my mind for life that we had left the store together, he took me into Longchamps and bought me a drink."

"No!"

"Yes."

We each knowingly cocked an eyebrow at the other and she continued, "You know he never bought a girl a drink just on a burst of generosity."

"Even Gloria," I admitted, "who conscientiously says only generous things of any man, confesses that he's unpardonably tight."

"Do you want to hear any more?" she asked.

"My tongue's hanging out," I said.

"As you know," she continued, and I suspected that this spree in disloyalty to a stooge superior was easing years of pent-up resentment, "Garry swore that the two keys which had been given him by the superintendent of the apartment were the only keys he had ever had, that one was on his key-ring and his Filipino had the other."

"So what?"

"He has another key. When he moved into his present apartment he gave his key to Sarah and had her take it to a locksmith on her lunch hour and get a duplicate. He can't do anything himself," she added caustically. "He was apparently afraid that the police would ask her so he told her that if she would not mention the third key, he'd give her a trip to Bermuda for her vacation."

"So," I said flippantly, "you want a trip to Honolulu in return for not mentioning that he can type?"

She looked so shocked that I added quickly, "Who had the other key? Whom is he shielding?"

"I couldn't swear to it because we have only indirect proof—but we're pretty sure that Mrs. Martin Cole had the second key."

"She certainly got around!" I exclaimed. Then added, "Why shouldn't she have had a key? They were very good friends for years."

"Do you have the key to any man's apartment?" Margaret demanded.

"Tut, tut," I admonished, "don't be personal."

"The rest of the story," she continued, "is that Garry received a small package also mailed from Queens Plaza. It came here to the office. Sarah gave it to him and he opened it in front of her, frankly wondering what it could be. It was the key Sarah had ordered for him."

I had to admit that it was all very baffling. Why hadn't he told the police that he had had a third key, had lost it and had received it through the mail? This would have given him a much better alibi than to have maintained so steadily that no other person could have gained access to the typewriter in his apartment.

"Do you have any explanation?" I asked. I certainly had none.

"I have no explanation," admitted Margaret, "but I wish that something could be done about it. Sarah has decided that Mr. Cole found the key, used it to write the letters and then sent Garry the key to shut him up—some kind of a threat. Sarah is an inveterate gossip and she'll have that story all over the store if she isn't stopped. I thought that you could talk to Mr. Holmes about it and something might be done. I can't keep Sarah quiet, but maybe he could."

I agreed to do what I could and left her. More than anything else in the world, I wanted a quiet place where I could sit and think. Try to find one in a department store!

12

"Mrs. Wood," called Ken's secretary as I passed his office, "Mr. Holmes has just come in and he wants to see you. He went at once to Mr. Cole's office and suggested that you follow him as soon as possible."

By the time I had reached Mr. Cole's reception room and Miss Deacon had announced my arrival and then ushered me, with due formality, into the sanctum sanctorum of our President, I was feeling definitely cautious. My three prize suspects included Mr. Cole's childhood friend, who had apparently been on too intimate terms with his wife; the most trusted lieutenant of his father's organization; and the ex-fiancée of his wife's intended second husband. A pretty mess and nothing to start babbling about just to relieve one's nerves!

"You're looking better," Mr. Cole said cordially, as I seated myself. "I didn't know that you were back so I sent for Ken, here. I don't want Mr. Fenton to have things too much his way at the conference this afternoon. And, of course, I won't be going."

For about fifteen minutes we talked about the plans which Mr. Cole wanted presented at the fashion conference that afternoon, and I began to fear that the engrossing subject of our double murder was going to be ignored.

However, Mr. Cole soon pushed the folders of work aside and said, "Sheriff Dodd tells me that he called on you yesterday. He seemed to get the impression that you are not very fond of either Mr. Otis or of Jane Kingsley. I was astonished," he added, teasingly.

"You'll be more astonished," I retorted, "when I tell you that right this minute I'm definitely fond of Jane. What's more, I'm going to talk to Carlson Dwight of Prescott and Black's in Kansas City and urge him to try to get Jane Kingsley away from you because I think she's exactly what he needs in his store."

"Woman in her infinite variety," said Ken. "Deborah, my dear, since there can be no advantage to you in such behavior, this must be pure altruism."

"It's just the kind of thing you men do for one another every day." I smiled sweetly. "Jane's in a tough spot," I added more seriously.

Martin Cole tilted back his chair and spun around toward the window, a favorite gesture which prevented anyone in the office from reading the expressions of a too mobile face. "I didn't tell you, Ken," he said, "but Jane has been engaged to Jim for three years. The Sheriff told me last night."

I outlined to them, as briefly as possible, the reasoning which I had followed upon my return to the store after lunch, ending with the question, "Why would a woman who is guilty of murder be trying to get a position in Kansas City?"

"I've heard tell," said Ken, "that Kansas City offers better possibilities for the future than Sing Sing."

Ignoring him, I continued, "The only thing which makes me still suspicious of Jane is that she denies pacing the floor while I was in the library. I distinctly heard her. It's silly to lie about it."

Martin Cole spun around and looked at me intently. "Did you tell Dodd?"

"Of course. Didn't he tell you?"

He shook his head. "No, but now I understand why he did something which puzzled me at the time."

"It's nice you understand," I said irritably. "I just go around handing people pieces of this puzzle and they smugly fit them into place and don't show me where. I wonder if anybody ever actually died of curiosity?"

"A perfect lady wouldn't," smiled Ken. And I knew by the way he looked at me that he loved me. It took me some time to adjust to this exhilarating knowledge and by the time that I had once more become a business woman with her mind on her surroundings, Ken was telling me that Martin Cole had just explained to him some details which, he thought, Mr. Cole might be willing to repeat for my benefit.

Martin nodded agreement and pulled out his top drawer, taking a pack of cigarettes from it. "I have just been telling Ken," he said, "the conditions under which Lissa inherited her stock. Of course, all this publicity has put me in a very bad light. People assume that I married her to gain control of the store and refused to permit her a divorce in order to retain that control. Naturally, my father and Lissa's uncle Bill were anxious that the control of the store should be kept strongly concentrated. Lissa and I were the only direct heirs in the two families. According to her Uncle Bill's will, if Lissa and I had not married by Lissa's twenty-fifth birthday, Dad, or I, if he were no longer living, had the right to buy her stock at a fair price. However, if we should marry, the stock and the income from it remained her property. The way the will is worded, I have the voting power of my wife's stock and the right to buy it at her death, the money derived from it to go into her estate. The difficulty arises from the fact that no provision is made for Lissa's being alive and not being my wife—once we have been married." He laughed shortly, "Uncle Bill died nearly twenty-five years ago. Lissa and I were children. Divorce simply wasn't accepted by such families as the Dexters and the Coles. Therefore, when Lissa wanted a divorce, I offered to buy her stock. That was certainly the spirit of the agreement into which her uncle and my father had entered. But Lissa wouldn't sell. So I refused to give her the divorce."

I said, "Thank you for telling me. I wish that you would give this version to the papers. Those of us who know you are more than willing to believe that you were justified in refusing Mrs. Cole a divorce. But the papers and the public are not so charitable."

He shrugged and the corners of his lips curled a little. I guessed that the aristocrat in him was deciding that the papers and the public could go to hell. Then he said, "As a matter of good publicity for the store, we'll have to make that gesture when the time comes." The store! It was bred in his very bones. Every act was predicated on the best interests of the store. For one soul-shaking moment, I could believe that even murder was not impossible to the man whose raison d'être of life was threatened.

We talked a few minutes with Mr. Cole regarding details of the impending conference in Jim Fenton's office and then I returned to the Advertising Department with Ken. Going down the hall I said in a carefully non-committal tone, "Garry and Lissa were very good friends, weren't they?"

He shot me a sidewise glance and said, "Go on."

I repeated briefly my conversation with Margaret Blake. I also told him of the sentence fragment which I had overheard in Mr. Otis's office and added, "You told me not to do any sleuthing and then keep the information to myself. To the best of my knowledge you know everything that I know and practically everything that I think."

"What do you mean, 'practically'?"

We had stopped before his door and he stood looking down at me. At his question, I raised my eyes to his and, under the penetration of his gaze, turned deliciously limp. "If you keep on looking at me like that," I warned, "I'll bury my face against that shoulder which you are holding so tantalizingly close and just sob my heart out."

"With joy?"

"With a combination of emotions. Do you like beefsteak rare or well done?"

"Rare."

"Isn't life wonderful? I like it rare, too."

"Debby," he said, "will you please turn around and walk quietly down the corridor and into your office? I haven't the will power to leave you and it would be impossible to kiss you here in the hall. What would those three people at the elevators think?"

"The truth," I answered, and turning, walked quietly down the corridor and into my office.

Gloria was waiting for me, eager to recount her luncheon conversation with Adele Bainter. We compared notes and found that Jane had given me a concise and accurate account of her affair with Jim Fenton. "She's had a rotten deal," said Gloria feelingly. "I don't blame her for killing Lissa. I wonder why she didn't kill Jim instead?"

"Maybe she hoped to get him back."

"Maybe she's still waiting for her chance—to kill him, I mean."

"Now tell me something," I said. "When I told you that Garry had kissed me on the driveway of the Cole home and insisted that he was in love with you, why did you discount the whole episode?"

Her black brows shot up inquiringly. "You haven't stumbled on anything, have you?"

"You answer my question. Why do you always say that Garry never was in love with you?"

"Because he never was," she said. "Look, Debby, Garry isn't in love with me but I do feel a great sense of loyalty to him and I don't want to discuss his personal affairs—unless, of course, you think there is some good reason for doing so. Actually, I don't know anything, but I do suspect a lot and I've just hoped that no one would question me."

"Just tell me one thing. When I said he had kissed me, did you assume that he had mistaken me for Lissa?"

"Yes, I did."

We sat in silence for a moment, each busy with her own thoughts. Then Gloria added, "Garry's in a tough spot. You won't do anything to make it worse, will you?"

"I'm still betting on Arthur Otis," I said. "And now, we'd better go to that meeting and let Jim drink his vichy water to impress us."

We were almost the last of the group to reach Jim Fenton's office. There were several buyers from the Fashion Department scattered about the room, and the whole atmosphere was one of such business-like normality as to be balm to my harassed spirit. Jane came in and, without hesitation or seeming self-consciousness, crossed over to Jim's desk and attempted to ask him about some fabrics, swatches of which she carried in her hand. Ken and Mr. Otis were near one of the windows talking to a buyer and completely absorbed in their conversation. Murder may come and murder may go, but the merchandising business continues on its relentless way.

Garry, standing by Fenton's desk, was urging him to sign a group of comparison reports before the meeting should start. He had them arranged so that the lower edge of each sheet was slid an inch or so below the preceding sheet. "You've seen all these," he was saying urgently. "Just put your signature on each page. It won't take a minute. You don't even have to turn the pages, you can sign every one at once."

"I'll wake up some fine morning and find that I've signed my life away," declared Jim with a frown. "How do I know what's on these pages?" He took his fountain pen from its holder and signed each one

obediently, then flipped one or two for a quick glance at its contents
and passed them back to Garry. "All right, old boy," he said, the indulgent tone in his voice shadowed by contempt. Garry put the papers on
the conference table behind Jim's desk and crossed the room to join
Edie Rothman who, smartly dressed and witty, was his favorite buyer.

Mr. Fenton turned then to the swatches in Jane's hand. He had
been permitting her to stand beside him as if entirely unconscious of
her presence. Now he demanded imperiously, "What are these for?"

She told him in a quiet, well-controlled voice, her expression betraying none of the emotion which must have been tormenting her. He
fingered the fabrics, holding them up to the light, his lips pursed and
sulky. Then he flung them on to the desk so that they slid across its pol-
ished surface and would have fallen to the floor if Jane had not leaned
forward and caught them. "The blue is the only one fit to consider." His
tone implied that she was a fool not to have known as much. "Can't you
make any decisions of your own?" he added insolently.

To my horror I said, in a voice shaking with fury, "If she had picked
the blue, you'd have claimed the green was the only one."

"Someday," he retorted sharply, "you may learn not to speak out of
turn."

"That would be a great asset to me," I admitted, smiling. After all, I
can alter my moods too. And this was no time to pick a fight.

And then something happened which will always remain in the
back of my mind as a subject to speculate upon when I'm in the mood
for a nightmare. He had looked up at me, his intense blue eyes dark
and sullen, but as I smiled down at him, his eyes changed. It was not
merely one of his lightning shifts of expression which shocked me. It
was the familiarity of the look. There was something in it to which I
responded with a surge of affection. He ceased, for an instant, to be
Jim Fenton and became someone of whom I was very fond. And in the
shock of this realization came the memory of Jane's desperate voice,
He hypnotizes the women who fall for him.

If this were hypnosis, it seemed imperative not to risk its charms.
Turning on my heel, I walked across the room to Ken and the hand I
laid on his arm was visibly trembling. "Can't the meeting get started?"
I asked. "My knees are still a bit wobbly."

And so the meeting got under way. Mr. Otis pulled up a chair to the end of the long conference table and Jim swung his swivel chair around so that he was seated in the middle of one long side. The rest of us drew up chairs and, after some confusion of shifting stacks of correspondence and trade journals and reports from the table, we were ready for work. Then Jim went into his act. He carefully rearranged the papers which were to be under discussion during the meeting. Then he took out a yellow scratch pad and placed it ready before him. He buzzed for his secretary and gave her instructions regarding an anticipated telephone call.

The rest of us waited.

And then came the crowning touch. He spun his chair about and reached for the siphon of vichy water, placing it before him on the table. Another spin and he secured a glass. Then with deliberate precision he squirted the vichy into the glass.

The rest of us waited.

With the air of a connoisseur he lifted the glass and watched the bubbles for a second. "Not the life it should have," he said. "It has seemed flat this last day or two. I'll have to write them." He looked so pleased with himself contemplating the arrogant letter he would write.

"Drink your damned water," commanded Otis sharply. "We can't wait here all day."

"To your health," Fenton laughed and, waving his arm in a gesture which included us all, he drained the glass.

Three minutes later he was dead.

13

As the Sheriff said later, there was enough poison in that drink to have killed a pair of oxen. Before Jim Fenton had so much as taken the glass from his lips, his body stiffened and he lunged to his feet, only to sprawl drunkenly across the table. Gloria, seated to his left, threw out her arm as he pitched forward and broke the fall so that his face did not crash against the surface but turned upward, the lips working grotesquely. She leaned over him to catch the muttered syllables, her bright hair for an instant blotting out that tortured face. Then Garry, from the other side, helped her to steady the relaxing body and ease it back into the chair.

Bedlam had broken loose in the room. Jane was screaming, shrill, piercing shrieks of hysteria, as she struggled against Edie's restraining arms. Mr. Otis had flung open the door into the outer office and was calling for the doctor, the police—for anyone. Beads of perspiration stood out on his forehead. His voice was edged with panic. A buyer flung up one of the windows and then, looking foolish, lowered it again. Gloria, her hand still on Jim's shoulder, was saying in a dazed way, "He said 'paper.' He said 'paper.'"

Ken alone remained self-possessed. He had caught up the glass as it fell to the table and sniffed at the liquid still remaining in the bottom. "Potassium cyanide," he said. Then he lifted the phone from its cradle and said, "Medical Department. Urgent." An instant later his quiet, un-hurried voice was giving the store's nurse concise instructions.

As if by a miracle, Martin Cole appeared in the doorway. Behind him was Sheriff Dodd who had been with Mr. Cole in his office at the moment of Jim's death. The two of them entered and the Sheriff, although having no official capacity in New York City, took charge of the situation with a brisk impersonality of manner which stilled the aimless flutterings of the others. Soon a sprightly nurse, her white cap flouncing with efficiency, hurried into the room.

As Jim was carried from the office, his limp body now decorously concealed by a sheet, Jane's hysteria became frenzied. The sight of her face, tear-stained and convulsed with grief, was more than I could endure and, still seated at the conference table, I was about to bury my own face in my arms when the Sheriff calmly picked up a carafe of water and dashed it into Jane's face. Her screams changed to strangled gulps as he picked her up and gently deposited her on the couch opposite the windows. She lay there gasping. Edie, who was taking Jane as her personal responsibility, seated herself on the edge of the couch and carefully wiped away the trickling drops. The rest of us watched as if we were mesmerized. It dawned on me that experience with murder does not apparently increase one's capacities to cope with it. We had all been much more efficiently useful at the time of Lissa Cole's death. Presently the door opened and the nurse reentered, a hypodermic syringe in her hand. She crossed over to Jane and, drawing back her sleeve, thrust in the needle.

"Not enough to put her to sleep," instructed the Sheriff. The nurse nodded, pressed the plunger gently and withdrew the syringe. Jane turned her face to the wall and moaned softly. The room was suddenly silent.

I looked around the office. Ken was once more sitting beside me and when I attempted a weak little smile of gratitude for his strengthening presence, he put his hand over mine. It was firm and steady and something which had been quivering within me was quieted. Martin Cole stood with his back to us all, staring out of the window. The sun was just sinking behind the Palisades. Our third sunny day was over. "Things do run in threes," I thought, "it isn't just an old wives' tale." And suddenly, as if a voice had spoken, I knew that our murders were over. They had run their cycle: Lissa and Jim, who had tried to flout the rules of good sportsmanship; Louella who had been an innocent scapegoat. But the accounting remained. Someone still had to pay.

The Sheriff was busy at the telephone. He had called police headquarters and the District Attorney's office. Until someone from the

New York Police Department arrived he could have no authority. As he had said at my apartment the previous afternoon, the investigation of the case had passed out of his hands, except as it was related to the murder of Mrs. Cole.

However, he did dispatch the buyers to the outer office where they sat forlornly grouped about Elsie Higgins, Mr. Fenton's middle-aged and, at the moment, completely nonplussed secretary. She had a bewildered air as if uncertain as to which drawer murder was filed in. Only those of us who had been present at the unfortunate week-end party up the Hudson now remained in the inner office. A sort of sheep and goat arrangement which in itself gave one a sense of guilt.

Suddenly I became aware that Gloria was still poking at the papers scattered over the desk and table. She had recovered much of her accustomed poise and when the Sheriff snapped, "Miss Trent, I have said nothing is to be disturbed," she looked up at him and explained with a kind of patient desperation, "But he said something about a paper. I thought it might be something that was here."

"Everything will be examined in due time," he told her. "Just find yourself a chair and wait for the police."

She sat down obediently in the nearest chair, which happened to be the swivel that Jim had occupied, and swung herself gently back and forth from desk to table and table to desk. Garry was slowly pacing the floor between the table and the windows. He had the air of a big-business magnate who is planning the details of his next billion-dollar coup. Martin Cole still watched the fading color in the western sky. I tried not to remember that less than an hour previously I had admitted to myself that murder might not be impossible to a man whose raison d'être of life was threatened. But surely that threat had been removed before the death of Jim Fenton. "He couldn't have done it," I whispered to myself and kept repeating the words over and over like a prayer.

A movement at the end of the table diverted me. Arthur Otis, seated in the chair which he had previously occupied, was now taking careful inventory of the occupants of the room, his hard brown eyes remote and impersonal. But it was noteworthy that his previous readiness to take command and browbeat the rest of us was lacking. That week had taken a heavy toll of the vitality of our Executive Vice-President. Watching him, I recalled that sharp command, "Drink your damned water!" which had hurried Jim to his death. I wondered if speed in the drinking could have meant anything. Would Jim, playing with his drink in his usual dilatory fashion, have been more likely to detect the faint odor of almonds which characterizes potassium cyanide? Abruptly Mr. Otis dropped his head into his cupped hands. He looked completely exhausted. I began to speculate upon the identity of his blackmailer. I wondered if Mrs. Otis had left the store.

The door from the corridor to the outer office opened and closed. Mrs. Otis appeared in the doorway between the two rooms. Her face had that same guarded expression which I had noticed when she stood looking at Lissa Cole's lifeless body. She seemed to be consciously refusing to betray surprise or horror or grief. Perhaps she had not yet decided which emotion was appropriate to the occasion. She came into the room and, without acknowledging anyone by so much as a nod, went over to Martin Cole, slipping her arm through his. Startled, he turned and looked down at her, then drew her closer in a half embrace. It was as if she had given him her allegiance and he had accepted it. Her husband did not move.

The next ten minutes were the most completely dismal which have ever fallen to my lot. No one spoke. Jane sobbed a little from time to time, the hopeless sobs of resignation and despair. It dawned on me with horror that I was hungry.

"At the risk of seeming irreverent," I said to the Sheriff, my voice sounding apologetic, "may I request a cup of tea and some toast? I don't seem to be over my experience of last Wednesday."

"How does a person get food up here?" Sheriff Dodd asked Ken.

Phoning the restaurant for tea and coffee broke the crushing silence. As Ken hung up the receiver, the police arrived. We were off to a grueling few hours.

Assistant District Attorney Hoffmann took charge of the case with the air of a man who has had enough of this nonsense and intends to put a stop to it. He was a large man, squarely built and pugnacious of jaw, with a brush of stiff dun-colored hair standing up from a massive brow. And one look at his pink-rimmed, light eyes convinced me that he'd break the case if he broke every one of us doing so. Here was no nice distinction, such as Sheriff Dodd possessed, regarding the breeding and social responsibility of a man like Martin Cole, no sympathy for the shattered spirit of Jane Kingsley, no masculine susceptibility to the charms of Gloria Trent. Here was a Juggernaut which would roll relentlessly over each of us, crushing the innocent with the guilty. But, in the end, he would know the truth. Assistant D. A. Hoffmann was there to get his man. One look at him convinced me that he would do so.

There was a bustle of activity as the police took over. The medical examiner was dispatched to the Infirmary. I was grateful for the fact that Jim Fenton had died in such a manner that he could be removed from the scene of the crime. A corpse, added to the belligerent efficiency of Hoffmann and Jane's whimpering sobs, would have taxed our nerves beyond endurance.

A crew of assistants went to work at once. Actually there was little to do. The siphon and the glass fragments were carried next door to Jane's office which, ironically enough, was to serve as the police laboratory.

It was the work of but a few minutes to establish the fact that Jim Fenton had died of a large dose of potassium cyanide which had been contained in his glass of vichy. The vichy remaining in the siphon was heavily charged with the poison so that there was no doubt as to its source. There were no finger-prints, other than Jim's, on the siphon. The glass had three sets of prints—Jim's, his secretary's and those of the cleaning woman who daily washed the glasses on the executives' desks.

The Sheriff, Hoffmann and a go-between whom they called Guffey, and whose function it was to run in and out of the room carrying messages, withdrew to a corner and held a whispered consultation. Then each of us was taken in turn to a washroom and our possessions examined scrupulously for some minute flake of the poison which might have clung to us. They even probed under our fingernails. But all the poison had gone into Jim Fenton's vichy or had vanished beyond the reach of the disgusted police. We returned to the office one by one and resumed our places as if we were the characters on a stage setting, waiting for the curtain to rise.

When, that Saturday afternoon, no direct evidence was to be found on our persons, Hoffmann installed himself at Elsie Higgins's desk in the outer office, the Sheriff at his side, and had the door closed to the corridor. Then one by one we were called before him and questioned.

I was the last one for whom he sent but by the time Guffey opened the door and bawled, "Mrs. Wood next," even the hot tea I had been consuming had not stilled the shaking sensation in the pit of my stomach. The expression of each one who had returned from that relentless fire of questions was mute testimony that what we had been through to date was a pink tea by comparison.

I sat down reluctantly and faced my inquisitor. When he had established the details of my identity to his satisfaction and had assured himself that I had been practically on the doorstep of every one of the three murders, he began probing for motives. Considering that I had none, other than the possible desire to marry Ken, he did magnificently with the little at hand. It made me realize what some of the others, whose motives were substantial, must have gone through. But it was soon apparent that he was not really interested in the idea of me as the murderer. What I knew about the others and their possible motives was his goal.

"Do you consider Mrs. Kingsley's behavior normal?" he demanded.

"Perfectly," I replied. "She was in love with him. You know that."

"She says she didn't know that Fenton was two-timing her," he said. "Do you believe that?"

"I have no reason not to."

And then, suddenly, I remembered Jane's face as she got off the elevator the Saturday noon before Lissa Cole was murdered. She had looked like a woman whose life had crashed before her very eyes. "I don't think she knew," I added stubbornly. It was my atonement for having said that I had heard her pacing the floor above the library.

"You're lying!" snapped Hoffmann. "What do you know?"

But I stuck to my guns and he finally went on to another question. This time he shifted to Mr. Otis and made me reiterate all of the suspicions which I had confided to the Sheriff. I regretted my past loquacity but was glad to get away from the subject of Jane. Whether or not she was guilty, I was inclined, after our luncheon conversation, to feel that a woman in her position was to be excused if she had indulged in some action more drastic than that of registering pique.

When we had roasted Mr. Otis to a nice brown crisp, my interrogator suddenly jerked his head toward the door of the inner room and said, "Go back in there and wait with the rest of them." Relieved that we had not touched upon the subject of Garry, I returned to the office and once more sat down beside Ken.

In less than a minute, Sheriff Dodd opened the door and came in. We all went rigid watching him. My stomach started to tremble again. He walked over to the end of the conference table which was across from Mr. Otis and to Ken's right. In his hand was an automatic pencil. He laid it on the table before him. "Mrs. Wood," he asked, "have you ever seen that pencil before?"

"I don't know that I've seen that one," I said. "Pencils like that were passed out to each person attending the last Amos Parrish Fashion Selling Clinic. They are semiannual conferences held here in New York and most of us attended one a month or so ago."

The Sheriff nodded, turning the pencil between his fingers. "Will everyone," he asked, "who has such a pencil either give it to me or tell me where it can be found?"

Gloria and I opened our bags and pushed our pencils along the table to Ken, who, not having attended the conference, possessed none. He handed them over to the Sheriff. Martin Cole crossed the room and laid his with the others. I pointed to Jane's handbag and the nurse, opening it, drew out a pencil and brought it to the Sheriff. Arthur Otis fidgeted about in his pockets and then turned to his wife, "Do you know what I've done with my pencil, dear?"

"It was on your desk this morning," she answered.

Her voice was that of a very tired woman. Apparently the morning spent with her husband, not to mention the effort of keeping track of his pencils, had worn her resistance to a thin veneer.

Guffey was dispatched for the pencil which, when it was placed before the Sheriff, had a grey elastic twisted about its erasure cap. That completed the collection. Garry did not own one, much to his disgust. The Sheriff, under our collectively interested gaze, gathered the six pencils into his hands, rolled them meditatively between his palms and then slowly laid them on the table, leisurely forming a six-pointed star. Then he looked around at our inquiring faces. "Thank you," he said.

Leaving the pencils to pique our curiosity, he started picking up the papers which were scattered about the floor. "Mrs. Wood," he requested, "will you please check through these and see if there is anything unusual about them?" He took a pile himself and pushed some across the table to me. In silence we leafed through them. I had finished my first sheaf and started on the second when I found it. There were three pages of white bond paper clipped together. At the top of the first was the heading: "To Sheriff Dodd." At the bottom of the second page, several inches below the edge of the typed message, was Fenton's scrawled, pagoda-like signature.

"To Sheriff Dodd," I read.

"Wait," said the Sheriff. He went to the door and called Hoffmann. Then the two of them stepped inside the room and closed the door behind them. They stood there while I read it. The others were as still as images carved from stone.

"To Sheriff Dodd [So the letter went.]:

"It is only a matter of days until you will catch up with me. I prefer this way out.

"As you have suggested, but really not believed, I quarreled with Mrs. Cole at lunch last Saturday. She told me that she had decided to abandon our plan of getting the stock away from Martin and that, instead, she was going to offer to sell it to him and then get her divorce and marry Garry Thorpe. I saw red. No woman had ever made a fool of me before and I didn't intend that she should. I cajoled and threatened but got nowhere.

"When I reached the Coles' home Saturday evening, I still thought it would be possible to persuade her. But all through the evening I had no chance to talk to her until just before we went upstairs for the night. Then she told me that Martin had found one of my letters and had raised hell. She was enjoying her little game and said that she'd let him worry awhile and then offer to sell at a better price than her stock was really worth. At the foot of the stairs, I overheard her tell Garry that she would meet him in the drawing-room at one-thirty A.M.

"Of course I had lost the chance to control the store but I was in a white heat of rage and I saw a chance to punish everyone who had thwarted me. The house was full of people who had motives for killing her.

Martin Cole was the first. I was about to jilt Jane Kingsley, which would have given her a motive for killing
Mrs. Cole. Martin had told the Otises, immediately upon
their arrival, of our supposed plans (Lissa told me that)
and they knew that they stood to lose their power in
the organization. And, finally, there was Garry who,
as everyone knew, was crazy about Mrs. Cole. And I
guessed, as later proved the case, that the police would
doubt his story that she had turned me down for him.

"So I got up about one-fifteen and went down to the
library and took the gun. Then I waited. Garry left his
room soon after I returned to mine. Mrs. Cole came out
of her room at the same time and they met on the landing and walked downstairs together.

"While they were still in the drawing-room, Mrs.
Holmes went down to the library and returned almost
immediately. She was still on the landing when Mrs.
Wood left her room. They saw each other but they didn't
speak. While Mrs. Wood was in the library, Garry returned to his room. About two minutes after Mrs. Wood
closed her door, Lissa came out of the drawing-room.
She saw me in the upper hall and screamed, trying to
turn and run toward the north corridor. I shot her and
tossed the gun into the hall. Knowing that I could be
considered the one person who had no motive for killing
her, I made a great show of being the first person in the
hall and behaved properly frustrated and outraged. You
must admit that it was a good act.

"Then, when Arthur Otis was questioning us in the
drawing-room later that night, Mrs. Holmes provided
me with the perfect scapegoat. I had, naturally, recalled
her attitude toward Mrs. Wood and had guessed, from
her trip to the library, that she had wanted to obtain the
gun. But I had assumed that the presence of her husband in the room would give her an alibi. He might have
been asleep when she went downstairs but he wouldn't
sleep through a revolver shot. When I learned that he

had been out of the room, I knew that fate had played into my hands.

"At the fashion show I saw the perfect opportunity to close the whole matter. I had learned—never mind how—that Mrs. Wood and Mrs. Holmes were attending the show together. Tuesday night I stayed late in the office of one of the buyers on the third floor and then went up to the fifth floor and got some potassium cyanide from the photography department. When I ordered drinks for the crowd at the show, I was trying to figure out how I could get the poison into their two glasses without throwing suspicion on myself. When Mrs. Wood ordered tea for the two of them, I saw my chance. Under the pretext of talking about advertising, I kept Mrs. Wood with me until the waiter brought in the tea. When she looked up at him, I passed my hand over the spout, which fortunately was the straight type, and dropped in the poison.

"You know the rest. Mrs. Wood recovered and talked too much. I still felt comparatively safe. You had so many good suspects that I figured you would never get around to me. Than I made my blunder. This morning Gloria came into my office. The carpet muffled her footsteps and she reached my shoulder without my hearing her. I was holding my Amos Parrish Fashion Selling Clinic pencil. I had disposed of the large vial of potassium cyanide after murdering Mrs. Holmes but I had been carrying enough for several more such episodes in the lead compartment of the pencil. Unfortunately, I had succumbed to the temptation to shake the powder into the palm of my hand. I was wondering if it would ever be necessary to use it again. When I saw Gloria looking at it, I knew it would be.

"I threatened Gloria, telling her that I had a hired gunman who would avenge me if she ever exposed me. I felt that she was sufficiently terrified to keep quiet for a little while but I knew that she would soon realize she was in greater danger from me than from anyone whom I might have hired to avenge me. Inevitably, she would confide in someone.

"Being a showman at heart, I was tempted to set the stage to make it look like another murder and hope that Gloria's story of the pencil would be doubted. But I have finally decided to make the one magnanimous gesture of a sinful life. There is the possibility that Jane will be suspected and, by confessing, I can save her any further suffering. It rather pleases me to go out of this world be-having in a noble manner. Such a pleasant change from routine!

"Of course, it would be perfectly possible to drink my poison quietly at home. But that is not my nature."

Then came the scrawled but unmistakable signature.

Positively, when I had finished reading, my voice seemed to have taken on something of the quality of Jim Fenton's voice. The letter was so completely characteristic that one could almost hear him speak. The straightforward thinking and clean-cut presentation coupled with that insolence of manner. A shrewd and clever mind thumbing its nose at decency. To the end, he had gloried in the dramatic. Not to save Jane had he confessed. The pride of the perfect crime had been upon him.

I laid the typed pages on the table and looked up at the two men by the door. Their faces were completely expressionless as their two pairs of eyes flicked from one to another of us. So I took an inventory too and was struck by the singularly impassive countenances about me. The merchandising business is obviously one of the better spots in which to develop a poker face. But the police learned plenty from that survey of expressions. No one was offering credulity or incredulity. They were nei-ther distressed nor relieved. They were not glad nor sorry. By their very refusal to betray themselves, they betrayed themselves. For they were going to let the police swallow this confession, if the police would do it.

There were, however, two exceptions. One was Garry. He took out a handkerchief and mopped a damp face, his lips pursed to emit a "whew" which was scarcely audible. The other was Gloria. She looked up with evident relief and said, "I'm glad he told it before I had to."

Dodd and Hoffmann came over to the table and stood looking down at the typed message.

"Where did Fenton learn to type?" the Sheriff demanded.

"Apparently he didn't," I replied. "There are lots of erasures, the margins are irregular, words are divided in the wrong places and the whole thing is too messy for even a passable typist. He must have punched it out letter by letter."

Hoffmann turned to Gloria and demanded truculently,

"Whyn't you tell us about the poison?"

"Because I was frightened," she said, and there was very real terror mirrored in her eyes. "He threatened me so terribly. He said that he had a man who would kill me if I ever uttered a word to incriminate him."

"He's been going to the movies too much," muttered the D. A.'s assistant. "And you have, too, if you believed him."

"I've always been afraid of Mr. Fenton," she admitted. "He was treacherous. When he threatened me, I was literally paralyzed with fright. Then when he was dying, I was sure that he said the word 'paper' as he was pitching forward on to the table. So I guessed that there might be a confession. I wanted you to get the story from the confession instead of from me because then no one could believe that I had given him away. If there hadn't been a confession or he had tried to pass the guilt to someone else, I would have told you the whole incident at once."

Hoffmann gave her a searching glance and then, apparently satisfied, carried the 'confession' into the outer office and asked Miss Higgins to copy off the first few lines. One of his assistants studied the two sheets for a moment and then returned it to his chief. "Both written on the same typewriter," announced Hoffmann, returning to the inner office and closing the door behind him.

Mr. Otis stood up. "Looks like the whole thing is pretty well settled," he said. "I suppose there is no reason why we should stay. You have your murderer."

"Yeah," said Hoffmann. He looked at Mr. Otis and Mr. Otis sat down again. "The Sheriff and I want to talk things over." The two men stalked out of the room together. At the door, they beckoned the nurse to follow them. The rest of us subsided into a nervous silence.

A few minutes later the door opened and the nurse reentered. She carried a glass of cloudy liquid and, crossing over to Jane, seated herself on the edge of the couch. Jane had fallen into a heavy sleep and it took several minutes for the nurse to rouse her. At last she sat up and drank the dose of aromatic spirits which were held to her lips. Then, swinging her feet to the floor, and steadying herself with a hand pressed against the nurse's knee, she looked about the room at the seven of us sitting there, tight-lipped and nervous.

"What has happened?" she asked, the syllables separated by little gasping breaths. "I mean what happened after—" She couldn't say after what.

For an instant no one moved or spoke and the atmosphere of the room, which had been so tense with uncertainty, suddenly was charged with sympathy and kindliness. But it was apparent that no one cared to undertake the responsibility of telling Jane just what had happened. Perhaps no one quite knew.

The nurse did the talking, and she had obviously been rehearsed. "Mr. Fenton," she said in her quiet professional voice, "was not murdered. You see, he had murdered the others. So he committed suicide."

"Oh, no," cried Jane, "not Jim! He'd never commit suicide. He loved life too much." She swept her hands out to us in a gesture of appeal. No one moved.

"According to the confession," continued the nurse, like an efficient child reciting her lesson, "Mr. Fenton and Mrs. Cole had lunch together last Saturday. She told him that she had changed her mind about marrying him. He was in a rage and that night he killed her. We have a full explanation and a signed confession here."

"I don't care what you have," screamed Jane. "It's a lie—a lie, I tell you. I know. I can prove it."

"Then prove it," commanded a harsh voice behind us and we all whirled to see the assistant D. A., his belligerent jaw thrust forward, standing in the doorway.

"Last Saturday," said Jane, and, like sightseers on a bus, our heads turned in unison to look at her, "last Saturday, I went to Tremaine's restaurant, alone, for lunch. Jim and I have been meeting there at least once a week for dinner. I had never been there for lunch before but I was in the neighborhood, so I just dropped in." She drew a long breath and stared off into space for a moment, as if organizing her thoughts. "There was a substitute head waiter and he didn't recognize me. I asked for the center booth at the back because that was the one Jim always reserved for us. Maybe," she shrugged ruefully, "I was feeling sentimental. The head waiter said that it was occupied and took me to a table along the side. I was scarcely seated when the doors of the center booth opened and Mrs. Cole came out. She closed the doors behind her and walked out of the restaurant without seeing me. I don't know why I assumed that the booth was empty, but I did. I got up from the table, walked over and opened the doors. Jim was sitting in there—alone."

"Well," prompted Hoffmann.

Jane moistened her lips, so blatantly crimson against the parchment white of her skin, and drew a deep breath. "Jim was smiling—that cruel, triumphant smile of his. I went into the booth and sat down opposite him. He was furious that I had caught him and Mrs. Cole but he was too completely pleased with himself to really care. He told me that he was going to marry her. He said"—the bitterness in her tone increased—"that he would keep me in my job and that I ought to be thankful to get that much. He promised to make my life hell if I betrayed him and I had no doubt of his ability to do so. He left me there and came back to the store. When I had pulled myself together a little, I came back too.

"Jim and Lissa didn't quarrel that day," said Jane, "they came to a definite understanding with one another. Jim didn't kill Lissa. Somebody killed Jim."

The most awful crawling sensation started at the base of my spine and crept along each vertebra until it burst across my scalp like a thousand sharp, little needles. Gloria's hand twitched convulsively in mine. At the end of the table Mr. Otis whispered, "Oh, my God!"

14

So we were back where we had been one week previously as we had stood looking down upon our murdered hostess, Lissa Cole—with the exception of two more corpses and a crop of clews which had the police dizzy. The eight of us who had managed to survive the week's carnage were left by Hoffmann and the Sheriff to sit and contemplate our sins in the gloomy half-light of Jim Fenton's erstwhile office. This we did in a mournful silence which was so solid it could have been cut into slabs and used for soundproofing.

In the meantime, the Messrs. Dodd and Hoffmann had their heads together in the outer office, checking through seemingly endless pages of our testimony, winnowing the grain from the chaff. They decided to make each of us testify to his actions before the entire group in the hope that someone, to save his neck, might tread on another's toes and force a contradiction; thus the police might gain an entering wedge.

So they returned to the office and went to work on us. Hoffmann with hammer and tongs, the Sheriff with less fireworks but more subtlety. They made a formidable team and put us through an ordeal, the subconscious memory of which still has the power to bring me out of a sound sleep, whimpering with fright.

However, it was neither of our two inquisitors who spoke first after they had settled themselves at the end of the table. They faced the windows and looked directly at Arthur Otis, seated opposite them. Behind him was Martin Cole, again lounging against the window sill. It was Martin who spoke first and he said a remarkable thing, when you stop to think of it.

"Gentlemen," he said, "I think that it should be brought to everyone's attention that the 'confession' purported to have been written by Jim Fenton was a forgery. Therefore its contents do not necessarily give a true picture of existing circumstances. It was written for the convenience of the murderer. Any allusion"—and here he came to his point—"to a relationship existing between Mrs. Cole and my friend, Garrison Thorpe, should be dismissed from the minds of all of us. We are all ready, I am confident, to regard it as the fabrication of someone in need of an alibi."

Even Hoffmann was stopped! For would not Garry, if innocent, have flown, outraged, to his own defense? And had not Martin Cole, sensing that Garry's plodding mind had not adjusted to this new turn of events, tossed out a life-line to him?

The look which the assistant D. A. gave Martin was one compounded of respect and annoyance. As for Garry, he looked up slowly, his mind adjusting to the new idea and realizing its import. "Thanks," he said, and the note of gratitude in his voice was touchingly sincere.

"O. K., old man," returned Martin briefly.

"Miss Trent," the assistant D. A. hunched forward, hurling the question at her, "what about this fine story of yours that Fenton was pouring potassium cyanide crystals out of a pencil into the palm of his hand when you walked in this morning?"

She regarded him with surprise. "Nothing about it," she said. "He had the poison in his hand just as I have said. Everything happened exactly as it was told in the 'confession.' Mr. Fenton had his back to his desk, and therefore, to the door. He was leaning over the table, just as I am now, and he didn't hear me come in."

"But if he didn't kill Mrs. Cole," Hoffmann pointed out, "there would certainly have been no point to his killing Mrs. Holmes. And if he didn't kill Mrs. Holmes, why would he have the poison?"

Gloria looked puzzled. "I wouldn't know," she said. "He didn't either admit or deny the murders. He simply threatened me, should I ever say that I'd seen the poison." She looked at the six Amos Parrish pencils on the table. "Maybe someone had taken his pencil and put the poison in it and he had just found it. Maybe he wanted to learn who it was for himself and didn't want the police in on his game."

"Or," suggested the Sheriff, "someone may have overheard your conversation with Fenton and made use of it by inserting it in the 'confession'."

"Miss Higgins would know better than I," said Gloria. Her expression indicated that she was shrewdly sidestepping a confirmation of his suggestion.

The Sheriff said, "Push the buzzer," and Gloria, still seated in the swivel chair, complied. A terrified-looking Miss Higgins entered. She closed the door gently and stood before it, her two hands behind her clasping the knob, as if not daring to lose this contact with an avenue of escape.

"At what time did Miss Trent come to this office this morning?" demanded Hoffmann.

"About eleven-thirty, I think it was."

"Who was in the office at the time—besides Mr. Fenton?"

"No one. He was alone."

"Which way was he facing when she entered?"

"He was working at the table. His back was to the door."

"Did you watch them while they were talking?"

"Certainly not!" exclaimed the secretary indignantly. "I was busy. And then Mrs. Otis came; I was talking to her."

Like so many automata we all shifted our eyes to Mrs. Otis. She was looking badly flustered. I wondered if she had failed to inform the police of her visit to Mr. Fenton's office—or at least his reception room—that morning.

"I see. You were talking to her all the time that Miss Trent was in the inner office." He made it sound as if such a circumstance would be very detrimental to Mrs. Otis and got the desired reaction.

"Oh, no, sir!" protested Miss Higgins eagerly, "I was talking on the telephone when Mrs. Otis entered and she sat down on the chair just behind me until I finished."

"How do you know she sat on the chair if it was behind you?"

The frightened girl blinked at him in bewilderment. "She was sitting there when I turned around. Then she moved over to the chair by my desk and we talked for quite a while."

"Were you still talking when Miss Trent left?"

"No. I had had to take some reports into Mrs. Kingsley's office. I didn't see Miss Trent leave."

"Of course," said Hoffmann, "Mrs. Otis left the office when you did?" Again he made it sound as if the fact of Mrs. Otis's leaving was very incriminating and again Miss Higgins fell into his trap.

"Indeed, she didn't," almost triumphantly, "she just sat there and waited for me to come back."

"And when you came back Miss Trent had left and Mrs. Otis was talking to Mr. Fenton?"

"Oh, no, sir! When I came back Mr. Fenton had left too. But Mrs. Otis had waited for me." She was plainly touched by such an honor as having the Executive Vice-President's wife wait for her.

"Then Mrs. Otis was alone in the room when you returned from Mrs. Kingsley's office?" questioned Hoffmann, as if that were quite the nicest thing he could conceive of.

"Yes," agreed the secretary happily, "she was alone."

"You may go now," said Hoffmann and little Miss Higgins retired in a rosy glow over having been so helpful to her friend, Mrs. Otis.

The D. A.'s assistant did not press his advantage over Mrs. Otis. Instead he looked at her husband. "Mr. Otis"—and the blandness which had come into his voice as he adroitly led Miss Higgins through her paces now gave way to sneering insolence—"how does it happen that you did not send out for any lunch today, nor eat in the executives' dining room, nor leave the building for your lunch?"

"I often go without lunch."

"Not according to your secretary. She says that, in the five years she's worked for you, you haven't failed to have at least a sandwich and a glass of milk at your desk regardless of how busy you are. In that same five years, your wife has never entered your office until today. Yet today, you and she sat closeted alone in your inner office from eleven-thirty until two-thirty. From one to two, Miss Phillips was at lunch and can only assume that you and Mrs. Otis remained in your office. But you didn't take an elevator and you didn't go to the restaurant."

He stopped and regarded Mr. Otis accusingly. For once that gentleman was out-classed in the matter of nasty facial expressions. He returned the look unflinchingly and remained silent. It was well done, indicating that there was no need of rushing to his own defense; he could afford to hear Hoffmann out and then answer at his leisure.

"It would take no more than an hour for even a poor typist to write that confession," continued Hoffmann, "and I suppose we can assume that neither you nor your wife are expert typists?"

"On the contrary, Mrs. Otis types very well. She has acted as my unofficial secretary at home for many years. She would never have produced a mess like that confession."

"Well," said the assistant D. A., and his voice grew more pleasant, "we've been looking for a good typist out of this crowd ever since the papers received those letters regarding Mrs. Holmes and Mrs. Wood."

Mr. Otis's jowls suddenly went a little baggy. "My wife would not stoop to writing such a letter," he replied, with quickly mustered dignity.

"Oh, there's no doubt," interjected the Sheriff humorously, "that we are up against a very high-principled group here. Everything but murder is beneath them. And they are so hide-bound by convention that they won't even admit to that."

Hoffmann looked down at the notes before him and struck one off. Mr. Otis took the opportunity to say, "About my wife's visit to my office—we were, quite naturally, concerned over the events of the past week. Her coming in to see me was perfectly normal."

He was ignored and the attention shifted to Jane. The two men dragged her relentlessly, step by step, over the events of the past week, attempting to trip her by backtracking and insinuations but, exhausted and grief-stricken as she was, her story stood up against their fire. The one thing which was most in Jane's favor was that she could account for every minute of her time from eleven-thirty, when Gloria had surprised Jim with the poison, until the moment of his death. However plausible were the counts against her on our first two murders, she had certainly not been personally involved in the death of her late fiancé.

"Mr. Thorpe," snapped Hoffmann, and the way his pale-lashed eyes narrowed made me thankful that they were not boring into mine, "you have stated that you were in bed when the shot which killed Mrs. Cole was fired. Will you explain how you were able to get up, put on your robe and slippers, tie the sash of your robe, tie a scarf into an ascot and appear in the hall in the same length of time that it took two other men, both of whom were out of bed and already wearing robes, to rush into the hall?"

"I don't know how I did it," admitted Garry, as if marveling at his own proficiency, "but apparently I did."

"When you went downstairs to meet Mrs. Cole—"

"What makes you so sure that I went down to meet her?" interjected Garry, adding with a note of triumph in his voice, "Martin had already said that everything in that confession is imaginary."

"You didn't go downstairs," mocked his questioner, "but your cigarette case went down and deposited itself on one of the chairs before the fire."

Good heavens! Were the police mind-readers?

Garry cast a scathing glance in my direction. "That was not my cigarette case. It was Lissa's. I gave it to her last Christmas. When Mrs. Wood picked it up I took it from her and later told Martin that I wanted to keep it. That was agreeable to him so I kept it." Like a small boy who has just vindicated himself of an unfair accusation, he half grimaced at me.

"In case you are interested," observed the Sheriff mildly, "it was not Mrs. Wood who gave us the information. It was Mr. Otis."

That was the first move the police made to drive a wedge between Garry and the Otises and caused Mr. Otis to say quickly, "I mentioned it on Sunday morning, Garry. Of course, I have since supposed they had learned the truth or I would have corrected the impression."

"What difference does it make when you mentioned it?" demanded the Sheriff.

"None," Otis assured him hastily.

"And how did you suppose that we had learned the truth? And how, incidentally, did you learn it?"

"Actually," temporized Mr. Otis, "the matter seemed of slight importance and therefore slipped my mind."

"Mr. Cole," Hoffmann asked, as if unaware of the Sheriff's questions, "is it true that Mrs. Cole attempted to get a divorce about three years ago?"

"Right."

"Whom did she wish to marry at that time?"

"As far as I know, she had no matrimonial plans."

The assistant D. A. laughed unpleasantly. "I see," he replied, "she planned to run Dexter and Cole all by herself. She wanted to be a big merchandising executive. That's why she refused to give up her stock."

"Was it?" inquired Martin, with mild interest. "I thought she refused to give it up because she really didn't want the divorce. Therefore she made an impossible stipulation. Unfortunately, my wife was subject to attacks of intense boredom. At such times, she'd think up domestic crises just for the sake of their nuisance value. As soon as something more diverting came along, her interest would shift and she'd forget about wanting a divorce."

Once again, District Attorney Hoffmann abruptly shifted his attack. "Mr. Thorpe," he said, turning to Garry, "where were you this noon—say from one to two?"

"I was around the store," replied Garry irritably. "I don't chart my days—part of the time I am here and part of the time I am there."

"Don't be so specific," said the Sheriff, suppressing a smile. "Just tell us where you were." It struck me that the Sheriff liked Garry. And suddenly, I realized that I liked Garry, too. It would be just awful for nice ingenuous, aggravating Garry to be proved a murderer.

"Well-l-l," he replied hesitatingly, "about one-fifteen, I left my office. I wanted to check on some merchandise in different departments in the store and I wandered about looking at things until nearly two. Then I went to lunch in the executives' dining room."

"That was a quarter of two. To whom did you talk on the selling floors when you were looking at merchandise?"

"Well-l-l," Garry again thought his answer out, "I didn't talk to anyone. I just looked at the merchandise."

"That's extremely unfortunate," observed Hoffmann bitingly, "for, of course, the merchandise can't tell us that you looked at it."

"No," agreed Garry doubtfully.

"It might interest you to know," pressed the assistant D. A. relentlessly, as he started hammering on the table to emphasize his point, "that a list of names was given to every section manager in the store and your name was on that list. Every salesgirl has been asked if she saw you between one and two today and not one of them did." He leaned back in his chair and regarded a wilted Garry triumphantly. "Were you, perhaps, invisible when you were looking at that merchandise?"

"I guess no one noticed me," said Garry weakly.

"Your modesty is equaled only by your morality," quipped Dodd. "You don't suppose," and his tone grew smoother, "that a handsome young man like yourself could pass unnoticed by five hundred or so young ladies?"

"Well-l-l," said Garry tentatively, his vanity piqued by this unflattering picture.

Suddenly Hoffmann sprang to his feet and hurled himself across the room. He towered above his victim, an accusing forefinger almost bumping Garry's classic nose, and shouted, "You know why no one saw you downstairs. Because you were here in the outer office. You were sitting at Miss Higgins's desk writing that phony confession. You were putting the blame on Fenton because you had to get rid of him. He knew you were the murderer of the woman you were in love with. He knew you were mad with jealousy and would rather see her dead than married to him. So you killed him. You sneaked in here at noon, closed the door, and typed out that story. When the meeting started this afternoon, you had Fenton sign that bogus confession along with those reports. Now don't," as Garry tried to stem the onrush of accusations, "don't try to lie out of it like you've lied out of everything else. We know you were here because we have evidence." He stopped gesticulating long enough to drag a paper out of his pocket. He waved it in Garry's face. "What do you think my men have been doing? Sitting on their fannies? No, sir, they've been getting evidence and it all points toward you. On this paper is the signed statement of one of the secretaries from this floor that she saw you enter Fenton's outer office about fifteen after one. You looked up and down the hall to see if anyone was watching and then you sneaked in and closed the door behind you."

He stopped. His face, with its pugnacious jaw and cruel eyes, was thrust almost against Garry's face. Garry was whipped! Beads of perspiration stood out on his forehead and upper lip, and he swallowed convulsively before his words came. "All right," he whispered, "I was in the office. But it wasn't as you said. Let me explain."

Hoffmann swung back to his seat triumphantly, "All right, big boy," he said. "You sure have something to explain." I took a peek at the piece of paper which he flung on to the table and could have wept to find it a dry-cleaner's bill.

We all sat and watched Garry expectantly. He took some time to assemble his thoughts and the police let him alone while he did so. At last, one foot pulled up on his knee, nervous hands gripping his ankle, he told his story.

This is what he told us: That morning, shortly before twelve, he had met Gloria near the elevators. She had said that she was going downstairs for a cup of coffee because she was very much upset about something. He had volunteered to go along and while they were drinking their coffee, had urged her to tell him what was worrying her. At last, upon his insistence, she had told him about seeing the poison in Jim Fenton's hand and of Jim's threat to her life should she betray him.

Garry had reassured Gloria to the best of his ability and, upon returning to his office, had cast about for a means of helping her. Finally, he had hit upon an idea. He would search Jim's office while it was empty at lunch time and perhaps find the pencil. With it as evidence, he would go to the police. Then he, and not Gloria, would be the target of Jim's wrath if his threats regarding vengeance had any basis in truth.

"But I couldn't find the pencil," he concluded plaintively. "Jim must have taken it with him. Or maybe he put the poison in the siphon and then threw the rest away."

"What makes you think that it was in the siphon instead of in the glass?" asked the Sheriff gently.

Garry looked surprised. "The glass was upside down on the tray."

"What makes you think that Fenton put it in?"

After considering that for a moment, Garry replied with an air of pleased surprise, "That's right! Martin said nothing in that confession was true."

"Oh, Lord!" muttered Hoffmann.

The assistant D. A. now devoted himself to making us all establish an alibi for the time at which the four identical letters had been mailed from Long Island City. Garry had, of course, been right on the spot. All the rest of us, with one exception, could produce an alibi. That exception was Nora Collins Otis. She had come into the city to shop—primarily for the unhappy purpose of purchasing a black dress to wear to Lissa's funeral the following afternoon. She had bought the dress and then had lunched alone at Schrafft's. At one o'clock she had gone to Radio City where she claimed to have spent the afternoon.

She steadfastly denied all knowledge of the letters but readily admitted that she was an efficient typist. "I have done secretarial work for my husband for many years," she explained. "However, we have never mentioned the fact to anyone."

The Sheriff looked at Hoffmann who muttered something under his breath and then began the puffing-out process which heralded one of his periodic onslaughts. Striding to the middle of the room, he stopped to glare at Garry and then at Mrs. Otis, shifting his bull-like head from one to the other. At last, when the strain had become almost unbearable, he bellowed, "All right you two! Make up your minds which one did it. Everyone else has a fool-proof alibi for when the letters were mailed. Everyone else has a fool-proof alibi for when the 'confession' was typed. Everyone but you two. One of you is the party we're looking for. One of you is going to confess before we leave this room if we have to stay here till you die of exhaustion. We're going to hammer at you till you drop—and we're going to get the one who did it. We still have some information that you don't know we have. It'll be a whole lot better for the guilty one to speak up now rather than to make us drag a lot more dirt out in the open."

He paused, and when no one answered he began again, "So you're not going to come clean? O. K., then, we'll find out for ourselves." And with a suddenness which took our breath away, he whirled on Arthur Otis. "Who's blackmailing you? And why?"

So Ken must have told the police of the sentence fragment which I had overheard! Our Executive Vice-President, who had devoted so many years of his life to trampling upon the spirits of those about him, resembled one of his own victims. His ruddy face had gone ashy and it was a full minute before he recovered sufficiently to stammer out, "Blackmail? Why-a, why-a, that's ridiculous."

"So ridiculous that your wife came into town to talk it over with you. So ridiculous that on the day you are discussing it, a third person is murdered. Murdered after a lunch time during which you sent your wife from your office to this office to type a phony confession and to put potassium cyanide into a siphon on this table."

Mr. Otis lifted his hand. "But," he pointed out, trying to make his voice sound more reasoning than panicky, "Garry has just admitted that he was in here, searching the office. Certainly Mrs. Otis couldn't have been here typing the 'confession' at the same time."

"I have the answer to that," snorted the assistant D. A. and again he swung over to Garry's chair to stand with feet apart and swaying slightly, like a ponderous bear, before his bewildered witness. "You," shaking his finger in Garry's face, "you walked into this office to find Mrs. Otis typing at the secretary's desk. You caught her red-handed and you're trying to blackmail her."

There was a sudden crash as Garry's chair shot back against the wall and he sprang to his feet, his face livid with rage. "You lie," he shrieked. "By God, I'll—" and he drove a clenched fist against his accuser's sturdy jaw.

It must be said in Hoffmann's favor that he took his punishment as well as he gave it. After the excitement had died down a bit and Garry, still shaking with outraged virtue, had been persuaded to resume his seat, the assistant D. A. stood in the center of the room rubbing his jaw reflectively. "That one seemed to backfire," he observed, almost as if he had enjoyed the whole episode. Then, to my complete consternation, he walked over to me and when he spoke there was no doubt in my mind that if Arthur Otis was not sent to the gallows, I was out of a job! "Mrs. Wood," said Hoffmann, "I promised to keep you out of this if I could, but I'm afraid that you will have to repeat exactly the words which you heard Mrs. Otis say."

"I heard her say 'blackmail becomes a lifetime proposition. It would be better—' That is all."

He nodded and walked over to Mrs. Otis. "Will you please give us your entire sentence?" he asked. "Better give us the whole paragraph."

Mrs. Otis had the look of a person who was doing some fast thinking. But she evidently got it done for her answer came promptly, "We were talking about what Mr. Fenton might have done if Mrs. Cole had not been able to get a divorce. Mr. Otis was of the opinion that he would have tried to create some compromising situation and then have attempted to blackmail her—or possibly her husband. Then I said, 'But blackmail becomes a lifetime proposition. It would be better for him to marry her than to blackmail her.'"

"Very interesting," commented Hoffmann as he walked back to his chair, "particularly interesting that in your conversation you used the future subjunctive to discuss someone who had been dead for a week."

"I'm not very good at grammar," said Mrs. Otis humbly. "My education was very limited."

The D. A.'s assistant sat down again and Sheriff Dodd shifted the six pencils before him to form two triangles. For a whole minute we had complete calm. Then the Sheriff looked up at Garry and asked, almost plaintively, "Mr. Thorpe, why have you persistently lied about the letters which were sent to the papers last Monday? You say that you did not and could not type them. We have learned that you type expertly." He paused, as if giving Garry a chance to volunteer some further information himself, but continued when nothing was forthcoming. "We have learned several other things in that connection. The substantial fortune which you inherited has been steadily dwindling, has it not? And you have become more and more pushed for money. For the past two years you have been supplying information about your society friends to one of the gossip columnists in order to earn some money on the side. Is that right?"

That it was right there could be no doubt. One look at Garry's abject expression was sufficient confirmation. Heavens, what a lot there is to learn about people! Here was the reason for Garry's seeming parsimony. And here, very possibly, was the reason for such arduous typing in his office the previous night. It was more than understandable that he would have hesitated to use his own typewriter so soon after its having been brought to the attention of the police. And perhaps the cocktail which Margaret Blake regarded with such suspicion had been, after all, a genuine gesture of good fellowship—unfortunately timed.

"Knowing of your financial difficulties," the Sheriff was continuing, "you can understand why, when the subject of blackmail was introduced, we suspected you." Garry was still looking unreceptive to the whole idea. At this point the Sheriff shrewdly decided to utilize some of the gallantry Garry was exhibiting, rather than combat it. "You have let us accuse others of writing and mailing those letters. A man who instinctively shrinks from the very thought of blackmail is not being fair to himself when he denies having written letters which he did write. Now I will make a bargain with you. If you will, on your honor as a gentleman, promise to tell me the truth about those letters, I will promise to believe what you say."

Garry regarded him doubtfully, but it was apparent that he felt anxious to do his part as a gentleman. "Are you sure you will believe me? And are you sure he—" nodding toward Hoffmann, "will believe me?"

"Yes, son," said Hoffmann, "go ahead, I'll believe you." I felt that he would. And I knew that I would. For the second time since Lissa had been murdered, I looked at Garry and thought, "Breeding does tell."

"Well," said Garry, drawing a deep breath of relief, "I did write the letters and I mailed them when I was going through Long Island City. I had thought about the whole thing very carefully"—it was easy to imagine his careful ponderings—"and I was convinced that Mrs. Holmes must have done the shooting. There were only two other people who would have had any motive (that was before I knew about Mrs. Kingsley's motive) and I was positive that neither of them could have done it. The papers had all the evidence against Martin and none of the evidence against Mrs. Holmes. So I sent them the information about her fight with Debby."

"Hardly a fight," I said coldly.

"Whatever you want to call it," he replied agreeably. I could have shaken him and cried over him all at the same time.

"What about the key to your apartment?" inquired Dodd smoothly.

Garry looked surprised. "I mailed it to myself," he explained. "I was going to use it as evidence that someone else had gone to my apartment. That was intended to show that I hadn't typed the letters."

"Very subtle," commented the Sheriff, trying to keep the sarcasm out of his voice. "Why did you not show the key to the police and clear yourself, as you had planned?"

Garry shifted uncomfortably. "I can't explain that," he said, with a return to his virtuous air.

"Who were the two other people who had motives? Mr. Cole and who else?"

Again Sheriff Dodd drew a blank. Garry wouldn't answer. So the Sheriff said, "In regard to your mailing the letters to the papers, it wasn't very gallant of you to put the blame on to a woman, was it?"

Garry looked up in quick agreement. "That's what I said," he exclaimed.

"To whom did you say it?"

The room was as hushed as a snowfall. No one seemed to so much as breathe, and when the Sheriff spoke again it was in such a soft voice that he seemed to be thinking aloud. "Someone suggested that you write those letters. Isn't that how it happened? You protested that it wasn't very sporting and the person talking to you persuaded you that since it was a choice between two women, you should be loyal to the one who meant more to you—and especially to Martin. Isn't that the way it was?"

Garry again failed to answer, but sat as if paralyzed, his throat working convulsively. Hoffmann rose and went over to him. But this time there was no hint of threat in his manner. He was exuding fatherliness. "Listen, son," he said, his harsh voice making one think of that good old cliché about the diamond in the rough, "you say that you were in bed when Mrs. Cole was killed. You know we can't believe that. Nobody could have duked himself out like you were and still have reached the landing as soon as all the others. So you must have been dressed. You probably were doing one of two things. At the moment the shot was fired, you were either looking out your door and saw someone shoot Mrs. Cole or you were looking out your window and saw someone who couldn't have shot Mrs. Cole. If you had looked out of your door, you would have seen the real murderer and you would not have believed it to be Mrs. Holmes. Therefore, you must have been looking out of your window at the time of the shot and have been able to see one of the Otises in their bath or dressing room. You suspected that the other one did the shooting. I doubt if you would have gone to all this personal risk to shield Mr. Otis so I guess it was Mr. Otis that you saw and you knew that Mrs. Otis was alone at the time of the murder. Now, I don't know what you did next, or how you did it, but one or both of the Otises found out what you knew. They inspired you to write those letters. You knew how devoted Martin was to Mrs. Otis so you tried to be a good sport and help her out."

The D. A.'s assistant stopped speaking. It struck me that the rest of us were like so many figures in one of our own Fifth Avenue windows. A window which could have been labeled, with no originality whatsoever, "What the well-dressed Executive—Male and Female—will wear this spring." The presence of the nurse was a discordant note. No nurse should be included in a window display of executives' attire. No models should look so nervous or harassed as the eight of us were looking. On second thought I realized that we didn't look like a group of papier-mâché figures, but like a roomful of people who were realizing, gradually, that Nora Collins Otis must be our murderer.

For my own part, it left me quite cold. But Martin Cole looked like a man who has had his last faith in mankind torn from him and Mr. Otis was really in a state of frenzy.

"It's outrageous," he spluttered, "a lie. The whole thing—we can explain—you have only Garry's word— maybe this is his way of giving himself an alibi—"

"That's enough, Arthur," said his wife, and her voice was charged with a cold and deadly loathing. If ever a woman hated a man, that woman hated her husband. "Garry," she commanded, "go ahead with your story. We might as well get this over."

"Well," said Garry, plainly relieved to be talking under orders, "you were right about it, Hoffmann. I saw Mr. Otis just at the time the shot was fired. I had gone downstairs in an effort to persuade Mrs. Cole not to marry Jim. She had promised to meet me in the drawing-room at one-thirty. After I came back upstairs, I was raising my bathroom window and I saw Otis in their bathroom. The light had just come on. Their window was open only about three inches and the way that I could tell it was he was because I later saw his robe and it was the same maroon. So I knew Aunt Nora had been alone, and I knew how devoted she had been to Martin, so that is why I claimed to be in bed. I didn't want to have to say anything about what I had seen. But Sunday evening after the others had left, Mr. Otis called me into the library. He tried to make me confess that I had murdered Lissa out of jealousy of Jim. I denied it and finally when he got really nasty I told him that I had an alibi—I had been watching him. He got all worked up—as he is now—and asked me to keep quiet about the whole thing. He suggested writing the letters about Mrs. Holmes, saying that she was probably guilty and that I owed that much to Aunt Nora for always having been so good to Martin and me when we were youngsters—after Martin's mother died."

"Did you and Mrs. Otis collaborate on writing that 'confession' today?"

"No," replied Garry definitely, "she wasn't in here when I was. But I wasn't here very long."

Assistant D. A. Hoffmann turned and strode over toward Mrs. Otis. Except for a bleak look in her eyes, she seemed less ill at ease than anyone else in the room. She looked up at the approaching investigator and said quietly, "There is no use questioning me. I have nothing to say. If you can indict me and get a conviction on the circumstantial evidence in your possession, that is your privilege. I admit to the truth of everything that Garry has said. Beyond that, you have to work alone."

"That's okay," Hoffmann assured her readily. "It's between you and Martin Cole now, everyone else is accounted for."

"He has an alibi for today," she answered quickly.

"Yeah. But how do we know that he didn't commit the other two murders and then you pulled this one to draw suspicion away from him?"

The two eyed each other with deliberation, and, at last, Mrs. Otis said quietly, "You win. I did them all. I'll give you a statement."

Dimly I realized, for my eyes were still on the rigid woman facing the D. A., that Martin's back was to us, his hands clenched behind him and that Arthur Otis, elbows on the table, had buried his face in his palms. "They must be suffering," I thought, "this is all very terrible. Mrs. Otis is a murderer. She did it to save Martin's store for him. I must overcome this awful sense of unreality and become conscious of what is happening."

Garry, too, was apparently only half aware of what was transpiring. He remarked musingly, his mind still on his conversation with Hoffmann, "He was," nodding toward Mr. Otis, "so startled when he heard the shot that he dropped a bottle on the bathroom floor. I heard it break. Didn't you fellows find it when you investigated?"

For the third time in that never-to-be-forgotten afternoon, things happened so fast that they left me breathless. Before Mr. Otis was halfway out of his chair, Hoffmann and the Sheriff were on either side of him, the D. A.'s assistant administering such a vigorous shove that he bounced back on to the seat and nearly overturned. Martin Cole had also darted forward and now stood directly behind his Executive Vice-President, an expression of such contempt on his face that I was amazed to see one group of features holding it all. Mrs. Otis let out a half-gasping sob and, rising abruptly, went to the window where, her contorted face turned from us, she pressed her forehead against the cold pane of glass.

It took some time to get things straightened out but eventually we learned the reason for all the excitement. For the broken bottle had been found on the bathroom floor and stains from its contents had been found on Mrs. Otis's slippers and the hem of her nightgown. Mrs. Otis and not her husband had been alone in the bathroom at the time Lissa Cole was murdered. Mr. Otis had been alone in the bedroom, well out of his wife's sight. As for the broken bottle—he had destroyed its significance by claiming that it had been broken soon after they had retired to their room.

Mrs. Otis had agreed to the deception only because she believed Louella Holmes to be the murderer. If not Louella, the choice seemed to lie between her husband and Martin, an intolerable solution in either case. But eventually, she had become convinced that Louella was innocent. Her trip to her husband's office had been for the purpose of trying to convince him that, since Martin was still a suspect, they should tell the true story to the police. Mr. Otis had refused to do this.

A detail which it required some questioning to clear up, was that of Garry's mistake in the identity of the occupant of the Otises' bathroom. We learned, finally, that Garry had not seen our Executive Vice-President's robe but a lounging jacket of the same material which had been hanging on the back of the door. His wife had lifted the garment down from its hook and it was this movement which Garry had observed. Her husband had let this mistake in identity go uncorrected. In this incredible betrayal, Nora Collins Otis had lost the last vestige of respect for the man whose career she had so faithfully been building these last twenty years. She had come to the scene of Jim Fenton's death convinced that her husband or Martin Cole was the murderer. And she had come ready to offer her own life to save either one of them. The impulse to save Martin sprang unquestionably from a deep well of gratitude and affection. I suspected that she would have died for her husband in a cold fury of utter contempt.

Now we had another murderer. Not merely a murderer but a man who had deliberately planned to let his wife pay the penalty. While I was still trying to adjust myself to this nauseating idea, I became aware of Mr. Otis's voice, raised in vigorous self-defense. "But you must realize," he was protesting, "that when I permitted Garry to believe that I, and not Mrs. Otis, was in our bathroom, I knew that I was not guilty of the murder. I insist—"

"Tell it in the courtroom," interrupted Hoffmann. "You'll get a chance to defend yourself. We've heard enough for today."

There was a general bustle of activity preparatory to our departure and I was about to whisper to Ken that I guessed I knew a murderer when I saw one, when the door opened and Guffey entered. He handed a telegram to Hoffmann. The D. A.'s representative tore it open, read it and said, "Well, I'll be damned." Then he handed it to the Sheriff.

"We'd better get the rest of this story," said Sheriff Dodd when he had read the brief message. He motioned us to resume our seats and the two men left the room, closing the door behind them. I had the dreadful feeling that the session was about to begin all over again. We lit cigarettes and I poured some of the cold tea from the pot before me and tasted it experimentally. Gloria reached over and, drawing the cup across the table, took a sip from it. "I'm dry as a bone," she whispered. "If this goes on much longer, I'll go screaming crazy."

We must have waited more than half an hour in that desperate silence. We were tired beyond speech; so shattered by uncertainty and exhausted emotions that conversation seemed like something in which we would never again participate—a social gesture belonging to a world we had once known but from which we were now exiled.

When the two representatives of the law reentered the room they at once seated themselves in their chairs at the head of the table. Then they looked at Gloria.

"Miss Trent, I have a question to ask you," said assistant District Attorney Hoffmann, in a harshly brittle voice, "Is your hair naturally red or is it dyed red?"

I laughed hysterically. Of all the silly questions! But one glance at Gloria told me that she was taking the question seriously. So seriously that she had caught the edge of the table to steady herself and in her eyes was a terror even greater than any terror we had yet witnessed in that room.

"Red," she whispered, moistening her lips with the tip of her tongue. "It's naturally red."

15

"So your hair is red, naturally red? Well, Miss Trent, that is very interesting for the real Gloria Trent, born in Walla Walla twenty-two years ago, was born with black hair. Her hair remained black until she left Walla Walla at the age of fifteen and went into show business. She teamed up with another girl who was a natural red-head. They decided to put on a sister act and Gloria Trent had her hair bleached and then dyed red. They called themselves the Dean Sisters although neither of them was named Dean. Do you want to tell them the name of the other girl, the one with the naturally red hair?"

"No," whispered Gloria.

"Then I will tell them. You are that other girl. Your real name is Doris Fenton and you are the illegitimate daughter of Jim Fenton who was murdered in this room less than three hours ago."

"He deserved it," said Gloria sullenly. "But I didn't do it."

Now, at last, I knew something of the tormenting fear which the others had suffered when their loved ones were threatened. For Gloria was my pet. It couldn't have been she who had put us through this week of agony! I was leaning forward, a horrified protest on my lips, when Ken drew my shoulders back against the chair. "Steady," he whispered.

Looking at Gloria, it was as if I were seeing her for the first time. In that few seconds before the assistant D. A. continued with his story, my mind was like a kaleidoscope in which scattered fragments suddenly shifted into new and related positions. I could hear Garry saying, "Gloria had a blond mother and a brunette father." I remembered my quick change of subject because of her hatred of the father who had deserted her. There was Jane's voice as she said, in the restaurant, "And there was another woman—he never married her. She was a fragile little blond and she had a baby." And the implication in Jim's voice when he had mocked, "Neither Mrs. Fenton blessed me with an heir." His inference had been obvious. Also, there was the moment at the head of the stairs: "Why, Gloria is young enough to be your daughter, Jane." How well he knew! And Gloria, whose religion it was to be ingratiating, had deliberately insulted him before the portrait of Benson Cole I, hatred written all over her habitually self-contained face. Why had I not been startled by such antagonism? For I had always been aware that moral indignation was not a part of Gloria's nature!

Nor was that all. They looked alike—barring their hair and skin coloring. They had exactly the same exceptionally large blue eyes, and had I not mentally compared their astonishing lashes on the very day of the first murder? Also, Gloria, in moments of strain, showed the same square jaw line and abrupt sullenness, followed by just as abrupt sunniness. Yes, unbelievable as it was, my Gloria could unquestionably have been the daughter of that reprobate, Jim Fenton. Now I knew why that overwhelming sense of familiarity had come to me when Jim had looked up from his desk that very afternoon. My inexplicable surge of affection had not been for the man at whom I was looking but for the daughter whom I saw in him. I put my head on the table and shut out the scene before me. But there was no shutting out Hoffmann's implacable voice.

"Oh, yes, you did it," he had retorted. "And you killed the others, too. Do you want to tell us or shall I reconstruct it?" There was no reply and he went on, "About seven years ago, you met a girl named Gloria Trent. You two became the Dean Sisters. Mrs. Wood dropped that information quite accidentally yesterday. The police have just located an insignificant notice in *Variety* stating that the Dean Sisters had separated and that one of them, Gloria Trent, had joined a vaudeville troupe, heading for Mexico City. A few months later there was another small notice in *Variety* which stated that Doris Fenton had died in Mexico City while playing with a vaudeville troupe. They wired to Mexico City and were informed that there is no record of the death of any American named Doris Fenton. There is, however, a record for the death of Gloria Trent. Her birthplace of Walla Walla was also given. We have learned that Gloria Trent's whereabouts are unknown but that she was born with black hair.

"Now the implications are obvious. Upon the death of Gloria Trent there is a good possibility that her belongings were sent to her recent team-mate, Doris Fenton. Doris, loathing her own name and wishing to conceal her identity and her past, took the name of Trent. She inserted the notice of her own death in *Variety*.

"With this new name she came to New York. Am I right, Miss Fenton?"

"The name is Trent," said Gloria. "Mother was never married to him, but she used his name. I hated it after I was old enough to understand. I was sixteen when I ran away. She was still tagging him from city to city and she used to take me to see him occasionally, hoping his paternal instinct would get the better of his greed. It never did. He kept on picking rich wives and we kept on starving. Gloria—the real Gloria—was an orphan. I knew that she wouldn't be missed by anybody and that no one would be trying to trace her, so I took her name. It worked out fine until Jim came here. If I had known ahead of time that he was coming, I'd have left before he saw me. But I was on my vacation when he arrived and I innocently walked into his office the day after my return. He hadn't seen me since I was fifteen—but of course he knew me."

"So when he decided to marry his third rich wife, you decided to stop him?"

"No," replied Gloria, "I didn't know a thing about it. Not until Debby mentioned it at our apartment. Debby can tell you that."

"She was stunned," I assured him, looking up and taking new courage at the sight of Gloria's face. She seemed quite back to normal, as self-possessed as ever. But she didn't seem so appealing as she had always been, now that I was aware of the shrewdness in those blue eyes.

Hoffmann shrugged. "Now, I can't reconstruct the whole thing," he admitted, "but I can do a pretty good job. We've been looking for someone who had a chance to know everything about every person and you just about fit the bill. Whether Fenton told you about his plans or whether you found them out, I don't know. Anyway you knew. And they interfered with your own plans. You'd been figuring on marrying what you thought was Garry's fortune. Then you found out that he didn't have a fortune. By this time, you were well acquainted with the Coles. They were bored with one another and you figured that Garry would take Lissa out of the picture and you would marry her husband."

Martin Cole, standing by the window, turned toward us and said, "Oh!" There was no astonishment in it nor was it a rude disclaimer. However, to my great relief, his expression was more that of a man who is making a quick readjustment in values than one who is suffering from heartbreak.

"You felt that your father had cheated you out of a decent childhood and you didn't intend that he should cheat you out of a brilliant marriage," Hoffmann continued. "You got the gun when you went downstairs for your evening bag. You did it so openly that no one was suspicious. You watched the others go up and down the stairs, just as Fenton was supposed to have watched them. While Mrs. Wood was in the library you paced up and down your room. She thought it was Mrs. Kingsley. If it had been Mrs. Kingsley, the pacing would have been done near the east windows, for the furniture of her bedroom was chiefly on the west wall. Your room, however, was directly above the desk." I had a shattering moment of revelation. Of course! Where had my powers of deduction been? The corner fireplace in Gloria's room! There was no fireplace in the morning room! One of the library's twin fireplaces must have been beneath Jane's room, the other beneath Gloria's.

"I wasn't pacing the floor," declared Gloria. "Debby was dreaming. She's as nervous as a witch anyhow."

"That's what she said about you," interjected the Sheriff dryly.

"As to the poison," Hoffmann continued, "you had a perfect set-up for obtaining it. The night before Mrs. Holmes was murdered, you went to a studio to be photographed, so you picked up a little potassium cyanide."

"How did I get it into the tea?" demanded Gloria almost insolently.

"There again," replied the assistant District Attorney, "you did the perfectly natural thing so openly that no one suspected you. You left Mrs. Holmes before the tea was served and stayed away until you could return in the company of her husband. You said you went to the powder room and the fact that Mrs. Otis found you there substantiated your story. But the tea had already been served to Mrs. Holmes when Mrs. Otis found you in the powder room. You have no alibi for the time during which the tea was being brought to the ballroom to be served. Now it is a very interesting fact that the service elevator used by the waiters serving in the ballroom is located just off the corridor leading to the powder room. A lot of cocktails and canapés were being brought up at the same time that the order of tea came up. Now it is possible that these trays were lined up on serving stands after being taken off the elevator. It is also possible that someone hanging about the service elevator and watching her chance could have slipped the poison into the teapot and have escaped the notice of a busy waiter."

"I don't know anything about the service elevator, or about the poison or about the tea," Gloria declared. There were tiny beads of perspiration on her upper lip. "I didn't even know that they were having tea."

Mrs. Otis made a little involuntary movement which she quickly stilled. My heart sank. At least three of us knew that Gloria had been present when Ken told Mrs. Otis that I had ordered tea for Louella. And I recalled, too, with a sickening sensation, that Gloria had been present when I had assured Ken that, if Louella would stay for Jim's cocktail party, she and I would have tea together.

"And," concluded Gloria, trying to look amused and succeeding only in looking defiant, "you certainly haven't proven that I poisoned the tea."

"I have only shown," Hoffmann conceded, "that you had an opportunity. But an opportunity seems to be about all you need."

"Well, anyhow," said Gloria, "I have an alibi for this noon, in fact for every minute from the time I was in this office this morning until I came to the meeting. And after we came to the meeting, I didn't come within ten feet of this table until we all sat down."

"I'll bet you didn't," agreed Hoffmann. "You knew you were going to need this alibi and you have it. I admit that. You didn't write that 'confession' today. You wrote it yesterday. Miss Higgins, by her own admission, left her office early yesterday—not later than four o'clock. Your father—"

"Stop calling him my father," stormed Gloria.

"All right," he conceded, "Fenton hadn't been in his office since noon. So you stopped in on your way home, closed the door and typed out the 'confession.' You messed it up with erasures to make it appear to be the typing of someone who didn't know much about typing. Then today you came into this office and acted out the scene you had previously written. You brought a lot of ads in here with you this morning and got the signature exactly as we accused Mr. Thorpe of getting it;

by having Fenton sign several papers at once. You can't deny that your purpose in coming to the office was to have him O. K. some ads. His desk is visible from the corridor and it was a simple matter for you to pick a time when he was sitting with his back to the door—especially since he usually worked at the table rather than the desk. Then when he was dying, you bent over him so that no one else could read his lips or hear what he was trying to say."

Gloria's poise was crumbling under his relentless fire but she still managed to reply, with some show of assurance, "You think that is what happened but you can't prove it. You have about the same evidence against me that you have against the others. You simply show that I had an opportunity to commit each of the murders. But you don't prove that I did them."

"You are the only person," Hoffmann pointed out, "who could have written that you saw the poison in Fenton's hand and could have testified to that later."

"I did see it," she persisted. "You haven't proven that I didn't. You haven't proven that he didn't write the 'confession', that he didn't commit suicide, or that he wasn't murdered by Mrs. Otis or by Garry. You haven't proven anything at all."

Hoffmann stood up abruptly. "We've proven things to our own satisfaction, and we'll satisfy a jury," he told her and scooping up the six pencils before the Sheriff he handed them to me. "Will you," he asked, "return these to their proper owners and give me the one that is left over. I don't know it from the others."

I took the pencils and regarded them dubiously. Then I gave the one with the grey elastic to Mr. Otis who put it in his pocket with a muttered "Thanks."

Jane said, "Mine had part of the date scratched out," so I gave her one on which the "1940" was blurred.

Mr. Cole took the remaining four in his hand and selected one. "It had no lead," he explained, and held it up for me to see the tip.

The one with the very small, almost invisible crack in the eraser cap I laid before Gloria. Then I said to the Sheriff, "You can have your choice of these. As far as I know, mine had no distinguishing characteristic."

"Is that yours, Miss Trent?" inquired the Sheriff. I should have realized that his voice had grown too gracious.

"Yes," I answered for her. "That is hers. It has a tiny crack on the eraser cap."

Gloria looked down at the pencil as if it had been a scorpion. "No, it didn't," she denied vehemently. "It didn't have a crack. There wasn't anything about it that could distinguish it. If it has a crack it is some-one's else."

The Sheriff looked at me. "How do you know Miss Trent's pencil was cracked?"

Regretfully I replied, "Because I cracked it. Last Tuesday night we worked late and just before we left I knocked her pencil on to the floor. As I picked it up I saw the crack on the eraser cap. You can only see it when the light shines across it. Otherwise it is invisible. It wasn't im-portant enough to mention at the time."

The Sheriff walked around to Gloria's side and picked up the pen-cil. He took off the eraser cap and laid it on the table. Then he pulled out the eraser itself. Finally, drawing a sheet of clean paper before him, he turned the pencil upside down to shake out the leads. But there were no leads in it. On to the paper fluttered about an eighth of a teaspoon of flakey white powder. Though I had never seen potassium cyanide, no one had to tell me that I was looking at it now. We all sat as if trans-fixed, staring at that damning little pile of crystals.

The Sheriff returned to his chair. "No proof?" he asked.

There was no answer.

16

Never, if I live to be a hundred, will I be able to erase from my mind the terrible half hour during which Gloria told us of the circumstances leading up to the murders and the manner in which she had accomplished them. She talked willingly enough and, by the time she had told the whole story, it was easy to see why she was driven to murder. It wasn't only the poverty and humiliation of her childhood, it was the trap which Jim had laid for her. For there was in his nature no conception of the debt he owed his child, only a realization that she offered him another pawn in his game of life. He had told her of his plan to marry Lissa Cole and had demanded that she collaborate with him in trapping Martin into a compromising situation upon which Lissa could base a divorce suit. It had all been planned very carefully and they were to use Lissa's key to smuggle Gloria into Garry's apartment on one of the nights when Martin was sleeping there and Garry was out playing around the night spots. Then Lissa was to stage a timely entrance with the unsuspecting Garry and other friends and Martin, however innocent, would have been definitely compromised.

Jim had promised to give Gloria Jane's job as stylist and a good payment in cash but Gloria knew from bitter experience just how much she could trust him to pay off his indebtedness. Nor was she anxious, at such a promising point in her career to become involved in a scandal. She had become increasingly conscious of Martin's regard for her and had herself planned to move into the Cole home and fortune. The thought that her detested father could not only ruin her career, but in so doing would take for himself the coveted plum which she had been carefully ripening—well, murder seemed the only way out.

Her voice was hard and resentful as she told her story and when I asked why she hadn't gone to Martin Cole and told him the whole plan, she looked up and demanded sneeringly, "What chance would Jim Fenton's bastard daughter have had of marrying Martin Cole?" Little enough I was forced to concede.

"I planned to kill Jim first," she admitted. "I was in such a frenzy that I could have killed him openly and gone to the electric chair feeling that I had done something good for society. But then I got to thinking it over. If I could get rid of Lissa, Jim couldn't marry her and I stood a chance of marrying Martin. Of course Jim would have blackmailed me with the threat of telling who I was—but that wouldn't have mattered once I was married to Martin—Martin would have paid just to protect his wife's name."

"Ah, Gloria!" I thought, "how like your father you are!"

"It was that incident in the library between Mrs. Holmes and Debby that gave me the idea. I was desperate. If I didn't play ball with Jim I knew he'd hound me till the day I died and thwart every chance I had in the world. If I did as he demanded, I stood to lose everything I wanted and he would have thrown me out the minute he was through making use of me. Not only that—Jim would win everything and I nothing. It's been that way all my life and I determined to stop him if I had to do it with my own life.

"I overheard Garry and Lissa plan to meet in the drawing-room. I didn't know why, for I hadn't learned that Martin knew of Lissa's intention to marry Jim. But I figured that they would go to and from the drawing-room separately and I could get Lissa in the hall. Having been brought up on a ranch, I can shoot with the best of them, but I don't discuss the fact because people ask where I learned. As you know, I dropped that part out of my life when I took Gloria Trent's name. Debby was the only one who knew of the ranch and I've been scared to death she'd mention it."

"I did," I said, "the other night. But it didn't click."

"I was horrified," she continued, "when I learned that Martin had quarreled with Lissa about Jim and that the servants knew of her refusal to give Martin a divorce. That made a much stronger suspect of him than I had expected. In fact, I was just hoping it would be an apparently inexplicable murder which the police wouldn't be able to solve. When

Martin was suspected of killing Lissa to keep control of the store and Mrs. Holmes was suspected of killing her instead of Debby, I decided that I'd take another chance and see if I couldn't fix it so that Mrs. Holmes would be considered the murderer. That would have eliminated the suspicion that Martin had killed Lissa; it would have eliminated the possibility of having the police detect me and it would have kept Jim from suspecting me."

The fact that Louella Holmes, Garry, Jane, Martin or either of the Otises might well have murdered Lissa had kept Jim from really suspecting Gloria, although, judging from the fact that he had accused her of double-crossing him that day before the washroom doors, he was aware of that possibility. However, he didn't take the idea very seriously for at the time Gloria obtained his signature on the ads and the confession, she had calmly unscrewed the top of his siphon saying, "Jim, how do these things work? I want to get Debby one for her birthday. Should I buy any particular kind?" Jim had delivered quite an oration on the subject of siphons and their relative merits and had then turned to reading the sheaf of ads which Gloria had laid on his desk. She put the siphon back together again, taking the opportunity to drop in a minute portion of the poison which she had rolled into a bit of Kleenex. Of course the Kleenex had dissolved and the poison did its work.

Characteristically, Jim had not signed the ads but had returned them to her unsigned. She told us that she walked part way out of the room and utilized this moment to slip the spurious confession from a second group of papers in her arm into the fashion ads. Then she had returned to the desk, told Jim to sign all the papers and had them arranged so that he saw only the lower margin of each page.

"How did you know," demanded the Sheriff, "that Fenton wouldn't drink his vichy before you got here this afternoon and could add the 'confession' to the other papers on the desk?"

"That was easy," she replied wearily, "yesterday I made a point of learning his schedule for today. He was going into the market at eleven-thirty and planned to be back just in time for the conference. I came in to the office at the time he was scheduled to leave it."

Exchanging the pencils had been easy too. Never guessing that this act would betray her, she had attempted to strengthen the fiction of her seeing the poison by planting her pencil upon him. He had been using his own Amos Parrish pencil when she came into the office and had laid it upon the desk. She had placed hers beside it and then, when leaving, had picked up the one belonging to Jim. And by this carefully planned ruse, she had sealed her own fate!

Her decision to murder Jim was based on several factors. One was the success of the other two murders which had not involved her in any way. She grew overconfident. Then there was the fact that Martin, having attended the fashion show, was still suspected by the police and she feared the power of the circumstantial evidence against him. But most important of all was the threat of Jim Fenton to her future life. Having failed to place the blame for the murders on Louella, she decided to place it upon Jim, thus using him for her own purpose as ruthlessly as he had attempted to use her.

There was another detail of our mystery on which I wasn't quite clear for some time. It was several months before I got up enough courage to ask Mrs. Otis about the blackmailing episode. We were having lunch together soon after she returned to Dexter and Cole's and she told me the whole story. No one was blackmailing the Otises. Mrs. Otis had been insisting to her husband that his threatening Garry was tantamount to blackmail and that it would be better to tell the whole story to the police. I felt pretty horrible when she told me about it but she never seems to hold it against me.

A pretty grand person—Mrs. Otis! She's back in the store now, being Martin's general assistant. She's hard and shrewd when necessary but she is also magnanimous of spirit. Her generosity is never more apparent than when Jane is in town on one of her periodic trips from Kansas City. Mrs. Otis tips Jane off to many a trick that she would never get next to if left to her own resources.

Mr. Otis has been disposed of most adroitly. He is traveling in South America for an indefinite period, ostensibly to locate new products for Dexter and Cole. It must cramp his style to have to bully people in Spanish!

I've often wondered what big-business executives find to do with the couches in their offices. Now I know. As soon as the stylist recovers sufficiently to be transferred to a chair, they stretch out the advertising manager and start all over again with the smelling salts. At least, that is what they did in Jim Fenton's office after he had ruined half a dozen people's lives and paid the penalty in his own agonizing death. Because, as District Attorney Hoffmann prepared to leave, and to take Gloria with him, I took one look at Gloria's face and a merciful blackness engulfed me.

The room was almost empty when I regained sufficient consciousness to grasp my surroundings. Ken was sitting on the couch beside me, solicitous and exhausted, waving a bottle under my nose. He looked up at someone and said, "She's coming around all right."

I struggled to pierce the haze and Martin Cole's features appeared fuzzily. Beside him was a worried-looking Garry. I did not flatter myself that he was worrying about me. Gradually all the horror of the preceding hours came back to me. I could feel the pressure of hysteria against my throat and the tears welled up in my eyes. "Steady there," said Ken. He took me firmly by the shoulders and shook me a little so that my eyes came back to his. "Don't think," he commanded. "Don't think anything. Keep your mind a blank."

From away down under all the grief and shock, my feeble words pushed through: "My mind a blank? Impossible!"

"She'll live," said Martin dryly.

Ken got out a big clean handkerchief—isn't it amazing the way a man always has a big clean handkerchief?—and gently mopped me up. Martin and Garry went over to the pile of wraps which someone had deposited on the conference table and put on their coats. Garry brought Ken's overcoat to the couch and held it for him. Then Ken scooped me up as if I were a rag doll, and for all practical purposes I might as well have been, and they poured me into my own single-breasted reefer. Ken regarded my hat dubiously and then perched it on my head. I took it off and hung it over my arm. The four of us made our way slowly to the elevator.

"There are two taxis waiting in the delivery entrance," said Martin. "That way we can avoid the reporters." He looked at Garry who had the air of a puppy waiting to be forgiven. "How about a drink?" he asked.

Garry's gloom vanished. "Swell!" he answered and drew a deep breath of relief. The two of them saw us into our taxi and then climbed into their own—as companionable as if Lissa Dexter had never lived.

Our ride up to my apartment was quite cozy, though it didn't start out very auspiciously. We hadn't gone a block when Ken said abruptly,

"I have a brother in Rio de Janeiro, you know. I think that I'll go down there and visit him for a year. Maybe work on some of the articles I always mean to write and never do."

I dragged my nose away from the shaggy comfort of his tweed sleeve. "If one of us has to leave Dexter and Cole's," I said earnestly, "let me go. Please do. I can find something else in another city."

"I've cabled Jack to expect me early next month," he told me, quite as if I hadn't spoken. "A couple of years of travel will do me good. You like to travel, don't you?"

"Oh, I love to travel. I always say there's nothing so broadening as travel. Don't you agree with me, Mr. Holmes? Don't you always say there is nothing so broadening as travel?"

"You're a nitwit," said Ken. His voice indicated that he was partial to nitwits.

We sat in silence for a few minutes. When a man has been a widower for only three days, there are limitations. At last he asked, "If you could pick the one place in the world that you want most to see, where would you go?"

"To the Temple of Luxor. Then I want to ride up the Nile."

"So does Hitler," said Ken.

I didn't feel equal to arguing it out with Hitler. "I'll compromise for Rio," I offered.

The taxi slithered up to the curb and the doorman came running. "Do you think," Ken asked me, "that you could get your things packed in about a year's time and make it to Rio without getting lost?"

I thought that I could.

MARRIED ONES ARE BEST

(*Collier's Weekly*, September 25, 1943)

MARRIED ONES ARE BEST

"And so," Mary Ann concluded, "I told her that you're married."

Rohr Carson looked at his sister and reflected that twenty-three years of experience had not equipped him to cope with her. Her snub freckled nose and wide gray eyes always looked so innocent and she had an annoying way of making her voice sound very practical, as if what she was saying were just good common sense. His mind reached out for anger but captured nothing more potent than exasperation. "So I am married," he said.

"It won't hurt you for a week," Mary Ann assured him, "and it's the only possible way that Tiffany could
enjoy herself."

"Someone should have told me that this furlough was for Tiffany's benefit and not for mine," said Rohr. He took out a cigarette and lit it, tossing the match into the fireplace. "The whole setup is impossible, sis, and here's why: San Francisco's full of fellows on furlough who know me, and we're sure to meet somebody who'll tip my hand."

"You don't understand," Mary Ann insisted. "You don't have to drag her all over town with you. While you're loafing around the apartment, it won't hurt you the least bit to have a wife and a couple of children."

"She doesn't require her married men to have children, does she?" asked Rohr.

"Raul has two children. I told her you're my married brother. She knows all about Jane and the babies and all you need to do is act as if they're yours."

"Now look, sis," his voice indicated that this time he was not to be cajoled. "I'll take your word for it that your friend, Tiffany, is a great

193

girl, even if she is a bundle of cockeyed inhibitions. But I'm here to forget my troubles, honey, not take on a new batch."

He pulled his carrot-topped six feet two out of the chair and gave his sister a friendly little clip on the chin. "You can leave her a note," he said. "Tell her I made plans on my way into town."

He was no sooner on his feet than the sound of a key in the lock made him toss his cap back on the table with an exasperated, "Oh, hell!"

A moment later Tiffany Russell entered the room, and Mary Ann's eyes twinkled mischievously as she introduced them and watched Rohr's transformation from an exasperated male to a man with a new interest in life.

Tiffany was a very tall girl and very slim, with long fine bones which gave her a willowy grace completely devoid of angularity. Her features were delicate and her skin had a faintly luminous quality. She was wearing a flame-colored suit, and all her accessories were a deep, flat black, even to the precisely tailored blouse. Blond hair shone through the open meshes of a black fascinator, the ends of which she had tucked casually under her collar. Rohr had time for just two fleeting thoughts. The first was: No wonder they call them fascinators! The other thought was a disgusted: And I'm supposed to be married!

"I'm so glad you've come," said Tiffany, holding out her hand. "Mary Ann has been living for this."

Rohr took her hand in his and noticed that it had a soft, crushable quality. Tiffany regarded him with frank but friendly appraisal. "You brothers must look as much alike as your names sound alike. I thought Raul was the married one. Now I find that you are the married one. But I must say that you look like the pictures of the single brother."

"If we hadn't been born two years apart," said Rohr, "they would have called us identical twins." From behind Tiffany, Mary Ann blew her brother a kiss and relaxed in her chair.

He again caught up the cap and beamed first at one girl and then the other. "Come on, you two," he said. "We'll go over to the Army-Navy Club and pick up someone for Mary Ann to waste her sweetness on. Then," catching Mary Ann's eye and ignoring its warning, "we'll go someplace for dinner."

It had been but little more than a month since Mary Ann, determined to be as close as possible to her two brothers while they were
still on this continent, had followed them to the West Coast and taken a
copywriting job in one of San Francisco's department stores. Seated at
the next desk in the advertising department was Tiffany Russell. "Mary
Ann Carson," Tiffany had repeated. "Mary Ann Carson. It seems to me
there was a girl by that name at Wellesley."

"I thought I recognized you," cried Mary Ann joyfully. After that it
was inevitable that when she moaned about the ghastly room she had
found, "the only empty one in the city, I do believe," Tiffany had invited
her to share her own small bright apartment on Nob Hill.

In the weeks that followed, their lives fell into a happy and congenial
pattern. They rode up and down the San Francisco hills in the clattering cable cars. They lunched together at the Claridge or El Prado or
went up Grant Avenue to Chinatown. They went to the Blood Donors'
Center together and spent one evening a week at the Red Cross. They
talked about school and shared their home and their confidences until
the day that Mary Ann hung up the telephone receiver and said, "Tom
and Bill Haskins are in town and I told them they could take us to dinner."

Tiffany's face had gone white. "I can't go with you, Mary Ann. I
never go on blind dates."

"Phooey," said Mary Ann. "I can vouch for both of them. Good-looking, witty, Yale—known 'em since I was a kid. Now what more can you
ask? Nothing blind about that."

"It doesn't matter," said Tiffany stubbornly. "I never go on any dates."

Mary Ann's nice gray eyes were thoughtful. After a moment she
said, "They're tall. Both of them over six feet."

Tiffany's pallor gave way to an embarrassed flush. "I don't go on
dates," she said flatly, and spinning about to her typewriter, wrote
across the top of the page: "Polka dots are new this year." Then she x'd it
out, muttering, "New, heck! They're old as the hills." She rolled the page
farther up, wrote "polka dots" and then sat staring at the words . . .

"You two wait here," said Rohr as he got out of the taxi in front of
the Army-Navy Club, "while I go fishing."

"Bring me a tall blond," instructed Mary Ann, "with the face of a
saint and the soul of a demon."

A few minutes later, Rohr found Hank Gleason dropping quarters in a slot machine. Although Hank in no way filled Mary Ann's specifications as to either face or soul, Rohr considered him particularly amenable to suggestion.

"I have my sister and her roommate outside." he said. "How about joining us for dinner and perhaps a spot of dancing?"

Hank deposited a final quarter, pulled the lever and then gathered in the coins as they clattered down. "Just as I've begun to win," he moaned.

"Before we join the girls, I want to explain something." Rohr attempted nonchalance but found himself stammering a little over his words. "This may sound crazy but if the subject of my being married ever comes up, just take it in your stride."

"Congratulations, fella!" cried Hank.

He attempted some violent back-thumping, but Rohr dodged with a hasty, "No, no, you've got it wrong. I'm not married. Come on." He drew Hank toward the hall. "Mary Ann's got herself in some kind of a jam," he explained. "She told this friend of hers that I'm her married brother. So when I speak tenderly of my family you just look as if it were the natural thing. And while you're at it," he added, "remember you're coming along for Mary Ann. The blonde belongs to me."

"I don't get it," Hank admitted. "I've known blondes who were interested only in married men. But you're neither old enough nor rich enough, me lad."

When the two men climbed into the taxi, Rohr had an opportunity to see what Mary Ann had meant when she said that Tiffany froze in the presence of eligible men. She had been so gay and happy and alive when there were just the three of them. Now she sat quietly in the corner of the seat, her fingers pressed taut and stiff against her handbag, her eyes intent upon the tips of her slender shoes. In the restaurant she concentrated on the dancers, her contributions to the conversation limited strictly to an occasional yes or no. Then Rohr asked her to dance and made two discoveries—that she danced divinely and that she could again chat without restraint. Later in the evening, he asked, trying to sound more casual than curious, "Why wouldn't you dance with Hank when he asked you? He's a swell dancer."

"I didn't dare dance with him," explained Tiffany, her manner suddenly diffident. "I'd have been all stiff and jerky with self-consciousness."

"But you dance marvelously."

"With you I do," said Tiffany. "After all, I've gone to the best dancing schools in New York and Boston. Mother thought it might help but it didn't."

"Help what?"

"Me." After a moment she added, "Mother's the dainty, fluffy type. She was always a great belle. That's the reason it's been so hard for her."

"What has?" asked Rohr.

"Me," said Tiffany again, as if that were a completely adequate explanation.

The music stopped and the couples started drifting back to their tables. "Come on up to the bar," said Rohr. "Mary Ann no doubt wants to get Hank under her spell and, anyhow, I have to get this thing straight." They pushed their way up the steps and across the lounge. "Tell me," he said a few minutes later, looking over his glass into Tiffany's clear blue eyes. "What's the connection between the fact that your mother used to be a belle and the fact that you can dance with me but not with Hank?" Tiffany's eyes had a faraway look in them.

"Hank's single," she explained in such a low voice that he had to lean over to hear her words above the hubbub of the room. "*You* know that I'm not interested in you."

"That," said Rohr, "is what could be termed a devastating compliment."

Tiffany laughed in a kind of happy embarrassment.

As the week wore on, it astonished Rohr to find how easily he fitted into his new role as his own brother. The fact that they had gone to the same college, been in the same business and lived in the same small Ohio town was a great help. He carefully kept Tiffany away from the places at which he was most likely to meet intimate friends and when forced to introduce her to anyone, he eased her away before conversation could become personal.

On the whole, he kept excellent track of his dual life although occasionally he was disconcerted to have Tiffany correct him on such intimate details as the exact age of his younger son.

Once Rohr said to Mary Ann, "How about whispering in Tiffany's ear that the slightest reference to my family leaves me devastated with homesickness? Tell her it's the better part of patriotism to ignore the whole subject. And," he added, "will you please tell me how we're ever going to end this deception? Raul will turn up here some day and then you'll be in a pretty mess."

"I'll just say he's single," retorted Mary Ann. "And Tiffany will go and visit her cousin in Berkeley for a week."

"That's not exactly what I mean," said Rohr bitterly. "This is a tough spot for me."

One evening while Mary Ann was building up the morale of the Marines, Rohr and Tiffany climbed the steps to the Coit Tower on top of Telegraph Hill. All about them lay the bay and the city, the one a wide curving ribbon of fathomless black, the other a dark carpet sprinkled with San Francisco's dimmed-out wartime lights.

They sat down on the broad, shallow steps encircling the base of the tower and Rohr gradually swung the conversation to Tiffany's life in New York. "I suppose," he suggested casually, "that you're working out here for experience so that you can go back and get a job on Fifth Avenue."

She fell into his trap readily enough. "I'll never go back," she said. "I deliberately moved as far from New York as possible. But," she added, and there was a note of surprise in her voice, "I can think of it quite impersonally now."

"It's an impersonal place," agreed Rohr.

"Not when you've grown up in it. Not when you're part of a definite crowd. New York is just a small town except that there are more people to watch you fail."

Her tone indicated that this was not the moment for a flippant reply, but Rohr, his attention caught for the moment by a tiny light dodging across the bay, said absently, "Yes, you're obviously a complete flop." A moment later he put his arm about her and fished for a handkerchief. "Now, listen, baby, I wouldn't have said it except for its impossibility. Why don't you tell Uncle Rohr all about it?"

"It was mostly Mother." The words were muffled behind the handkerchief. "She wanted me to be the most popular deb in New York and from the time I could talk she was coaching me about what to say to boys and how to smile at them and how to be coquettish." A strangled laugh came from behind the square of linen. "Imagine me being coquettish at dancing school, looking down on the heads of all those nasty little boys. When I danced with the shortest ones, the others would say, 'Why don't you get a ladder?'"

He swung around bracing his elbow against the step above them, his long legs stretched out ahead. "I don't understand it, Tiffany. Here you are, a beautiful, clever, intelligent girl and you're letting a complex carried over from your early teens ruin your whole life."

"There was more to it than dancing school," said Tiffany. Her face was just a pale oval in the soft darkness but her voice betrayed her agitation. "Can't we forget it?" she asked. "I've decided what kind of life I'll be happiest living and I'm very nicely adjusted to it."

"You wouldn't deliberately cripple yourself physically," said Rohr. "Why cripple yourself psychologically?" To release her from a sense of scrutiny, he tilted his head back and looked at the stars. "I suppose you blame your mother for all this."

"Mother really wasn't to blame. She couldn't help it that I was just the wrong daughter for her. I finally persuaded her to let me go to a girls' college and in return I tried to live her kind of life during vacations. To please Mother, I tried to make the boys like me but the harder I tried, the more I scared them off. Then during my senior year, one of them started taking me out quite regularly. It was the first time anyone had ever asked me for even a second date and I was pathetically grateful."

"And what became of him?" asked Rohr.

"I went into the powder room at one of the hotels and overheard something I wasn't intended to hear. Or maybe," she added, her voice little more than a whisper, "I was intended to hear it. Don't make me tell you."

"Things are hardly ever as important after they've been honestly faced," said Rohr.

Tiffany took a deep breath like a swimmer about to plunge into cold water. "My father was paying his tuition for two years of postgraduate work."

Suppressing an impulse to take her in his arms, Rohr lighted a cigarette and inhaled deeply before he spoke: "So you came to San Francisco."

"Yes."

"You showed enough courage to walk out and make a new life for yourself. Why not make it a full life?"

Tiffany looked away from him to the west where a string of amber lights spanned the Golden Gate. "Do you think you'll be sent some place in the Pacific?"

"Could be."

They were silent watching the searchlights which had come on about the horizon, their shafts relentlessly searching out a plane until they held it imprisoned in their converging beams. It was a startling reminder of the war. He said, "Someday you may see a convoy going out and weeks later you'll learn that I was part of it."

She stood up suddenly and turned her back upon the panorama before them, tilting her head upward as if she were looking at the tower. "Until now convoys have always seemed thrilling," she said, "but they're really terrifying, aren't they?" Her abrupt movement and the quiver in her voice made him forget the plane in the lights. He sprang to his feet with the sudden urgent need to comfort her. The blond hair was on a level with his lips, and he put his arms about her and found that her shoulders had the same soft crushable quality that her hands had. There was just time to catch a hint of what it might be like to love Tiffany when she became a slim rod of steel in his arms. "Come," he said somewhat shakily, as he released her, "we'll go over to Julius' Castle and have a nightcap. Then I'll take you home."

The next day over the telephone Rohr inquired of his sister in an embittered tone,

"When a married man makes passes at a single girl, what does that make him?"

"A wolf."

"Then you two girls can entertain yourselves tonight," retorted Rohr. "I'm going out and eat Grandma."

He was, of course, waiting for them that evening when they left the store. "You'll never guess what I have." He patted the package under his arm affectionately.

"It's butcher-shop paper," said Mary Ann. "But it's probably wrapped around fish."

"A thick juicy steak," Rohr declared. "The hospitals are crowded with the women I had to knock down to get it."

"Much as I need some good red beef to stave off anemia," said Mary Ann, "this is my night at the USO. So you two will have to eat it by yourselves."

If Rohr had cherished any visions of Tiffany bustling about the kitchen and preparing a cozy meal, he was doomed to disappointment for, upon their arrival at the apartment, she took him out to the kitchen, made a sweeping gesture with her hand and said, "There it is and it's all yours."

"Oh!" He took a moment to adjust himself to the idea. "I'm cooking dinner, am I? Well, it's luck that steak is my specialty."

Rohr prepared the dinner that evening to a running accompaniment of under-breath comment which would have startled Tiffany if she had heard it. "This pretty little courting scene," he thought, "has the proper setting but the casting is in reverse." He snatched up the singing tea kettle and dumped some water onto the peas, muttering, "I think I've been had." *I really should bake a pie,* he decided as he sloshed the greens up and down in the sink, *because if this scene is going to be authentic I need a daub of flour on my cheek.* He rummaged around in the cupboard for the oil and vinegar. *If that girl's sitting in the living room reading the newspaper, I'll shake her.*

"Hey, Tiffany!" he shouted. "Do you have an apron?"

Tiffany returned to the kitchen and took an apron from the lowest drawer. "I suppose this is how you won Jane," she said.

"If anything makes me nervous," he said, "it's having people in my kitchen while I'm cooking. Will you please get out of here?"

After dinner, during which they discussed the arts and sciences because Tiffany considered that intellectual conversation was stimulating to a married man, Rohr opened all the windows to chill the room and then built a fire in the fireplace to warm it up. "Cozy, what?" he asked, sprawling comfortably in his chair. "With a setup like this, marriage wouldn't be half bad."

The doorbell rang, two sharp urgent peals.

"Who could that be?" Tiffany wondered. She went out in the hall and a moment later Rohr shot to his feet, for Jane's voice was saying, "Is Mary Ann here? I'm her sister-in-law, Jane Carson."

There was a confusion of greetings and a childish voice piped, "Does my Aunt Mary live here?" Then he heard Tiffany urge them to come in.

"Let me take the baby," she said; "you must be exhausted from carrying him. Mary Ann isn't here, but," she added, as if offering a priceless treasure, "Rohr is."

"Why, how nice," said Raul's wife in a cordial sister-in-law voice.

Rohr reflected that he was here only because going out the window would be certain suicide. "Offense is the best defense," he murmured and dashed into the hall exclaiming, "Jane, darling! How are you?"

"Dead," said Jane and submitted to his kiss. "Why didn't somebody meet me? I wired Mary Ann when I left Chicago."

"The telegram never reached her," said Tiffany. She had taken the baby out of Jane's arms and was holding him against her shoulder. "Mary Ann will be surprised to see you," she added and led the way into the living room.

"I don't know why she should be," said Jane. "She wrote me to get here before Raul does and he arrives tomorrow morning."

Tiffany turned to Rohr. "Mary Ann's been keeping this as a surprise for you," she exclaimed.

"So she has, the little devil," Rohr agreed. He was not looking pleasantly surprised. Tiffany glanced from him to Jane, and Rohr saw the question in her eyes. Does she suspect, he wondered, or does she think we are prospective candidates for Reno? He picked up Raul, Junior, praying that the child would confine his remarks to the weather, and said, "These youngsters had better get to bed immediately, Mary Ann probably has some hotel room reserved and is keeping that a secret too. You can take over the apartment, Jane, and the two girls can go to the hotel later." He herded them toward the bedroom, hoping he was doing a convincing act as the masterful family man. "You brought more luggage than that didie bag, didn't you?" he asked.

"It's at the station."

"Come on, Tiffany, we'll grab a taxi and go down and get it."

Tiffany looked at him in astonishment. "You don't need me," she said.

Rohr disappeared into the hall and came back a moment later with her coat. "Come on," he insisted. "Jane'll get along better alone with the children. They always act up in front of strangers." He held the coat for her and managed to wink at Jane over her shoulder.

"Sure," said Jane, remembering that she too had once been single. "Go along with him. I won't be fit for human companionship for a while anyhow."

"It seems so inhospitable," protested Tiffany as Rohr eased her toward the hall.

They had reached the front door and Rohr was drawing a great deep breath of relief when Raul, Junior, called out in his baby treble, "Uncle Rohr, when is my daddy coming here?"

"That does it," said Rohr. He opened the door, pushed a paralyzed Tiffany through it and closed it behind him. "Now, young lady," he said severely, as if the whole thing were her fault, "you and I are going to have a long talk."

Half an hour later, once again on the steps of the Coit Tower, Rohr said furiously, "How much longer do you expect me to keep up this monologue? What do you think this is, a Senate filibuster? I've told you how it happened. I've told you that I didn't intend to go through with it until you walked into the room and I fell in love with you on sight—" he broke off suddenly. The spotlights had come on again searching for a plane, and they watched them in silence. "I don't know," said Rohr, after a while in a voice that was suddenly quiet, "but it seems to me you're doing an awful lot of thinking about Tiffany and not much about Rohr. There's a war to fight and this may be my last leave—" He let the words trail off. Just then, her hand slipped into his.

"I don't know what to say," she whispered, "because I haven't had any practice."

"Say yes," said Rohr.

Murder in a Walled Town
Katherine Woods

MURDER IN TEXAS

Ada E. Lingo

"The story of a big-time murder in a small town, with the atmosphere of a hard-boiled newspaper office, a background of 'hot oil' and sudden gushers, and the intensity of a Texas heat wave."

Murder in Texas
Ada E. Lingo

Murder in Style
Murder on the Face of It
Dressed to Kill
Emma Lou Fetta

COACHWHIP PUBLICATIONS
COACHWHIPBOOKS.COM

ALSO AVAILABLE

Blood on Her Shoe
Who Killed Aunt Maggie?
Medora Field

Murder Ends the Song
Alfred Meyers